Just Passing Through

Just Passing Through

Short Stories

Jack Eugene Fernandez

authorHOUSE®

AuthorHouse™
1663 Liberty Drive
Bloomington, IN 47403
www.authorhouse.com
Phone: 1-800-839-8640

Published by AuthorHouse   12/03/2012

ISBN: 978-1-4772-9507-6 (sc)
ISBN: 978-1-4772-9508-3 (e)

Library of Congress Control Number: 2012922604

Contents

Foreword

Having recently entered my eighty-second winter on Planet Earth, I wish to celebrate both that milestone and my second career. After nearly fifty happy years as a chemist, I moved towards fiction, which has been every bit as happy and satisfying. I must confess that I've injected science into several of these stories, for which I ask no forgiveness.

My first story, *The Outlander*, came to me over thirty years ago while working on a chemistry textbook. The protagonist in that story, a chemistry professor, soon became a close friend. *The Outlander* and two other stories included here, *The Confession* and *Seeing Is Believing,* appeared in a previous collection, *Professors And Other Misfits*. All the remaining stories make their first appearance between these covers.

Perhaps our most compelling vision as we pass through this life is its end. Whether young or old, willfully or passively, forcefully or meekly, happily or angrily, we will all face it. Perhaps these stories will brighten the way.

I dedicate these stories to family and friends who have so graciously read my fiction, and especially to Sylvia, who for sixty-one years has offered endless love and understanding without which both my life and my careers would have rattled an empty can.

Finally I note that having family and friends read my fiction is a bonus of my second career that my first career rarely provided. That is why I will keep writing as long as my computers (the one on my desk and the one between my ears) continue to boot up each morning.

Jack E. Fernandez, Sr.
Tampa, Florida
2012

The Last Supper

The black brocade dress was not designed to hide her figure. Nor did her dark, silvery streaked hair, combed back into a tight bun in the Andalusian style, reveal her age. Wealth sparkled through the diamonds on her neck, wrists and fingers. Wrapped in an air of serene dignity, she drew every eye as the waiter escorted her to a table by the large window. Beholding the expansive Bay of Rosas, and without looking at the waiter, she said, "Bring a bottle of good French champagne and some Beluga caviar. My son will be late." Never breaking her meditative gaze out the window she reigned over one of the most enchanting coves on La Costa Brava: to the north, the site of Empurias, settled twenty-five centuries ago by Greek merchants, and beyond that, Rosas, sparkling like gems sprinkled across its ancient hills; to the south, the suburban beach of L'Escala rising seamlessly into the starry sky. Spread across the rocky amphitheater that surrounds the Bay of Rosas, L'Escala looks out over the opaque Mediterranean behind monolithic sentinels rising just beyond the water's edge.

The woman nibbled caviar and sipped champagne for well over half an hour before her companions appeared. Her son, perfumed, pudgy, and wearing an open collar and jacket, was in his early fifties; the woman was twenty years younger.

"I hope you have not waited long, Mamita," her son said as he held the chair for his younger companion.

"No more than usual."

The younger woman said nothing, but her large, watery green eyes searched out the man's in expectation. When she sat, her short, brown hair bounced lightly in rhythm with her nervousness. Soon, the beautifully curved fingers of her left hand were playing silent scales on the table. Robust, well proportioned and pretty, her neat, loose-fitting dress and wedding band as only adornment revealed that she cared more for comfort than for fashion.

"I'm glad we decided to stop here for the night," he said. "It is good to be where I was born and where God still walks the earth. The view from the Hotel *Nieves Mar* is superb and, as you will see, so is the chef."

His mother's voice snapped like a whip: "And you know them all, do you not, Carlito."

"Cataluña is my spiritual home, her every village a welcoming hearth, her inhabitants my brothers and sisters."

Moved by his own words, Carlos had risen on his toes as his mother watched with disdain. "My heart revels in the beauties and wonders of Cataluña." He sat. "Now, what shall we order? Something substantial, I think, after that long drive."

"L'Escala is the anchovy capital of Spain," the younger woman said.

"Of the world!" Carlos said. "Fresh anchovies, then, for our first course."

"Anchovies after caviar? Are we to have beer after champagne?" his mother said.

"Did you rest well, doña Esther?" the younger woman said.

"I could not sleep. Ah, but you, María, have little interest in sleep."

"We will rest in Barcelona," Carlos said. "María and I watched television and talked."

With mock surprise doña Esther said, "Television? Talked?"

Reaching for the caviar Carlos said, "I'm famished."

"I've never liked caviar," María said.

"I know," doña Esther said. "You should cultivate the taste, my dear. Caviar is one of God's great gifts."

"Do not forget the sturgeon, Mamita. She provided the eggs." Drollery radiated from the vibrating mass of sandy curls surrounding Carlos's cherubic clown's face. His V-shaped smile pushed his eyes behind slits.

"Have your little joke, Carlito. Too bad you have not developed more useful talents."

"Please, Mamita. We are on vacation."

"You cannot vacate responsibility."

"What can I do? Spain is in financial crisis; people are not buying . . . especially cars."

"I see new cars everywhere."

"Remember Juan Vila from Tarragona, Mamita? We did our military service together. He's the chef here. I shall ask him to make us paella. You will never taste better."

"Very good," María said.

"One thing you are good at, Carlito, is changing the subject. Paella is a trite conglomeration, but we shall see if it is as good as you say."

Standing he said, "I'll ask him to use lobster." Then, squeezing out a smile, "It is sure to win him the Nobel Prize."

Carlos pushed open the kitchen door. The two men embraced amid steaming kettles and hanging pots. "It has been too long."

Juan Vila's muscular frame pressed itself through his white uniform; a mass of red hair seemed to be bursting out of his tall chef's hat. Feeling Carlos's frail, bony shoulders, Juan said, "You look terrific, Carlos."

"It was very serious, but the doctor tells me I'm recovering."

"Good. Are you staying a while or just passing through?"

"I am on my way home from Paris with my mother and my wife."

"Too bad. I thought we might do the town. It's not Barcelona, but I know a neat disco."

"For sure next time."

"Still have your beach house near Tarragona, Carlos? We had good times there."

"O yes. María and I have missed few weekends since our wedding two years ago. We leave Barcelona on Fridays after lunch and return Monday nights. We sleep as late as we want and do the restaurants and bars in the evening."

"Hard life."

"What's the point of being boss if you can't take off when you want? Between us, Juan, business is so bad it doesn't matter whether I'm there or not."

"How's your mother? Still fit?"

"She's fine—I suppose," Carlos said shaking his head. "María is my salvation: strong, understanding, intelligent, talented, beautiful, loving, supportive."

"Sounds perfect. But then, you've always excelled in that department."

"María's different, Juan."

"So, Carlito has finally settled down."

"Absolutely. Now, how about making us one of your marvelous lobster paellas, like you made in Tarragona?"

"It will be my pleasure."

"Can you recommend wines to go with the escalivada and then the paella?"

"Amador has two superb whites. I'll send a Chablis with the vegetables and a Chardonnay with the paella."

"*Perfecto!*"

When Carlos left to speak with Juan, his mother had turned to the younger woman: "Carlito does not look well, María, and he still smokes. He cannot hide it from me."

"He has one or two a day; not enough to hurt."

"But physical exertion can kill him."

"I make him rest every day and follow the doctor's diet."

"He needs more than a cook and a nursemaid."

"I do all I can."

"He is not young and strong like you. He cannot maintain your pace."

"Carlos sets his own pace, doña Esther."

"He thinks he can please everyone."

"You're the one he most wishes to please."

"If that were true, he would take me and his job more seriously. He is shameful, getting to work after noon each day. No wonder our employees are slackers." The older woman's fury sliced through hissed tones.

"Carlos is having a difficult time. Feels powerless and even detests the place."

"You would do better to encourage him to work instead of making excuses."

"Right now his health comes first," María said. "He needs tranquility."

With laser eyes doña Esther said, "What he needs is for you to leave him alone. You brought on his heart attack with your insatiable demands."

"What an awful thing to say."

"I do not sleep as soundly as you think."

"With respect, doña Esther, that is between my husband and me. We have a normal married life."

"Abstinence is more normal. It is Christ's way."

"Are we to ignore God's gifts?"

"God's gifts are for creation, not recreation. Young people these days live for one thing only."

"Carlos is not a teenager! He's old enough to know how to live." Doña Esther had not noticed Carlos returning from the kitchen. Though the women did not raise their voices, Carlos could see the anger in María's face. He stopped behind his mother to listen and motioned for María not to reveal his presence.

"I do not doubt that you know how to live, María." The older woman's frigid gaze and voice rumbling with anger gave the younger woman a chill. "My son is a weakling. He falls in love with every woman who gives him what he wants—and there have been countless. Why he married you, I'll never know, but it is clear why you married him."

"Carlos is the only man I have ever loved. I would not have left the conservatory otherwise."

"Ah, yes. You love a sick, stupid old man. Perhaps you love him precisely because he is sick and old, and, I might add, potentially wealthy."

The earth trembled beneath Carlos's feet; he turned slowly and walked to the lobby. María, completely focused on his mother, barely noticed.

In a surge of power María said, "You're judging me by your own dark past, doña Esther."

"My past is pure, and beyond discussion with a nonentity like you."

"Your malicious opinions do not interest me, but your disdain for your son is shocking."

"I can be realistic and still love him more than you ever could."

"You should love him, but as his mother," María said as she stood and walked away.

The world had dissolved into the cavernous space that swelled beyond the streetlights. Only the flicker of a distant ship marked the horizon. Doña Esther could not make out the line separating water and sky. After several minutes her son returned. Standing by his mother he asked where María had gone."

"She went outside. Have no fear; she will not abandon you."

Without responding he walked out and found María standing on the hotel porch looking into the black, velvet night. She was contemplating the wispy halos that graced the streetlights when Carlos came up behind her and put his hands around her waist. "Don't let her upset you, my love; especially tonight." She turned revealing wet cheeks. "Give me a cigarette."

"You know you shouldn't."

"It will relax me." He lit the cigarette and exhaled a long plume of smoke. "When I was a child, she could make me shudder with a raised eyebrow or a curled lip. But I could never get angry; she sacrificed everything for me."

"Why does she hate me?" María's chin trembled.

"It is not you. She is a lioness guarding her cub."

"You mean a lion trainer with whip and gun."

"She will come to accept you."

"How could your father live with that?"

"He was a quiet man. As long as I could remember he had another woman. I hated him for it, until I grew up and began to understand the desolation in his life."

"So he found tenderness somewhere."

"He was happiest at work. I used to spend entire days with him. He talked mostly about business, but my best memories are his stories about his childhood on his father's farm. My mother is different; she never talks; she moralizes." Carlos thought a moment. "If only he had stood up to her."

"Perhaps no one could have."

"My father was a huge, powerful man, but my mother was much stronger." After a moment he said, "At least she respected him. She sees me as a weakling."

"How do you see yourself?"

Carlos shrugged. "She was good to me. She let me do whatever I wanted . . . as long as I didn't become involved."

"Perhaps what you took as weakness was your only way to survive."

"You're good for me, María." He kissed her.

"Go back to your mother. I'll join you in a minute."

Carlos flicked his cigarette into the street, removed a can of mouth spray from his pocket, used it with an embarrassed shrug, and returned to the dining room.

"She'll be right in," Carlos said as he sat.

"María is not for you, Carlito."

"What did you tell her?"

"We discussed your health."

"I won't let you drive her off the way you did Lourdes, Mamita."

"Lourdes, Magdalena, María; they are all one. They never cared for you."

"Of course not. Why would anyone care for me?"

"All they want is your money."

"I have no money, except what you dribble out to me."

"The way you live leaves the impression that you are rich. You should be actively managing the family business. Even moderate success would bring great rewards."

"The business is sinking, Mamita. Every manager has turned out to be a thief."

"For the hundredth time, you do not need a manager; you need to get your hands dirty as your father did, greet the workers when they arrive and say goodbye when they leave."

"Times have changed, Mamita. It is no longer a one-man operation. Papa worked himself into the grave trying to do it all. I need help. There is not time to do everything."

"There would be plenty of time if you didn't waste it on that woman."

"María's my wife." After a few moments, he said, "I have tried, Mamita. I can sell, but deskwork makes me crazy. Papa understood that."

"Your life style takes money, Carlito. There is your financial crisis."

"Am I not entitled to a decent wage?"

"You were entitled to an inheritance until your father came to his senses."

Carlos looked down at his caviar and reached for the bottle of champagne.

"And that's another thing. You drink too much."

"It calms my frustration."

"I did not know you cared enough about anything to be frustrated."

"How long will you keep me dangling, Mamita?"

"Self-pity is cowardly. If you really want to seize control of your life, throw out that woman and get to work."

Carlos looked down into his glass as if embarrassed. "I love her, Mamita."

"Don't make me ill. Your father and I did not have to spend all our time in bed proving our love. He was a decent man, content to live a celibate life. His years with the Jesuits prepared him well."

Her simplistic assertion shocked Carlos. She looked away with icy composure. Heavy makeup and painted eyelashes reinforced the ancient hardness. Many men had mistresses, but his father's deception now took on new meaning: he had twisted his life to fit a wife's warped morality. Her candor and cruelty seemed normal, yet strangely new, deeper, darker. She had always pampered him, going to extremes to satisfy his childish whims. Now, fragments of other incidents popped into view: times when she would divert his inquiring spirit from things she had no taste for, times when she surreptitiously pinched his tiny arm when he did something she did not like and others were looking; he dared not cry or complain. With a heavy foot she had cleared his path of every flower as she pulled him along by the arm. For the first time in years, he remembered a childhood dream in which he was drowning. He looked at his mother and softly said, "Mamita, I cannot touch bottom."

"I can accept your lack of business sense and your lavish life style, but I cannot forgive squandering your life on one unworthy woman after another. After giving you everything, this is my reward."

"I was looking for the wrong things in women."

"The Blessed Virgin should have been your model."

"I'm beginning to see."

After a long silence he said, "Mamita, why don't you like her? She has tried to love you."

"I do not need her love, and neither do you."

Her seductive gaze twisted her face into a dark caricature that sent a shudder through him. Feeling like a little boy he turned away, poured another glass of champagne, and leaned back in his chair and took a sip. "Mamita, do you remember the day I was born?"

"How can a mother forget the birth of her only child?"

"Tell me about it."

"It was horrible."

"Not joyful?"

"I was only seventeen and terribly confused. The pains woke me. By noon, they were excruciating. I had no idea what was happening. I panicked. If my mother had not been there, I would have died." Tears were running down the grooves in her shallow cheeks. "I knew God had inflicted that pain for a reason. I promised Him I would give up all worldly pleasures to devote my life to you."

"That wasn't necessary."

"I did not know how ungrateful you would be."

"After a long silence he said, "Is it true you married Papa after I was born?"

"Who told you that?"

"It is a simple question."

"I do not like the insinuation."

"Then it *is* true?"

"It was not what you think. I did not even know I was pregnant or how it happened."

"How could you not know? Did you think it was a miracle?" Her morbid glare revealed unfathomable anger. "Such an old trick, Mamita, so unworthy of you. When I overheard that story years ago, I could not believe it. But the venom in your words tonight makes me believe." After a few moments he said, "Was Papa my father?"

"You filthy son of a . . ." Doña Esther stopped when she saw María returning. Gripping her son's hand and with an imploring smile she said, "Please, Carlito."

"Welcome back, my love. We've been discussing my lineage."

Looking around for the waiter, doña Esther said, "I am tired of waiting. When are they going to bring something?"

"Here come the anchovies," María said. "Carlos, isn't there something you wanted to tell your mother?"

"It can wait. We've just spent two wonderful weeks in Paris. I want to celebrate our last supper." A grin pushed his eyes behind rolls of flesh.

The waiter brought out a bottle of wine, grilled anchovies, and a platter of *escalivada*—a sautéed medley of red *piquillo* peppers, onions, and eggplant.

"Is this the Chablis Juan Vila recommended?"

"Yes, sir."

"This is one of Juan Amador's best white wines, Mamita."

"It's excellent," María said. "Remember, Carlos? We met at the winery while my mother and I were spending the summer there." He reached for her hand.

"Juan is a great success, I hear."

"Yes, doña Esther. He has one of the largest vineyards in Cataluña, and he's expanding overseas. Juan and his younger brother, Manolo, have bought a winery in California. Manolo has already moved there to manage it."

"The escalivada is good; the anchovies are too fishy," doña Esther said.

Maria pointed to the sky and said, "Look: the crescent moon. How beautifully it hangs almost touching the water."

"Like a chalice, pouring light upon the world." Lifting his glass, Carlos continued, "To the moon that shines everywhere, even beyond Cataluña."

"A beautiful thought, Carlos."

"The moon is barren rock. Your life is on earth, Carlito, here in Cataluña."

"And I love Cataluña, but all the world is beautiful."

A smile crept over María's face.

After a long silence, doña Esther said, "Here comes the paella. Now we shall see if it is as good as you say."

The trio ate quietly for several minutes. The smiles that bounced between Carlos and María intensified his mother's scowl. As she ate, her eyes darted from one to the other. The couple's intimacy irritated her even more than her son's inquisition had.

"What are your plans, Carlito?"

"Plans, Mamita?"

"For dealing with your so-called financial crisis."

"We shall save that for Barcelona."

"Do not try to talk me into selling. The answer will be the same."

"I know better, Mamita. You are sole owner and monarch."

"It could still be yours, Carlito."

"Uh-huh."

"I can still change my will, but I will not live forever."

"Nor will I, Mamita."

"This subject is too morbid, Carlos, especially over such exquisite paella. I have never tasted better."

"Mediocre," doña Esther said.

For dessert, Carlos ordered crema Catalana and a bottle of Port. "A perfect finish for the last supper."

"Must you blaspheme, Carlito?"

"I mean it in a special way. Enjoying the delicate flavor the lobster imparts to the rice shows that disparate things often harmonize. And that inspires me to make an announcement." María looked up. "María and I are going to America." The younger woman looked for doña Esther's reaction.

"Good," his mother said. "A rest will help you recuperate."

"I'm glad you like the idea, but we are not going to rest. We're moving there."

"Your place is here," his mother said, slamming down her spoon.

"My place in Cataluña has crumbled, Mamita."

"So she has finally managed to take you away from me?"

"No, Mamita. I'm taking her away."

"I will not fund an open-ended vacation."

"Nor would I expect you to."

"Enough! You may have your vacation, but then you will return and manage the family business. That is your duty. It is what your father expects."

"Papa is dead, Mamita, but I am certain that he wanted me to enjoy life more than he did. Business doesn't bring me the happiness it brought him; it has brought me little money and less hope. All I have to show is a weak heart."

"And you expect to find health and happiness in America?"

"I can't be what you want me to be, Mamita."

"You will fail there as you have here."

"I never realized how much you depend on my failure, Mamita."

"Liar! I want only what is best for you."

"But we cannot agree on that, can we?"

"I want you to take charge, do something with your life."

"But Mamita, you would lose control."

"Ingrate! Is it not enough to be a failure? Must you be mean and spiteful too? You can go to the devil for all I care. You will return on your knees soon enough, begging me to take you back."

"You have not asked what we plan to do in America, Mamita."

"It is of no interest."

"Juan and Manolo Amador have offered us jobs in California and a house in their vineyard until we get established."

"Juan and Manolo have a rare kindness and generosity," María said.

"Manolo is very handsome," Esther said. "Is he married yet?"

"Not yet, Mamita."

"He is about María's age, is he not, Carlito?"

"They're María's first cousins; she grew up with them, and they're good friends of mine. They want me to work in sales and public relations. María will help in the office for a while. Besides our fluency in English they're impressed with my ability with people."

"I am glad somebody is impressed with you." She turned to María. "So, María will take over their business, what she could not do here."

Exasperated, he said, "Mamita, María will work for them for a while to help me. In time she will find something in music, a university position perhaps." For the first time, María was not tapping finger scales on the table.

"You think you are frustrated now. Wait till you have a boss who expects you to report on time every day. And you, María, do you think you will be able to live the way you live here?"

"I hope not. There should be more to life than waiting for someone to die. I want to wake up happy each day, looking forward to a day of useful life."

The older woman looked past them at the moon's image on the sea, imagining slimy aquatic creatures slithering beneath the shimmering surface. After a few moments, her eyes filling, she said, "What about me? Who will care for me when I am old and alone?"

"You'll manage," her son said. "You're strong and resilient."

"But the business . . ."

"Perhaps you can devise a plan," he said, grinning.

"I hope you are happy now that you have spoiled my supper. I am going to my room. We will discuss this matter no further."

"*Buenas noches*, Mamita."

"We will discuss improving the business when we return to Barcelona. Good night." Standing and straightening her back, doña Esther made a regal exit looking at no one.

"Would you like to walk along the beach, María?"

"I'd love to."

Carlos signed the check as they left the dining room, then turned and opened the kitchen door: "Wonderful meal, Juan. Keep in touch."

"I didn't know we had decided to move," María said as they reached the porch.

"We haven't."

"I don't understand."

"She will reconsider selling if she believes I'm leaving."

"You mean we're not?"

"So anxious to see Barcelona?"

When he looked at his mother, his eyes overflowed. "She's gone, Mamita."

Doña Esther smiled sympathetically, put her hand on his, and whispered intimately, "It is God's will, Carlito."

"Yes, Mamita."

The Confession

Father Otis had been sitting in the confessional for almost an hour with his shoes off and the door open. St. Timothy's was the coolest place in town on summer mornings. Fanning himself with a missal, he was studying the stained glass windows. "Twenty," he thought, "one for each year of my priesthood." Unlike the classic figures of the older churches he grew up with, St. Timothy's abstract images evoked only chaos.

Shafts of light stood like giant luminous planks leaning against the walls. They slid upright as the sun climbed into the sky, as if they too were slowly waking. Always fascinating, the dancing dust that gives substance to the slanted light pillars never settle—always moving, suspended in the vastness, like his soul. Morning confessions offered repose, a time when he could finish waking. He thought of it as meditation, but in truth it was more an attempt to erase thought, to make his mind empty, like the vast space in the church. That great dark angular interior had always felt to Father Otis like another expression of God's mystery: enveloping, yet hard, inscrutable. But lately he had wondered about his role in God's plan. While the walls and pillars of gray granite seemed to absorb the leaning light beams, only the gilded altar's gleaming arabesques and holy icons reflected their rays. Like a golden moon in a deep sky, the altar shone brilliant in the otherwise bleak vault reminding Father Otis of Jesus's message to a deaf, stony world. But unlike Jesus's simple words, that gilded tableau spoke in arrogant stillness. Father Otis had never reconciled the church's wealth with the plight of its poor. Perhaps those riches could wake the poor to God's glory, but they could not ease their hunger.

Unlike his other duties the confessional allowed Father Otis to fill his own emptiness with the emptiness of others. A life of repetitious ritual incantations and deadening routine was far from the thrilling expectations of his youth, and hearing others' problems seemed to lighten his own. The relief was only temporary but welcome, like swimming in a cool spring on a hot summer afternoon. As pastor of St. Timothy's he kept busy, but the administrative work of running a parish—raising money, overseeing the parish school, courting politicians—and the masses, baptisms, funerals, and weddings left him mentally numb and tired to the bone without the pleasant fatigue that physical exertion brings.

"Bless me Father, for I have sinned. It's been almost a year since my last confession."

"Yes, my son."

As Father Otis prepared to listen he leaned back against the back of the confessional, smoothed back his thinning black hair with one hand, and continued fanning himself with the other.

"I cursed at my wife."

"Why did you do that, my son?"

"She made me mad with her nagging. Can't stand me around the house."

"Love the good in her, my son. You loved her once. Concentrate on what attracted you to her. And while you're at it, try to get out more, see friends. It'll give you some new things to talk about."

"Yes, Father."

"Is there something else, my son?"

"I guess not, Father."

"Say five Hail Marys and one Our Father, and try to replace your anger with love for her as a human being. I absolve you of your sins. Now go and sin no more."

As the man left mumbling to himself, Father Otis mused on the poor man's predicament, "Retired: a life sentence with a hostile cell mate."

Engrossed in his mental rambling he didn't notice the man that had entered the confessional. The man remained standing for a moment before sitting and seemed out of breath.

"I'm sorry. I didn't hear you come in." Hearing nothing, he said, "Well?"

"Father, I've done something unspeakable."

"How long has it been since your last confession, my son?"

The man gasped, "I'm not . . ."

"That's all right. Go on, my son."

The man began to sob violently, bent over with his face in his hands. Father Otis sat up and saw that he was an African-American.

"Come now, you'll feel better when you start."

Whispering, the man said, "Father, I have just murdered my wife and daughter."

"My God!" With pounding heart and labored breath, Father Otis felt as if someone had poured ice water over his shoulders. Fighting to control himself he again said, "My God!"

Both men were silent for several seconds before Father Otis could collect himself. The resignation and agony in the man's voice assured the priest that he was telling the truth.

"How could you? How could you murder . . . I can't . . . You're not human. How dare you come to beg forgiveness?"

Father Otis was nearly shouting. Before he turned to look at the man, he was gone.

"Wait. Come back."

By the time Father Otis could put on his shoes and walk around the confessional, all he could see was the church door slowly swinging closed. Hoping to get a better look at him, Father Otis jogged to the front of the church, pushed open the massive front door that had almost closed and saw the man running down the street. Though he hadn't seen his face clearly, Father Otis thought he might have seen him at a recent mass. "Must be crazy; probably didn't kill anybody. Some people make up stories like that as outlets for their guilt," he thought as he let the door shut out the morning heat.

The rest of the day dragged by as Father Otis wondered what he should do. *If he really did it, who knows what he'll do next? I'll call the police. I'll ask if there were any deaths reported today, but they would want to know how I . . . If only he hadn't stormed out I might have talked him into turning himself in.* His duty to his church and to society crossed like bloody swords.

By late-afternoon Father Otis had calmed down. Listening to a Public Radio music program as he read through his mail, he froze when the hourly news blurted: "Harold Pitt, his wife, and their six-year-old daughter were found dead in their home, victims of an apparent murder-suicide. Pitt is a chemistry professor at the state university. Mrs. Pitt is a former member of the City Council."

My God! He went home and committed suicide. Compounded the sin. Maybe it's better that way. At least he won't do any more harm. " Father Otis tried vainly to imagine a more sinful act, shuddering that he had sat in the shadow of such evil. *How can there be forgiveness for such an act?*

The housekeeper came into his study to find Father Otis standing before a mirror fastening his collar with his jacket draped over his arm.

"Mrs. Olivera is here to see you, Father."

"Tell her to come back later, Agnes."

"She says she wants to talk about her will."

"Not now. Be polite, but I have to go to the police station." Thrusting one arm through his jacket sleeve he said, "I might have been the last person to see Pitt alive."

"Who?"

"Professor Pitt, the man who killed his wife and children this morning."

"How awful!"

"I might be able to absolve his wife of wrongdoing and perhaps help clear up part of the mystery."

The slow traffic afforded him time to meditate. But the sun blazing down like a giant, spectral demon distracted him from serious thought. At one stop light the glare off the car ahead nearly blinded him. Stopping, starting, twisting through the business district he finally reached the police station, but had to park two blocks away. The sun's raging breath blasted down like retribution. Averting his eyes from the angry sun, he longed for the cool darkness of St. Timothy's. Only the rare exhilaration of such an important act—murder—could have drawn him out of St. Timothy's that hot afternoon.

The air-conditioned building offered a welcome reprieve.

"I'm Father Thomas Otis of St. Timothy's. I'd like to speak with someone about Professor Pitt, the man who died this morning."

"One moment, please." The desk sergeant walked into one of the offices, and in a moment returned with a stocky man in his early forties, adjusting his tie as he approached Father Otis.

"Thanks for coming in, Father. I'm Lieutenant Garcia. We were about to pay you a visit. I understand you saw Professor Pitt this morning."

"How did you know that?"

"Tell us what happened, Father."

"It was my morning to hear confessions. I had heard one earlier, just before an African-American man came in panting; he had been running. I couldn't get a good look, but he sounded excited."

"A parishioner"

"No. I have few Black parishioners, and I know them all."

"How did you know it was Pitt?"

"I didn't. I figured it out when I heard the four o'clock news on the radio."

"Go on."

"I knew right away that he wasn't Catholic; he didn't know the ritual."

"Right, but what did he say?"

"That he'd murdered his wife and daughter. When I tried to talk to him, he ran away."

"What did you say to him?"

"I was shocked beyond words. I asked how he could have done such a ghastly thing."

"Thanks for coming in. You've been very helpful." The police lieutenant politely escorted Father Otis to the door.

On the way out Father Otis said, "It was terrible. Very disturbing. Horrible, horrible. What a monster."

"Thanks again, Father."

"Can you tell me if he has family in town?"

"A sister named Petula Pitt. It'll be in the papers tomorrow."

"Did he leave a suicide note?" Father Otis asked as he opened the door and felt the wall of hot air lean against him.

"We're not at liberty to discuss details."

"Of course. Well, please call on me if I can help."

"We will. Thanks again."

Father Otis would not be so easily pacified. He went directly into the rectory office to search the computer file. Always intimidated by the computer, he searched, moving and clicking the mouse, and mumbling, *Dumb, insensitive, inhuman machine. So damned efficient if only I could figure it out.* Finally in the membership file he found no Harold Pitt. Sally Pitt appeared as a member of St. Timothy's Parish; her husband, Harold, was listed as non-Catholic, and their daughter, Pearl was listed as Catholic. *I was right: he wasn't Catholic. Unusual for a non-Catholic to come to confession.* Then he looked up Petula Pitt in the telephone directory.

"Father Otis, supper is ready," the housekeeper said.

"Not now, Agnes. Got to go out again."

Petula Pitt's house was nearby, so Father Otis walked. By now his curiosity was soaring. This rare excitement in his otherwise dull life had generated a surprising surge of energy. He was enjoying the riddle and his connection to a murder investigation. He didn't relish going to a wake, but he walked on.

Parked cars filled Petula Pitt's neighborhood. Her front door opened to reveal a slim, middle-aged Black woman. Behind her, the living room was filled with people.

"Ms. Pitt?"

"Yes."

"I'm Father Otis, pastor of St. Timothy's Catholic Church. I hope I'm not intruding. I've come to offer condolences."

Petula Pitt began to cry. After a few moments she said, "Come in, Father. It has been a terrible shock. I didn't realize how bad it had gotten for them."

Father Otis sat on an overstuffed chair across a coffee table from Petula Pitt, a large, white leather-covered Bible lying on the table between them. A young woman passed among the crowd offering coffee.

"I saw your brother this morning. He was beside himself. What a ghastly thing."

She began to cry again. After a few moments she regained her composure and said, "Did you know his wife was terminally ill?"

"No, I didn't. They were not regulars at St Timothy's. Perhaps I could have helped if I had known."

Petula Pitt looked into his eyes with a vacant expression that made him uncomfortable. "Perhaps so, Father." She opened the Bible on the coffee table and extracted some folded sheets. "The police took the original and made me this photocopy. Harold left it."

"Are you sure it's all right? The police . . ."

She nodded, and Father Otis began to read, as Petula Pitt rose to speak with one of the mourners.

Dear Petty,

I hope you can forgive what I have done and what I am about to do. As you know, Sally's pain had become unbearable. The thought of spending her last days in agony terrified her as much as death itself. Eventually she resigned herself to the awful reality and began talking about ending her life. Imagine that girl who loved life so much. She felt she could not do it herself and asked me to do it, but how could I? She would smile at me through the excruciating pain and softly whisper, "Please, if you love me . . . but not yet . . . when the time comes." I saw her decline day by day into the gray world between life and death. One night she told me her life was ending before her body died, and that she wanted to erase that last interval. She knew the doctors wouldn't help. When the abyss of death had become more a promise than a condemnation, God help me, I agreed. That quieted her, and in a way she looked more beautiful than she ever had. She asked only that I not tell her when I was going to do it.

Last evening I brought ten grams of sodium cyanide home from the lab. It's quickest and least painful. I didn't sleep thinking about what I was about to do and wasn't at all sure I could do it. This morning I dissolved the cyanide in some orange juice. I planned to leave one glass with Sally at her bedside as I always did for her to drink later in the morning, and then take Pearl to school before she could know what had happened. I couldn't bear to be there when Sally drank it. I would return home to write this note to you explaining what had happened and attaching it to the will that Sally and I prepared weeks ago. Then I would drink the second glass of juice because I knew I couldn't live with what would be on my conscience. Without thinking, I left my glass of juice on the kitchen counter and went into our bedroom. I put Sally's juice on the night table and kissed her knowing it would be the last time. I told her I would give Pearl her breakfast and take her to school and go to the University for a while. When I walked into Pearl's room to call her to breakfast as I always did, she wasn't there. At that instant, horrified, I ran to the kitchen and found my poor child on the floor. She had drunk some of the juice thinking it was for her. The glass was half full and still on the counter. I tried to revive her, but it was no use. The next thing I remember was lifting my forehead off the floor and trying to get up. When reality again hit me, I ran out of the house not knowing where I was going. Somehow I ended up at the church. Sally loved St. Timothy's. I thought I might find her there or at least find some understanding. I found neither and returned home to write this and found Sally lying by Pearl on the kitchen floor. She must have heard the commotion, come in, figured out what had happened, and drunk the rest of Pearl's juice. I moved them both to their beds and found Sally's untouched glass by her bed. I can't stand another minute of the evil I have done. Forgive me.

Harold

Father Otis left the unfolded paper on the Bible that still lay open on the coffee table. Petula Pitt watched him walk to the door, open it, and walk out dazed.

"Poor man," she whispered.

Thomas Otis walked through air that felt like syrup. A low-lying branch scraped his head; he barely reacted. The temperature had fallen slightly with the setting sun. The brief red glow in the sky was yielding gently to deep blue night. Thomas Otis saw none of that. Like a deaf, blind man he walked along the deserted street past St. Timothy's wondering where he could go.

Goals

He was at his desk writing when I walked up. Without waiting, I said, "Mr. Lazzara, I'm interested in working in stocks and bonds and would like to talk with you about a job."

"How old are you, son?"

"Twenty-two."

"No brokerage house hires brokers under twenty-six. But it doesn't matter because we don't have any openings. Sorry." Lazzara resumed his writing.

"I knew that when I asked to see you, but when I tell you about myself, you might overlook my age. I can help your business. Merrill Lynch made me an offer, but I'd rather work for this firm."

"Is that a fact? What's so great about your background?"

"I have an accounting degree from Notre Dame University, and I can sell."

"Tell me how you got to be a red-hot salesman."

"I worked at Tampa Dodge my first summer in Notre Dame. At first they said the same thing, but they hired me, and that summer I sold as many cars as their top salesman. For the next three years I paid all my university expenses selling new cars in summers."

After staring at me a few moments, Sam Lazzara said, "Come back tomorrow morning at 8:30 and be ready to start training. Oh, and call me Sam."

With three months of training, exams, and two trips to Wall Street, I was finally cold calling to people on a list Sam gave me. I had been on the telephone all morning, all week actually, calling total strangers trying to get their business. Rejections and hang-ups never get me down; if one out of fifty calls leads to a new account, it's worth it. And I can do it in a comfortable, air-conditioned office with other people around to break the monotony, not in some dinky bookkeeper's room in a packinghouse or citrus concentrate plant. I don't know how I stood that accounting job as long as I did. It was boring and confining, and it would take years to get anywhere. I spent days without talking to anyone, just poring over balance sheets and columns of numbers. Don't ask me why I went with Price Waterhouse. Probably because everyone was dying to work for a Big Seven firm; it's the grand prize for accounting majors, you know. But the stock market has always fascinated me. It's a gigantic garden, filled with candies, fruits, goodies of all kinds. You just pluck what you like and sink your teeth. You need never go hungry in the market; whether people buy or sell, whether stocks rise or fall, commissions come in.

It was early September. One week of cold calling had netted me eighteen new accounts. And finally I was meeting girls. Some of my best cold calls were single working women who were as lonely as I was. There was one, Diane. I really liked her. We went out a couple of times to a really neat bar near the office, but she was too cautious, too worried about getting into a relationship. Well, it didn't matter. They're out there, and if there's one thing I can sell, it's myself.

On my first Friday of actual selling, I passed Sam's desk on my way to the coffee pot, and he stopped me.

"Jesse, I want you to meet Lucius Helling, a client of mine. I told him a little about you, and he wants to meet you."

At first I couldn't take my eyes off his thick red hair, neatly trimmed red beard, and green eyes. Otherwise, Lucius was not unusual; he was reasonably well-built, medium height.

"My friends call me Lucky. Sam tells me you're a recent Notre Dame graduate, Summa Cum Laude, and that you're a first-rate salesman."

"I'm doing OK, I guess."

"And you're an accountant?"

"Well, I majored in accounting, but I didn't really plan to be an accountant. I just figured it would be a good foundation for a business career."

"Good thinking. Sorry I don't have much time right now, but the way Sam's been bragging about you, I'd like to get better acquainted. Why don't you have dinner with my wife and me? When would be a good day for you?"

This guy was only a few years older than me; early thirties, I would guess. I wondered if he was on the level. "I have a pretty loose schedule; just about any day, Mr. Helling."

"You'll have to call me Lucky. How about Monday evening: sevenish?"

"Fine. Thanks."

Lucius reached into his coat pocket and pulled out a printed set of directions for getting to his house in a new, posh subdivision north of town. "See you Monday, Jesse."

"What's with this guy?" I asked Sam after Lucius walked out.

"Lucky's a good client and a very nice guy. He's new to Florida and wants to meet people and make business contacts. He's OK."

To tell the truth I'd forgotten the invitation when the phone rang Monday morning. It was Lucky calling to confirm. "See you tonight?"

"I'll be there." Lucky's relaxed, sincere demeanor was hard to resist. I figured I might as well go; who knows, I might learn something. And it was a free meal.

I felt foolish standing at the door of the sprawling, beige stucco house, wondering whether to ring the bell or turn around and leave. Before I could do either, the door opened. Lucky was wearing a short-sleeve shirt with a western string tie, cowboy boots, and jeans.

"Good to see you, Jesse; glad you could make it; I saw you standing out here and decided not to wait for the door bell."

"Hi, Mr. Helling."

"Please. My friends call me Lucky. Here, let me take your jacket. Barbara will join us in a minute. What'll you drink? We don't use alcohol, but we'd be glad to fix you a cocktail if you like. Barbara, this is Jesse; Jesse, Barbara." Barbara was a pretty brunette, though a little chunky.

Walking into the spacious ranch house I felt I had been transplanted to Texas or New Mexico. With cactus plants and flowers sprouting out of clay pots scattered over the tile floor it could have been a model for Better Homes and Gardens. The Spanish, rough-hewn furniture fit in with the Southwest look and was arranged to focus on the huge

43

fireplace crowned with an enormous pair of Texas long horns. Flames added brilliant color to the beautiful room. I was impressed.

"The fire feels good even on a hot day," I said. "You'd never know it was summer."

"We keep the air conditioner set cold so we can light a fire in the evening. Like Nixon used to do in the White House," Lucky said, laughing.

I walked toward the rear to look out of the large windows. The whole back yard was a rock garden complete with cactus, sea oats, and grape vines. Sculptured hedges, splashes of wild desert flowers, and carefully placed wooden lawn furniture surrounded the far side of the kidney-shaped swimming pool.

"Barbara, why don't you show Jesse the pool area," Lucky said. "I'll put the salad together." Barbara took my hand and led me out to a thatched hut that overhung the near end of the pool and served as a bar. Rising from the bottom of the pool along the bar were three raised tile seats.

"In the evening, when we aren't working, we like to sit waist-deep in the pool, have a limeade, and talk about our plans for the future," she said. She looked into my eyes, squeezed my hand, and pulled me close. I didn't know how to react; you know, whether to shake loose or squeeze back. I held on and she smiled. I figured I could have her in the sack in no time, but wouldn't try. "Maybe next time I can bring my swim suit, and we can go for a dip," I said.

"That would be wonderful."

"Shouldn't we see what Lucky's up to?" I said.

"The salad'll keep him busy for a while. Don't you like our patio?"

"Sure. I like the atmosphere, and the company, too." I could be wrong, but I'd swear she was coming on to me. We walked around the pool and went inside. The family room came into view with a large-screen television dominating one corner. On the opposite corner a glossy black grand piano captured my attention. I walked over to it and saw the famous Steinway name. A small vase of artificial yellow wild flowers stood over a red Spanish mantilla. On one wall hung a Mexican serape with a guitar hanging on one side and a wooden piece cut and painted to resemble a totem pole on the other. It had no strings, only flowers sprouting from its opening. It looked bizarre but interesting. On the wall behind the piano hung a large contemporary painting of a desert sunset with lots of reds and yellows.

"This is beautiful, Barbara. Your house is outstanding. Maybe some day I'll have a place like this." After a pause I said, "If the offer still stands, I'll have whatever Lucky's drinking."

"Another limeade, please, darling."

In a moment Lucky approached me with the limeade. "It feels like Arizona or New Mexico. Are you from out west?"

"No, we're both from New Hampshire. Never been out west actually. One of these days, maybe. We both like the Southwest ambiance, though. It's relaxed, yet classy; don't you think, Jesse?"

For a while Lucky and I juggled topics like light colored balls; I'm sure neither of us could say later what we had talked about, pleasant though it was. I had to stifle a smile when he said he was the Chief Administrator for the City Sanitation Department. He either caught it or maybe explained out of habit that his office is just down the hall from the Mayor's: "My job is very demanding; I'm responsible for a department of 780 employees. Barbara teaches hygiene and health in a high school in south Tampa. She loves her job, even with the long drive every morning and afternoon."

"That's right," she said as she joined us. "Ninth graders; the real challenge is dealing with all the snickering and giggling."

Barbara sat on the armrest next to her husband with her arm around his shoulder. "Dinner will be ready in just a few minutes," she said as she smiled and winked at me.

Lucky reached for a magazine, opened it, and showed it to me with a broad smile. "What do you think?"

The Ferrari ad showed a long-legged blonde in the passenger seat and a tall, handsome young stud, complete with black, drooping moustache, sliding in behind her. "I like sports cars too. "I have a Dodge Challenger."

"I drive a Honda," Lucky said, "but I'm going to have one of these babies. You have to order them months in advance, you know. Must feel great to drive one."

"Been interested in sports cars long?" I said.

"Actually no. Cars are a recent addiction. One of our goals is a classy red one. You know, Jesse, if you want to get anywhere, you have to set goals. Without goals you're a ship with no tiller, a car with no steering wheel. Goals set you on a path; they give you something to work toward."

"That's certainly true," I said. "Right now I'm looking forward to having a thick account book of clients, so I won't have to spend my days making cold calls. They get awfully tedious and aggravating."

"When Barbara and I got married, our first goal was to own our own home. We both worked, but even with out combined incomes it wasn't easy. Then we heard of Amway."

"Is that why you invited me over?" I said. "To talk about Amway?"

"To be honest, partly. You're a very impressive young fellow, Jesse. Intelligent, good looking, outgoing personality, and you obviously like people. You're the perfect type for Amway. But even if you told me right now you were interested in joining the Amway family, I wouldn't encourage you."

"Why not?"

"Because it's bad policy to recruit people in transition. You've just embarked on a new career. We wouldn't recruit someone who was recently married, or divorced. We want people with your qualifications, but who are well along in their careers, sort of gliding along on a plateau, people who are looking for a special challenge and aren't afraid to set goals and aspire to great things. But we can talk more another time, when you're ready." With that, Lucky, showing a new intensity, leaned toward me and said, "What do you want in life, Jesse?"

"Success, of course."

"OK, but specifically, where would you like to be in ten years? What would you like to be doing?"

"I haven't really thought about that; I guess I should though, huh?"

"See what I mean? You just graduated from college last year, and you've already changed jobs. You're about 22, and you're probably still trying to figure out where you'll live, with whom, and what you'll be doing next year. You have a good bit of short-term, unfinished business to work out, so your long-range goals are vague. Don't get me wrong; that's natural for someone in transition. In a year maybe you'll be ready."

I was starting to feel a little uncomfortable listening to this guy who seemed to know everything about me, so I tried to take control of the topic: "I met the president of Amway a couple of years ago at Notre Dame. He was on our lecture series."

"No kidding? What's he like? I've never met him; a great man. Everyone in the company idolizes him." Lucky rose and we moved to the dining room.

"He's the most persuasive person I've ever heard," I said. "I waited to meet him and told him he should run for president of the United States."

"Wow! You actually talked to him? He'd win, too," Lucky said.

An embroidered off-white tablecloth covered the antique looking, Spanish, wooden table. The severe, tall, leather-backed chairs felt more comfortable than they looked. Barbara brought out beef fajitas with refried beans, Mexican rice, salsa, corn chips, and Caesar's salad.

"Lucky made the rice and beans yesterday afternoon; I did the rest. We share household work and everything else in our lives."

"I also made the salad, Darling," Lucky said smiling.

"That's right, dear."

I didn't tell them I don't like Mexican cooking very much. I can't take all the hot spices, but it wasn't bad; it wasn't too hot at all.

"You can add Jalapenos or Tabasco if you want," Barbara said as she helped herself to some. "We love spicy Mexican food, but some people don't, so we don't add hot peppers when we have guests."

"This is fine."

Dinner conversation never drifted far from the subject of goals and finances. For dessert Barbara brought out fresh fruit in a sweet sauce. "Barbara and I have earned enough money this year to make a substantial down payment on a new house with professional landscaping."

"But this house is beautiful. How long have you lived here?"

"A little over a year," Lucky said. "But we're ready to expand our horizons; you know, move on. Our next house will be Polynesian style. This one doesn't really work in Florida. With all the rain, it's hard to maintain the desert look. Weeds and mold insist on spoiling our rock garden. We consulted our banker. He said we can easily afford a bigger mortgage with our combined incomes, so we're going for a bigger house."

"You asked the banker how much you could afford?"

"Absolutely." His eyes sparkled; he seemed happy to have caught my interest. "We incur as much debt as we can afford. The greater our financial obligation, the harder we have to work. Always keep in mind, Jesse, that the road to success is narrow but simple: hard work."

The logic was sound but unconvincing. It had never occurred to me to get into debt as a way to get ahead and said, "I'll have to think about that."

"We're also planning a weeklong trip to Europe next summer: England, France, Germany, and Switzerland," Barbara said.

"Isn't that a lot to see in one week?"

"We can't afford more time."

"I'd like to go to Europe some day," I said.

Lucky smiled, "You will if you set it as a goal and work toward it."

"Of course, the trip will depend on how well our business goes this year," Barbara said. "If things go well, and they will if we give it our best, we'll be able to get the Ferrari the following year."

"How do you do all this Amway business with your full-time jobs?"

Lucky smiled. "It isn't easy. Our long-range goal is to quit our regular jobs in a few years and devote ourselves entirely to Amway. By that time, our business should be at the level where we can sustain ourselves entirely from it. Then the sky's the limit."

"Sounds like you have your lives all planned out. What do you do for fun?"

"We don't have time for extracurriculars," Lucky said. "We plan to start a family after we leave our regular jobs. In the meantime, we take a golf lesson once in a while. In a few years we'll join a country club and take up the game seriously."

"I was on the Notre Dame golf team for four years."

"Surely you don't have time to play now," Barbara said.

"Once in a while. I try to make time for things I like."

"Maybe some day we'll be able to afford that luxury." Lucky said. I think I saw Barbara's face droop.

"Well, I only play once a month or less," I said, feeling guilty. These people were making me feel I was cheating on my job. Hearing and seeing how they organized their lives was inspiring, but a little scary. I had never seen such total commitment and planned to do some serious thinking when I got home.

The conversation gave me some ideas to ponder, but it also depressed me a little. Somehow, I felt I was slipping into a pit. Don't get me wrong. They were nice, but their lives seemed robot-like; you know, programmed.

After dessert I said, "I noticed the Steinway in the family room. Which one of you plays?"

"Neither of us. Do you play?" Barbara said

"Yes, but I'm a little out of practice. I don't have much time to practice these days." That was a lie; I make time to play almost every day. "I have an old tinny upright. One day I'll have a grand piano. The sound is so much richer."

"I wish I could ask you to play for us, but I'm afraid you couldn't play this piano. We bought it at a warehouse closeout sale. The sound was only fair, but the woodwork caught our eye. Lucky had the lovely idea of refinishing the exterior and taking the works out and installing our new sound system equipment in it. He also took out the old, yellowed ivory keys and replaced them with new, white plastic keys. Aren't they beautiful? When we want to play a CD, we just raise the top, and the sound comes out of the piano. It sounds simply grand," she chuckled.

As Barbara removed the mantilla and raised the lid, I walked up. "Come look inside," she said. As I came near, Barbara put her arm around my waist. I must admit, I felt a little revolted by her smile; it looked more like a sneer. And I felt uncomfortable standing there with her arm around me. I peered into the piano. A tuner, speakers, CD player, and other electronic equipment with tangles of electric wires interconnecting them had replaced the regular, parallel array of piano strings. The electric wires were randomly strewn about like the guts of a dead animal on the highway. I felt sorry for the piano. It was the victim of a senseless, brutal assassination.

"What would you like to hear?" she said.

I didn't answer. How could they destroy a magnificent instrument to play recordings? Someone could have played it even if the sound wasn't great. Reminded me of a revolting TV commercial in which a grand piano falls from a tall building and crashes on the sidewalk. I can't stand to watch it. They ripped out part of their humanity when they gutted this piano. It was like trading in your heart for a new suit.

Unable to contain my revulsion I said, "It's a shame to ruin a Steinway."

"Don't feel bad," Lucky said. "It's not really a Steinway. I had the logo put on when it was refinished. It's really just an old Chickering."

I didn't tell them that Chickering was a great piano, too, in its day. The ridiculous flower-pot guitar was bad enough, but defiling an instrument like this was unforgivable.

Lucky inserted a CD into the player. I figured that at least the music would offer a respite from the onslaught of their sermonizing. Without knowing it, Lucky had chosen one of my favorite piano pieces. The glorious sound of Vladimir Horowitz playing Liszt's Second Hungarian Rhapsody crashed out of the Steinway.

"Sounds like Horowitz is actually playing right here in the room, doesn't it?" Lucky said. We all sat down. Lucky would say something every few minutes while I tried to listen to the music. I was as anxious to avoid talking as I was to hear the music. The evening spun down with the musical crescendo.

Finally I looked toward the door and said, "I've got a lot of work to do tonight; I should be on my way."

"Happy to have you in our home, Jesse. We'll have you again soon," Barbara said.

As the mutilated piano strained to offer up the vibrant climax, I tried to smile, but I knew it wouldn't hide the emptiness I felt. I stood at the door a moment. The house looked different now. The light seemed brighter and hotter; I now saw that the walls weren't plaster or adobe, but dry wall; the taped joints showed through in the shattering light. And the furniture looked hard. The imitation adobe house was really more barren than any desert; I had the strange sensation that it might crumble into a cloud of dust. I opened the door and turned. For a brief moment no one spoke.

"Thanks for dinner and the advice," I said. Together, we conducted the small talk to its coda. The Hellings stood at the door hand in hand, smiling, framed by the hot glow of the interior lighting. I heard the resolution of the great C sharp minor cadence as I walked down the stone path toward my car. The humid air felt like warm arms. The stars sparkled cool and comforting, more beautiful than I had ever realized. They looked perfectly poised and balanced in the deep, dark sky. Two thoughts squeezed into my mind: try to get in a round of golf after work tomorrow, and call Diane; maybe she'd like to help me look for a grand piano.

The Ball Player

He was fighting sleep and losing. His father could see it, but continued reading. The next time his father looked up from the book, Joey had gathered his ten years and his baseball glove and bat to himself and had fallen asleep locked in a running position. Smiling the smile children never see, the father stood over his small son in the large bed for a few moments and tip-toed out, turning off the light and closing the door behind him.

As the batter swung and missed, bringing the inning to a close, Joey stood, socking his fist into his glove. A home run or even a base hit would drive in another run for the Orioles.

The Orioles were up in the ninth inning. Cal Ripken was first up to bat. After two swings and misses, Ripken delivered a tremendous wallop, and the ball seemed to go straight up into the sky. For a moment Joey lost sight of it in the blinding haze. Now it was coming down toward him.

His heart pounded, his glove ready. As if from heaven it seemed to be falling a little in front of Joey. He didn't have room to step forward. As the seams became clearly visible Joey stretched his left hand over the head of the fat man in front of him. The man was talking to the man next to him and had not seen the ball. It was falling directly at the fat man. Joey stretched and reached as high as he could above the man's head. As the ball hit the glove, Joey closed his eyes. He opened them to see himself waving it back and forth for everyone to see. He threw the ball into his glove a couple of times so everyone near him could see it. It was his first fly ball ever, and he couldn't stop grinning.

At first he didn't notice the fat man talking to him.

"You might have saved my life, young man," he said.

"What? It's my ball; I caught it."

"I know, I know, and I thank you for catching it. If you hadn't, it would have hit me on the head and probably knocked me out."

"Oh; gee. Thank you, Sir."

"No, thank you."

"Uh, well yeah, I guess so," said Joey, still not fully comprehending.

"How'd you like to have a couple of season passes to the rest of the Yankee games this season? It's the least I can do by way of saying thanks for saving my life," the fat man said.

"Wow! Thanks."

The conversation continued for a while leading the man to marvel at how much Joey knew about the Yankees and baseball in general. Joey confided after a while that he planned to play major league baseball when he grew up. "I play little league ball now and don't mind saying it: I'm the best hitter in the league."

"How old are you, son?"

"Ten."

"You're big for your age. Say; I have an idea. I'm with the Yankees, and I happen to know that the team is always on the lookout for talented boys who want to play ball. You're a little young, but . . . how would you like to try out for the junior team?"

"I never heard of it, Sir."

"Not many people have. We don't publicize it. But we have a group of young boys who are good ball players and who want to learn. Interested?"

"You bet."

Joey walked to the plate not as nervous as he expected to be. He hadn't noticed that the leadoff pitcher, Dwight Gooden, was already at the mound. "Oh no!" he thought. Gooden wound up and threw the ball. It made a loud clap as it hit the catcher's mitt; Joey never saw it. "What have I done?" he thought, as he looked at the pitcher. Joe Girardi fired the ball back to Gooden, who threw it into his glove a couple of times, adjusted his cap, spit, stepped back, and started his windup again. This time he decided to take it easy on the kid. The first pitch was just to introduce him to the real world. The ball came at Joey. This time he saw it. As it neared the plate, Joey guessed it would be a strike. He gave it all he had with his undersized bat, felt a tremendous connection as if body, bat, and ball were, for a split second, a single unit. He watched the ball rise, up and up until it hit something. The scoreboard lights shattered followed by the sound of falling glass.

Joey stood there for several seconds unable to move. Joe Girardi, slapped him on the shoulder and said something he did not understand. Gooden again wound up, feeling slightly sheepish. Another fastball shot across the plate, only this time Joey saw it clearly. Again he connected and sent the ball into the center field fence. By this time, the entire team had surrounded Joey. He heard words that barely penetrated his brain; things like, "Nice work, kid," and "Where did you learn to hit like that?"

"OK, kid. Go out to third base," shouted Joe Torre. "Let's see what you can do in the infield." After a few pitches and foul balls, the batter hit one that bounced once and fell into Joey's glove. Without thinking and with a perfectly fluid motion, he shot it to first base like a bullet.

Tino Martinez caught the ball at first base then took off his glove to look at his hand.

There was no end of the amazement in the locker room, especially with Joe Torre and the bald, fat man, who said, "That boy's ready."

Joey was fourth in the batting lineup. The Orioles were already warmed up and the first pitch would come over the plate as soon as the Star-Spangled Banner and cheering were over. The first three batters were the best on the team: Tino Martinez, Paul O'Neal, and Derek Jeter. Each one went to bat and struck out with Mussina's first three pitches. Joey was angry that he didn't get to bat, but he was also relieved that he wouldn't have to face that monster Mussina for another few minutes.

In the top of the second inning Joey caught a short fly ball near third base and put out a runner who was trying to steal second base. The third out came on the next pitch when the batter hit a line drive to third base and Joey caught it, stinging his left hand.

Mussina wound up and sent his fastball across the plate. Joey did not swing—a strike. He swung at the second pitch and missed. After staring at the catcher for what seemed to be minutes, Mussina hurled a ball, then another, then another. The count was three and two. A drop of perspiration rolled down Joey's back and gave him a strange chill. The pitcher began his windup and stopped in the middle of it.

He looked at the catcher, who was signaling a change in strategy. As the pitcher wound up, his left leg rose, his right arm seemed to reach down into the earth, and Joey felt a tug at his shoulder.

"Not now," he said.

"Come on Joey. Time to get up. Didn't you hear me calling?"

Eyes rolling, Joey was holding his bat with both hands lying on his side in bed.

The Immigrant's Son

With a canvas bag in each hand and a bundle of fig plants under his arm the teenage boy stepped down the gangplank. After three weeks in steerage he felt liberated stepping on hard earth. The people looked strange, nothing like his uncle in Sicily, who had driven him to the ship in a horse-drawn wagon. He had packed everything he planned to use for the rest of his life, all his worldly possessions, in two cloth bags. But most important was the bundle of fig plants he nestled under his arm. Throughout the trip he had kept the roots moist and wrapped. The sacred fruit from the old country would nourish his new family and neighbors. He knew none of the Tampa relatives he would meet that morning.

Decades later that immigrant's son, now a young father, remembering his recently-departed father, planted a magnolia tree that eventually produced a deep green halo over his house. Yearly that deep green halo would burst into giant white flowers.

On a cold morning years later this immigrant's son, now well into his fifties, awoke flush with tragic insight and methodically felled that magnificent magnolia tree. Slick with sweat, he hacked it down, for only he had the right. With blade screaming in his breast he hacked sturdy limbs and finally the trunk, then stacked the pieces into piles to be hauled away. That evening he sat alone by the fireplace. Knowing him well, no one dared ask why; he offered no explanation.

On a crushingly hot day years later, now feeble and stooped, this immigrant's son stopped talking. During this time of silence his now middle-aged son Charlie would sit beside him on the sofa after supper and talk to him, vainly hoping for a response. On one of these evenings with his arm around the old man's shoulder, he said, "Please, Papa, talk to me. It's been months." But the old man sat silent, unmoved, lips pursed, face calm, and continued to look out the window. "I love you, Papa. Please, let me hear your voice again."

After a long pause and without turning to look at his son, the old immigrant's son said, "Don't bother me. I'm playing with my brother and sister."

A Fleeting Fragment

Nothing helps—neither aspirin nor Tylenol—nothing. My head feels like it'll explode. I try not to move and lie down with a rolled up towel under my neck. That sometimes helps . . . Ah, that's better.

I think I slept . . . my neck and back feel relaxed finally. I'll lie here a while longer. I don't want it to start hurting again. I can move my head now; my neck doesn't hurt.

Why is everybody staring? "Don't worry. I'm fine; just a little tired, and the pain's gone." They look so sad. Sybil's crying. "Please don't, Honey. I'm fine; really."

"Professor Jackson! How good to see you. It's been fifty . . . no, sixty years. I'd forgotten how tall you were. And you're not dragging your leg the way you did then.

"Good morning, Lad. Don't get up yet. There's no hurry."

"The campus looks green and bright, Professor; even more beautiful than I remembered. And it's so quiet and peaceful. Look, there's Leigh Hall."

"All things change, Lad. This is the campus you remember. It looked greener and brighter then. You see clearly now as you once did, when the university was smaller and life was simpler. But . . . everything changes."

"There's Dad! Hi, Dad."

"You look fine, boy."

"Uh-huh. Just a little tired, that's all. That ache in my neck was getting me down, but it's OK now. Still work in your shop?"

"No. I can take it easy now."

"Mom! You look wonderful! It's been so long."

"Come, Sonny. We're going to the five and ten cent store."

"They still have the toy department in the basement?"

"Of course."

I reach up for her hand as we walk toward the bright city center.

Jesse's Sin

Where is she now? After all these years her image surfaces, sitting beside him in senior English class. Two months before graduation he asks the angelic, strawberry blonde to a dance. He doesn't expect her to accept. She does. They have great fun. Yes, and he tingles each time he takes her hand. He smiles; she blushes. On their way home she wants to park by the bay. She loves the watery view by moonlight. They walk along the cloud-covered shore. Returning to the car he starts the engine. Letting her head fall back as if to relax, she says, "Let's talk a while." He turns off the engine and turns to her. She stares back strangely, imploringly. He reaches to kiss her. She pulls him to her with strength he cannot believe. Suddenly they are doing what he has not planned or even imagined—an insane moment. They both lie back exhausted, not knowing if what has happened has happened.

He cannot recall the thoughts and feelings that flood the next moments. After a long silence he says, "Are you all right? I hope you're all right."

Tender tears trickle. "Did it happen?"

Confused, he starts the engine. No words pass between them until he stops at her house. With the engine still running he says, "It was a great dance. Hope you had a good time."

The sadness in her face saddens him. She gets out, walks to the front door, opens it, glances back, and enters.

The rest of the school year they speak little to each other; they never date again. She moves to a distant desk in English class, and they only 'hello' each other until the week before graduation, when she texts him, "Lets talk—chapel."

He responds, "ok."

The next two hours flow like heavy syrup.

He smiles weakly as she emerges from the chapel door.

"I skipped last period. I was praying. I wanted to talk with Father . . . but couldn't . . . I'm pregnant."

Her stony, calm voice frightens him.

"What'll we do?"

Gazing straight ahead she says, "I'll lose it . . . after graduation . . . before it shows."

"Please, no. It's a life."

She erupts into violent sobbing. He leads her to a shady spot under a broad oak on a quiet side street.

Mired in soggy conflict he offers marriage; he pleads, but weakly. He feels strong, but he is weak. She feels weak, but she is strong. She shakes her head with determination. "I will not let a stupid moment ruin our future. It'll shatter both our lives . . . your seminary . . . priesthood, my college . . . No."

He remains mute. He knows all the right words, but they do not emerge. Does he love her? He takes her hand; it is warm, limp, damp. He releases it.

She proceeds alone, without him, without parents, without priest.

With sealed lips he fills his vocation with dry confessions and abandons his unlived life of human love in return for a life of divine love and its deprivations. He buries his deceit and seals the bargain with hollow words of silver. Thus does Jesse inter his sin in a box lined with white lilies and draped with black rosary beads.

The Bota Maker

Everyone called him Uncle Jacinto, I suppose, because so many people were related to him. This was not hard to believe; he had lived most of his eighty-nine years in Seo de Urgell and had filled the town with descendants.

I first heard of Uncle Jacinto during our visit to Madrid in the mid-1960s. Our friend, Juan Font, had dropped in from Seo de Urgell and noticed the bota hanging on my wall.

"Where did you get that?" he asked.

"In a department store."

"A good bota will last for years, and after it is broken in, it improves the taste of the wine. There is a man in our town who has been making botas since the last century when he moved there from Aragón."

"How about this one?"

"It is not authentic. The ones Uncle Jacinto makes are made of goatskin with the hair on the inside. He seals the seams with a resin that never hardens." Looking into the mouthpiece he said, "This one has no resin. It will leak soon, and the wine will always taste leathery. These are made for tourists to hang on their wall."

"We'll be in Seo next month; I'll buy one of Uncle Jacinto's," I said. "I'd like to have a good one."

"I bought one for my father a few years ago. After a few days it began to leak, and I took it back to have it repaired. Uncle Jacinto looked at it, took his knife, slashed it to pieces, and threw it into the pile of cuttings on the floor. He gave me a new one, all the while swearing and muttering that a rotten bota could not be fixed and that he would have caught the flaw earlier if his vision had not deteriorated so badly."

I knew I had to meet this man.

We drove to Seo to visit Juan and his family for Easter. The morning after we arrived I went out for a solitary stroll hoping to find the old man. His shop was dark and dusty and showed few signs of life. I would never have noticed it if I had not been looking for it. Seven or eight botas hung from nails on a horizontal board that went around the entire gray-walled room about five feet above the worn wooden floor. In addition to the ordinary half-liter, liter, and two-liter botas, he also had a few large ones made of whole goat skins. The room was otherwise bare except for a small desk just inside the door, a cutting table in the center, a bench, and a couple of chairs. The room was drenched in the heavy light of a bare bulb that hung mid-way from ceiling to floor. Bent over with the wooden vise between his knees sewing a bota sat Uncle Jacinto. The stocky old man was wearing a cap snapped down in front and a magnificent Kaiser Wilhelm moustache that was slightly long, yellowed, and drooped. He did not look up.

"I'd like to buy a bota," I said.

His surprised look turned into a scowl. He raised his head and asked curtly, "What size?"

"I don't know. One liter, I guess. How much would a one-liter bota cost?"

"Coño," he mumbled, lifting himself out of his chair. He walked slowly to the little desk, where he searched among a pile of tools, papers, and other items until he extracted a small, worn, spiral-bound notebook. Thumbing through it with shaking fingers he finally answered, "One hundred and fifty pesetas."

I wondered why he would need to consult a price list with so few items, but what impressed me most was his voice. It's deep resonance belied his age. His Castilian was slow and musical. Seeing how slowly and painfully he maneuvered, I went to the wall and took down a one-liter bota.

"I'll take this one," I said, and offered him the money.

"Coño, they don't even let me test them anymore," he growled as if talking to a third party. He grabbed it out of my hand and with some difficulty unscrewed the cap, put the opening to his mouth, and inflated it. He screwed the cap on again, walked to his bench, and sat on the bota bouncing on it several times to be sure it was air-tight.

Grudgingly, as if reciting, he said, "Never put beer or carbonated wine in this bota; the pressure will cause the seams to leak. Don't keep it empty; it will dry out. Also, don't leave the same wine in it too long, or it will sour."

I thanked him and paid him the hundred and fifty pesetas. As I left the dark shop, the bright day forced my eyes to close; I walked down the street squinting.

Juan's mother, Rosita, was surprised and amused when I told her.

"How did you find his shop?"

"It was no trouble; Seo is not a big city. I just walked around window shopping."

She was especially amused and pleased that I had found him to be such an interesting character. She said he is well respected and well liked in Seo and insisted on taking me back to introduce us formally.

We returned to the shop after lunch and found him still bent over his vise sewing a bota. I couldn't help feeling sad watching his frustration: he would make a hole in the skin with the awl and then pass both needles through in opposite directions but only after poking blindly around the hole with the needles.

"I'd like you to meet a cousin from America. He was here this morning and bought a bota from you," she said in Castilian. He grunted and said he was not feeling well. Then he lapsed into Catalán. He and Rosita carried on a lively conversation, which I did not follow.

As we left the shop, Rosita explained that he was having dizzy spells: "He has been working as fast as he can. He wants to have a bota hanging on each nail—at least fifty. His age and maladies slow him down and frustrate him; every time he finishes one, someone comes and buys it."

"But isn't that the object, I mean, to sell them?" I asked, divulging my American upbringing.

"Of course, but he has his heart set on covering the walls with them," she said.

When she told the rest of the family about our visit with the old man, it was clear she enjoyed my strange curiosity.

A few days later, hoping he felt better, I returned to watch him work. He was marking a goatskin with a pencil using a cardboard pattern. Somewhat friendlier now, he answered my questions and said he was arranging the pattern to avoid the skin's weak spots and to be sure that the grain was in the right direction. He was also trying to maximize the number of botas from the skin. After laboring quietly for several minutes he began to mark it all over again explaining that the way he was going one of the botas would have a weak spot. He would rearrange the pattern to avoid that spot while wasting the least possible. I had to leave before he finished.

The day before leaving Seo I returned to buy another bota to take home to a friend. Rosita and I entered his shop and again found him bent over his vise. Rosita asked him how he was feeling. He replied that he was much better and again lapsed into Catalán, so I missed most of the conversation. Finally, she told him in Castilian how much I was enjoying the bota. I agreed heartily and said I wanted to buy another one to take to a friend in America.

"I don't make botas for tourists to hang on their walls," he said in a strong voice. "They are for wine." He resumed his sewing and said no more. Rosita smiled at me and continued her small talk for a few moments. She assured me I would get the bota.

As we were about to leave, a middle-aged woman entered from the back door of the shop and told the old man his coffee was ready. He rose slowly and left the room through the same door. Rosita introduced her as his granddaughter and told her of the old man's refusal to sell me a bota. Obviously embarrassed, they laughed at the old man's cantankerousness. "Poor Abuelo," the granddaughter said. "Until recently he had the wall covered with botas.

But lately he cannot make them fast enough. Poor man. I think he feels the world has passed him by." A tear ran down her cheek as she lifted a one-liter bota from the wall and shoved it at me moving me towards the door. "Is that the right size?" I nodded. By that time we were out on the sidewalk.

"Take it before he returns," she said.

"I don't think I should."

"Please. He means no insult; it is his age."

I took out my wallet.

"I don't know the prices. We can take care of that later."

I pushed 150 pesetas into her hand, and Rosita and I left. Down the block she said, "Do not worry. He'll never notice."

A few months later I noticed the bota hanging on the kitchen wall was dried and cracked. The following year a friend of Juan Font from Seo dropped by to bring regards and news from Juan and the family in Seo. During the evening he noticed the bota and its condition. I told him about Uncle Jacinto, whom he knew well. A few weeks later I received a new bota from Rosita. This time I resolved to use it regularly. At least twenty gallons of wine passed through that bota that year, a half-liter at a time.

The following summer we were away on vacation for six weeks. On our return I found the bota had opened up at one of the seams. The resin had dried out and cracked.

We returned to Spain five years later. Uncle Jacinto had died, but the shop was still open. His granddaughter now made the botas and ran the business. The shop was brightly lit; nearly every nail on the wall held a bota like the ones the old man made. She also had bullhorns closed off with skin at the big end and fitted with a mouth spout at the point. They resembled old powder horns but were made for wine. I held one and shook my head. She said, "You do not want that. It is for tourists."

Doing business with her was smoother than with Uncle Jacinto. She was amiable, showed me her merchandise, and, to my surprise, had not raised the prices.

I bought one, took it to a bar nearby, and filled it with a delicious local red wine. Throughout the rest of the trip I carried it with me and used it regularly.

I have learned that you can keep wine from souring in a bota if you squeeze out all the air before you cap it, and then store it in the refrigerator. Without oxygen the alcohol cannot oxidize to acetic acid, which imparts the sour taste to spoiled wine.

I used the bota almost daily for about a year after we returned home. About once a week I emptied the contents and refilled it with fresh wine. Wine will last almost indefinitely in a bota if you keep it cold and air-free.

It has been three years since I took a sip from my bota, but I'm sure it's still good. And it's not hanging on my wall.

Dangling

He finds himself dangling in a vast darkness. He cannot see his hand before his eyes or walls or limits of any kind.

"What's holding up this cord?" he mumbles to himself. "What'll I do if it breaks?"

A voice nearby mumbles and finally says, "Hello. Are you dangling too?

The first man feels a strange comfort in the voice of another in the same predicament and says, "I can't see you. Where are we?"

"I don't know. All I know is this darkness, and now your voice."

The first man lets out a loud shriek.

"What's the matter? Are you hurt?" the second man says.

"No. I just wondered if I would hear an echo, but didn't. This place must be very big."

"Uh-huh."

"Where are these cords attached?"

"I don't know that either."

"What's down below?"

"Can't you see I don't know?"

"I can't see anything. Who would know?"

"Please stop asking dumb questions I can't answer. Just be quiet."

Another voice from beyond the second man says, "Pay no attention to him. He's always grumpy. Doesn't seem able to accept his fate."

"It's the same as yours and mine?"

"Apparently, but being grumpy doesn't help."

"Well, then, if you don't mind, what's above us? I mean where the cords are attached."

"It must be a light and clear place. Otherwise, how could anyone have managed to dangle us here?"

"Light and clear! How wonderful! Think we can get up there?"

"I haven't figured out how, but we can't just dangle here forever without purpose. There must be something or someone up there controlling this . . . what-ever-it-is . . . place."

"Where did you come from?"

"I don't know."

"Me neither."

They dangle a long while before either speaks. "What makes you think it's light and clear up above?"

"Has to be. Let's think this out: we're dangling, right?"

"Right."

"How did we get here?"

"I don't know."

"Nor do I, but it stands to reason that we didn't hang ourselves here. Someone else must have done it. Right?"

"Seems reasonable."

"You're dangling by a cord that isn't moving, so we can assume the cord is attached up above somewhere."

"Right."

"How else, then, could this have come to pass? There must be a plan, a purpose."

"Reasonable."

"A plan implies a planner. Right?"

"I see what you mean. But where does all this logic lead us?"

"Only that if we're ever going to get up there, we'd better be nice to the planner."

"Makes sense."

"Bunk!" the pessimist says. He had remained quiet during the preceding dialog and could hold his silence no longer. "Has that so-called 'planner' ever spoken to you or given any evidence that he's up there? Have you ever heard his voice? Has he ever jiggled your cord or given any other evidence that he's up there?"

"Of course not. We're talking logic, not evidence," the optimist says.

"Logic be damned."

"What else do we have, my friend?"

"First of all, I'm not your friend. We just met, and I can't even see you. Second, we have absolutely nothing to go on. We're dangling, and that's all there is to it. None of your logic or anything you can say or do can change that."

"You're quite the pessimist, friend. I suggest we do have something even if we can't communicate directly with the planner."

"Oh? Well, by all means, let us in on it; don't keep it to yourself."

"I believe we should do everything we can to let the planner know we believe in him, that we believe he has a plan for us, and that we want to help him any way we can."

"Are you kidding? We're dangling in this abyss, and you want to help the guy who put us here?"

"Why not? What else can we do?"

"Self-respect isn't much, but it's more than you seem to have."

"I don't understand," the first man says.

"I mean I'm not going to butter up the guy who's dangling us like puppets. That's stupid and unmanly."

"I hope he didn't hear that."

"That's not my intent. It would serve no purpose to offend him."

The optimist speaks up: "So you're afraid to offend the planner."

"Bunk! I'm not afraid of him or anything."

"What would you think if we followed my suggestion and he rescued us and left you dangling?"

"I'll let you know when it happens."

The first man suddenly blurts out, "Wait a minute. If you try to be nice to the planner to prove a point to this pessimist, won't that make the planner angry? He'll know you're using him."

"I don't see why."

"Because you'd just be doing it to show this fellow. If you're going to be nice to the planner, you'd better do it sincerely with no other purpose than to help the planner."

"On second thought, I agree," the optimist says.

"But how do we go about being nice?" the first man says.

"How about singing something beautiful and flattering to the planner."

"I've never heard anything so stupid," the pessimist says. "With your screechy voice, the so-called 'planner' would cut your cord." He laughs aloud.

"What other choice do we have?" the first man says.

With a broad grin, the pessimist replies, "I have a better idea. Let's bounce on this cord and see if the planner responds. He might react by tugging or letting us drop farther down."

"That sounds dangerous," the first man says.

"Maybe, but at least we'll know he's there."

"Good point," the optimist says. "Let's try it. Let's all three of us bounce on our cords at the same time. Let's stay together and keep synchronized, though."

They all begin to bounce up and down. With the elasticity of the cord they begin to move slowly several feet up and then several feet down. They move together at first, but soon, the pessimist is moving more strongly than the other two. After bouncing a while, as the pessimist moves down and the other two move up they lose hearing contact with the pessimist. On their way back down, the other two do not hear the pessimist moving up from his bounce. The optimist stops bouncing, and soon he and the first man come to rest. They call out to the third man, but hear no answer. The first man waves his arms and legs wildly trying to find and grab the pessimist's cord. He finds it, but it is hanging loose. He pulls it up and feels the end; it's frazzled.

"Must have bounced too hard and broke the cord."

"Or the planner let him go."

"Wait a minute. How do we know the planner hasn't brought him up to the light?"

"I can't believe the planner would repay such arrogance with freedom. No, he's down there somewhere. I'd bet on it."

"Poor guy! I wonder where."

"I don't know, and I don't want to know. All I know is I'm not moving anymore."

"What'll we do then?" the optimist says.

"What can we do? Are we to dangle here forever, not knowing why?"

"I'd sure like to know where the pessimist went . . . I'd sure like to know how he's doing down there . . . or up there; wherever he is."

"You ask too many questions," the first man says. "Be satisfied you're here. We may be dangling, but we're still alive."

"I have an idea," the optimist says. "Let's swing gently so we can touch."

"I don't want to anger the planner, just in case he did cut the other guy loose."

"Why should he mind that? We'll swing gently until we touch, and then we'll at least be able to feel each other."

"No! Hearing you is enough."

"Please, it would be good to touch someone. We'd know we really exist."

The first man thinks a while and finally says, "OK."

They begin to swing, very gently at first, with their arms extended. "Not too hard," the first man says. "Got you," he says, grabbing the optimist's hand. "Wow! That's great. Hold on. Don't let go. Oh, it feels good to hold your hand . . . I feel better already."

"And we're still dangling. We haven't fallen. Maybe that's what the planner wanted all along."

"Think so?"

"Let's sing something."

"What?"

"I don't know; something beautiful. Anything."

Love Story

First Meeting:

In a silent eddy of a nearly deserted street, late afternoon poured darkness into the small downtown restaurant. The restaurant owner flipped on the lights. The man standing outside looked at his watch and paced to the end of the block, looked down the street in both directions, and walked back. A shock of white hair belied a youthful, ruddy face and athletic build. He stood erect, a bright green tie brightening his charcoal gray suit. Peering again into the restaurant window he wondered why he remembered it small; it now seemed cavernous. The only sign of life was the owner at the rear talking with the waiter, both wearing white, open-collared shirts and black trousers. The man outside adjusted his tie in his window reflection and passed his hand over his hair and again lifted his watch into view. After a few minutes a car drove into a space across the street and the woman got out. She smiled and crossed the street in a lively step and hopped onto the sidewalk. Her recently bleached short hair bounced lightly as she walked. He noticed that she had lost weight since he last saw her. Not pretty, she had a pleasant face. He had always noticed that her eyes smiled when she talked. In fact, he had always thought her eyes were her most attractive feature. As she approached, her make-up seemed excessive. To avoid an embrace he extended his hand and said, "How are you, Wanda?"

"Great, Bill! How about you?"

"All right, I guess."

"It's been way too long," she said, interlocking her arm in his.

The relaxed look of her loose-fitting shift clashed with her rapid, clipped speech.

After a seemingly endless silence he said, "Shall we go in?"

Posters of Venice, Rome and Florence facing a mirrored wall filled the place with memories. As they waited for the owner to greet them, Bill looked around as if trying to recall something. Wanda watched his expression, but said nothing. Each table had a red tablecloth and a white vase containing a single red rose. Too much red, Bill thought. The door closed behind them, and Italian mandolin music began to play; at first too loud, then it diminished.

"I can't remember the last time I was here," he said. "It was one of Bea's favorites."

The owner, young, dark, and handsome, with menus in one hand, led them to a table by a window that faced a tiny side garden lined with blooming bougainvilleas. The owner smiled then motioned sternly to the waiter, who was still standing near the kitchen.

As Bill held out the chair for Wanda, she said, "I'm glad you asked me out.

"You invited me."

She smiled, "You don't remember."

"You said we could go out; I asked when, and you said whenever. I said how about this evening."

"And a beautiful evening it is."

By this time the balding, middle-aged waiter was standing by their table, note pad in hand. Bill turned to his companion, "What'll you have?"

"A glass of Pino Grigio."

"Martini for me."

"Ah; you still drink martinis, sir."

Bill ignored the waiter's comment and turned to Wanda.

"So . . . how have you been?"

"Surviving. What about you?"

"Fine . . . sometimes I think I retired too soon."

"Really?"

"Just one more thing to get used to."

Leaning toward him she said, "We should've done this sooner."

He nodded ponderously.

"So how has it been, really?"

He shrugged.

"I know."

"Well I have time for baseball now. Bought Rays season tickets."

The waiter set their drinks down. She lifted her glass, "To survival."

They touched glasses. She looked into his dark eyes; he looked away.

"To Bea and George," he said, looking into her eyes for the first time.

They repeated the gesture, this time solemnly. He looked down into his glass.

"She still haunts you. It was the same for me when George died."

"Tell me about the girls. How's Katie doing in New York?"

"Typical star-struck kid. Hasn't seen her first actor, but thrilled at the prospect."

"What does she do?"

"Sales, promotion, advertising, that sort of thing."

"And Susan?"

"Get this: she's planned her wedding on the beach, right out on the sand in a formal wedding dress and barefoot, 'Where earth, water, air and sun can fill our souls.'"

Without smiling, he said, "Far out."

"I already bought my outfit: sea foam green. We're asking everyone to go barefoot. We'll have lunch on the sand too. I think it'll be beautiful . . . Ah, your first smile."

"Sorry."

"For smiling?"

He smiled again, this time dutifully.

"You're on the guest list if that's what you're worried about. Hope you don't mind a little sand between your toes."

His smile broadened. "I can't imagine George in his tux and barefoot."

"He'd have loved it. Susan was his baby."

After another sip he said, "Bea doted on our boys too."

"You must be proud to have two more chemists in the family."

"Billy graduates in June, and he's lined up several job prospects already. Charlie's another story." He shrugged. "Changed his major to accounting; that means two more years. Can you imagine Charlie as an accountant? I tried to talk sense into him, but . . . it's his life."

"Kids! They never doubt."

"Hungry?" he said.

"I wouldn't mind another glass of wine if you're not famished."

He caught the waiter's eye and motioned for two more.

Leaning toward him she put her hand on his and said, "I'm a good listener if you want to talk."

Withdrawing his hand he said, "We're talking."

"She smiled the smile of understanding."

As the waiter set the drinks down they both leaned back and looked out the window. After a long silence she said, "Are you all right?"

"Fine." He picked up his glass and took a sip.

"You must see our condo, actually my condo; poor George never really got to enjoy it."

"Shame."

"Twenty-three days after we moved in."

After another long silence she said, "You and Bea were talking condo too."

"Bea talked; I listened."

She laughed. "I remember. You didn't want to be cooped up."

"I need freedom and open space. I can't imagine living so high, isolated, like a cliff dweller. Sorry, I didn't mean . . . I'd have moved if she'd insisted, but Bea never insisted. Wasn't her style."

"Why didn't you call?"

"It was just after . . . I would've been terrible company. And then when George . . . it just didn't feel right."

"Is that why we met here instead of my place?"

He shrugged.

"We could've helped each other."

"How about supper?"

"Sure."

He called the waiter and she picked up the menu, "How's the lasagna?"

"That's what I'm having."

Neither spoke for a long while after the waiter departed.

"Sorry you came?" she said.

"Of course not."

"You coping?"

"Can't you see I'd rather not?"

"I've been through it. I know what you're feeling."

"I'm fine. Look, I don't want to be rude, but . . ."

They both looked up as the waiter laid their salads before them.

She picked at hers without speaking. Suddenly she looked up and said, "Sure, we can drop it, but I'm not sure you can."

He dropped his fork, laid his napkin on the table and said, "Sorry, but I'm miserable enough. I don't need this."

He stood and walked to the owner, laid a bill on the counter and left. She sat dazed, tears welling.

Ten days later:

Bill pushed the heavy glass doors halfway open and looked into the lobby. It was sparsely decorated with four large earth-toned vases, several deep green plush chairs, and a deep purple sofa. He stopped to appraise the white marble columns, crystal chandeliers and large wall mirrors as he walked in. Standing tentatively before the elevator, the doors opened abruptly and a young man in a tennis outfit bounced out with his tennis bag and disappeared out the back door. To his left, through heavy glass French doors, spread a dining room and beyond, windows that framed a garden and pool. Seeing her waving there Bill walked to her table.

"Hi."

"You've kept me waiting almost three minutes."

"Sorry."

"Just kidding. Thanks for coming."

"Thanks for calling. I didn't expect to hear from you after last time."

"That was ten days ago; I couldn't wait any longer. I was hoping you'd call, but . . . anyway, I wanted you to know I understand."

"I wish I understood. There was no excuse."

"Stop hammering yourself. I said I understand. And to prove it: lunch is on me."

"I couldn't . . ."

"This is the twenty-first century; drop the male chauvinism. It's dead."

He frowned at the word "dead." Then catching himself, he smiled and shrugged.

"And I'm celebrating with a martini," she said.

"For lunch?"

"Twenty-first century, remember?"

"Well . . . why not?"

"I've thought a lot since the other night," she said.

"Oh?"

"I'm glad we finally got together after so long. I couldn't remember my last date."

"Date?"

"Anything wrong with that?"

He forced a smile.

As the waiter stopped at their table she said, "Two martinis, up and with an olive." Then to her companion, "OK?"

"You're the hostess."

"Another thing: I want to show you my condo. It's only twelve floors up."

"I have a consulting appointment right after lunch. Maybe next time."

"I'll hold you to it. You'll love it; it's high, bright and airy. From my terrace you have the entire city in your arms. I have afternoon shade, and there's always a breeze, and sometimes a good rain to wash away bad thoughts."

"I will."

The sullen waiter approached, set down the drinks and walked away.

"To us."

He looked down into his martini.

"We were all good friends, weren't we?"

He looked puzzled.

"I mean the four of us."

"I guess so."

"Usually the men are friends and the women are friends. But I felt we were all friends." She lifted the glass to her lips.

He nodded.

"You were always a thoughtful and interesting man." She fondled the stem of her glass. When he sat back in his chair, seeming to withdraw, she said, "What now?"

"This is too . . ."

"Don't assume."

He looked at her wondering if he had misread her.

"We're both alone now, and we're both mature adults. What's wrong with remaining friends? We share lots of memories and fun too."

"Why don't we order?"

"You're upset. Friendship between a man and a woman is tricky. Even if neither wants to act on it, there's always an unspoken sexual dimension."

He said nothing.

"For heaven sake. I'm not coming on to you."

"I don't want to think about things like that."

She put her hands on the table with a look of desperation.

"It's just . . . I can't get Bea out of my mind."

"Not an hour passes that I don't think about George, but he's gone and I can't bring him back. Should I spend the rest of my life thinking about what might have been? I'm trying to make it without him. Is that wrong? Whatever the answer, it doesn't blot out the past."

He let out a deep sigh and finished his martini.

"Another?" she said.

"I guess not."

"She called the waiter.

"Look, it's not you, Wanda; it's me."

The waiter stood by their table looking past them at the garden through the large window. A bird was bathing in the fountain.

"What do you like?"

"The broiled snapper sounds good," he said, looking at the menu for the first time.

"The Del Monaco steak is good too," she said.

"I'll have the snapper."

After another long silence he said, "You've always been easy to talk with. Most of my friends are too busy."

"Mine too."

"But I'd prefer to keep it light and go with the flow."

"Meaning?"

"I don't know. Please, I appreciate what you're trying to do, but I just can't."

"So you'd rather ignore what's going on inside?"

He shook his head in exasperation.

"You can't base a friendship on chit-chat and small talk." She took the last sip of her martini and set the glass down. "When I lost George I felt dead, like you feel now. I couldn't think straight. Even my daughters couldn't make contact. It took months, but I'm finally coming out of it. You're still fighting it."

"What do you suggest?"

"Talk. You have a future, you know."

"I've abandoned my career, and my wife of twenty-five years is . . ."

"You might start by saying the word."

He frowned. "What word?"

"She's dead. Accept it. George is dead and so is Bea. They're both dead and gone, and we're here."

"When his eyes filled he turned away. "I'll be back."

She tapped her fingers on the tabletop.

In a few minutes he returned and sat down. After a moment of silence he said, "Of course you're right, but it's tough." He took another sip of his drink and, looked down into his glass.

Finally she said, "So the boys are doing well?"

He looked at her and smiled, "Oh, yes, I guess. Neither needs fathering by a tired, old has-been."

"Stop beating yourself."

After a long pause he said, "You talk about the future, but all I see is the past and loneliness. My life is over."

"Lighten up. You'll never be twenty again, but you're not ninety. We're both drifting somewhere between. I've got a good twenty years ahead of me, and I won't spend it moping about what I can't change."

"I don't know how to change."

"Find something good and beautiful to think about; something that was fun."

"Sounds peachy."

"Don't trivialize me, damn it! Soak in self-pity if you must. I'm doing my best to stay alive." She turned to the window to watch the bird. When another flew down, she assumed it was its mate.

"I'm sorry. That was rude. The last thing I want is to hurt you. I just . . . it's pointless. Maybe one day I'll be able to think clearly like you."

"Why not today?"

He shook his head and looked into his empty martini glass. "You won't give up, will you?"

"I think you're dying to talk about Bea's death. Tell me I'm wrong and I'll quit."

Through clenched teeth he said, "I don't know. I don't even know how I feel right now. I know you're trying to help, but . . ."

Her face was blank, not a smile, not a frown, as if she were peering inside his soul.

"All right," he said. "I feel trapped. My house drowns me with memories. They come out at night . . . I feel claustrophobic, like it'll all fall in on me. I try to read, but the words make no sense; I have to reread every line. Finally I turn on the TV."

"It's been fourteen months."

"Isn't it odd, both of them . . . the same month?"

"Both of them what?" she said patronizingly.

"OK, OK. Died."

"Better. Why didn't you call? I called several times, but I had the feeling you didn't know who I was."

"Those days are a blur. My brain was squeezed dry. I spent hours looking at our wedding pictures and old snap shots. Bea had them filed neatly in boxes with the negatives. I tried to put them back in order, but finally got so mad and frustrated I just threw them all in the box and kicked it into a corner. I couldn't find the order."

"In your life?"

They stopped as the waiter set the salads before them.

"Bea was organized and meticulous, but never fussy," she said.

"Every time I remember how I laughed at her neatness I hate myself."

"You got along better than any couple I know."

"We argued; everybody does, but never anything serious. At first it was about trivia. Like the time I said Nixon was a crook, and she got furious. What a thing to fight over! Years later we laughed about it."

"Couples have to stake out their territories. Like dogs peeing everywhere."

He laughed aloud.

"Isn't that why they do it?"

"So I've heard. So we were just peeing on our principles?"

"Probably."

After picking at his salad he said, "After Bea's funeral I was so angry I couldn't stand it."

"Why?"

"Don't know. Sounds crazy, but I was furious at her."

"I felt the same about George."

"Anyway I got over the anger, but not the depression, so I tried not to think about her . . . it."

"Time works if you let it. But you have start by accepting the fact."

The waiter walked by to see if they had finished their salads; they had barely touched them. They both looked at him apologetically and began to eat. After a minute Bill said, "This is pretty good."

She smiled.

"That appointment this afternoon is to be an expert witness in a lawsuit."

"What about?"

"Four men caught in an explosion in the hold of a ship where someone had left a welding torch on the floor the night before. When one of the men saw a fluffy flame at the top of the escape hatch, they all scrambled up. As the last man got half way up, the room exploded and he was killed. The widow is suing the gas company for damages because the torch valve had been left open."

"One of the workers could have left it open."

"It would still be the company's fault."

She shook her head. "How?"

"Because none of the workers smelled the gas, the gas company's lawyer claimed the oxygen caught fire. Seems lawyers don't know freshman chemistry. Oxygen doesn't burn; it had to be the welding gas. The plaintiff's argument rests on the fact that none of the survivors smelled it. Law requires flammable gases to contain a strong smelling component so even a small leak can be easily detected."

"Did you convince them that oxygen doesn't burn?"

"Oh yes."

"Do you think she'll win?"

"I don't see how she can lose."

"Sounds interesting."

"At first I took the job because it sounded entertaining; it would give me something to do. But when I learned about the poor widow; well, she's destitute and the gas company was at fault."

"It must feel good to help someone like that."

He nodded. "But I've been hogging the conversation. What about you?"

"I'm on the arts council. There was an opening; I've got the time. It seems they needed somebody who was idle and conscientious."

"You're a good choice," he said, picking up the empty glass. "I was going to offer a toast to good friends."

She smiled. "Bea was my best friend. I wouldn't do or say anything to soil her memory or George's."

"Tell me about the arts council."

"We're trying to expand the art museum. It's tough prying money out of people. Our next project will be a resident chamber orchestra. What a boost that'll be for the city."

"I'd buy a season ticket."

"Thanks. I know you're not a music lover. George wasn't either, but he humored me."

"Most of my friends don't know it, but I played violin when I was a kid. I wasn't very good. I preferred Mom's Jascha Heifetz records."

"I never knew."

"Dad did everything he could to discourage me. He thought it was sissy stuff."

"What a shame. Is that why you quit?"

"I don't know. I was good at math and Dad pushed me into science."

"There's room for both. I was lucky; my parents encouraged me to follow my passion."

"Teaching?"

"Art. I've always loved it. My parents took me to every art museum in every city we ever visited."

"But you taught school."

"I got my master's in teaching later. This arts council is my first job in art."

"I never got into art, but I have a good Heifetz CD collection."

"He was wonderful, but I prefer a full symphony orchestra with its range from faint to bombastic with cymbals and gongs and trumpets. A good symphony is the ultimate in musical freedom."

"Wow!" he said. "I never knew you felt so strongly about it."

"It feels good to air our secrets, doesn't it? Especially with a good friend."

The waiter brought lunch and walked away.

"I'm hungry," he said. "How about you?"

"Famished. Then my condo."

An Hour Later:

Holding the door open as he walked in, she said, "What do you think?" The light flowing through the large living room windows bathed the tropical space. A white, medium size grand piano grabbed his eye at the far end near a ceiling-high bookcase. Flowered pastels covered white wicker furniture, and white floor lamps and a white overhead fan lent the space an island glow. Prints of Gaughuin, Renoir, Degas, and Van Gogh adorned two walls, and large windows opened to a balcony that overlooked the city skyline. The living room flowed through a wide archway into the dining room and beyond that, the kitchen.

"Wow! Looks like a magazine ad. Feels like we're flying." Then, stepping toward the balcony, "What a view! I don't blame you for liking it. It's beautiful."

"Feel cooped up?"

"Not at all. I apologize for the stupid comment."

"No apology needed. You hadn't seen it."

As he stood at the balcony door taking in the panorama, she took his hand and led him out. "If you like this, wait till you see it by night. The city lights sparkle like diamonds sprinkled over stone and glass."

Looking down to the sidewalk below he said, "A little scary."

"You get used to it."

"If I lived here I'd spend the day out here."

"You're not built to spend your life as a spectator."

He looked at her seriously and said, "Maybe you know me better than I know myself."

"I'm a people watcher. I like to know what makes them tick."

"Got me all figured out, eh?"

"I'm working on it. Now sit and I'll get us some drinks."

He started to object, but her open, friendly tone stopped him. Standing on the balcony he tried to identify the buildings in the skyline and was doing well when she returned with two small glasses.

"George liked this port. I thought you would too."

An hour passed as they talked and sipped port on the balcony. They chatted about the view and the various buildings where he had worked. "That's the school where you taught," he said.

"Remember that trip the four of us took together to Cancun?" he said.

"It was a nice four days. I've always loved the beach. First time I'd ever snorkeled. What a sunburn! Couldn't sleep for days."

"It wasn't that bad on Bea and me with our complexion. Remember that little dive that served only beer and wine and had the best music in town?"

"Sure. We danced till way past midnight. It was something we never did before or after."

"I know," he said. "People get crazy when they're away from home. In this setting above the city I feel like I'm on vacation."

"Good! Go with it."

That Evening:

"You must be sick of me by now," he said, as they walked to the same table.

"I'll let you know."

"After seeing your condo I wish I'd let Bea talk me into one."

"When the lights come on the whole city twinkles like a Christmas tree. I don't mean to go on so, but it's been a long time since I showed it off."

"That can't be, with all your friends."

"That was then."

He nodded. The waiter stood over them looking into the distance over their heads, waiting.

"You're probably getting tired of martinis," he said.

"I feel so good," she said. "How about some champagne?"

"A bottle of Mumms, waiter," he said.

"Tonight is on me," she said.

"Next time. It's the student's turn."

Within minutes the waiter had brought the ice bucket and champagne, lifted out the bottle, wrapped a napkin around it and, with great pomp, popped it open, poured the glasses and returned the bottle to the bucket.

"It's been years since I walked the downtown area," he said. "It was nice seeing it together."

"I walk it a lot," she said.

'Then, just as I got home, the phone rang. It was Charlie."

"How is he?"

"Didn't say. Just kept asking about me. Thought I was still miserable until I told him we'd had dinner several times."

"He's a kind boy."

"Know what? He laughed! I thought he was poking fun, but he was just glad; happy about . . . you know. I didn't realize how worried he'd been."

"Being so far away, he probably imagined all sorts of scenarios. Kids know more than we think."

He took her hand.

"To our children," she said, raising her glass.

"They're growing up, it seems."

"Their future is spread before them. You know, I don't dread the future anymore. It's still out there, waiting for me."

He hesitated, then, "Every once in a while, when I think about Bea, I panic; I'm paralyzed. Even looking at you she's still there. I don't like walking alone into that dark house."

"Me too, but it's better now."

"I'm ruining a beautiful day for us both," he said. "I propose a toast to the future."

"Nice. It's the only time of value."

"What about the past?"

"It's more beautiful the farther it recedes, but we live on the thin edge between was and will be."

"Maybe you're right." Then holding up his glass, "To the edge."

After taking a sip he said, "Trouble with the edge is sometimes it feels like you'll fall off, or it'll cut right through you . . . I don't know if I can eat. I'm getting nervous."

"Then pour another glass of that wonderful wine. I've never tasted Mumms before."

"Bea and I first drank it in Paris."

"I'd forgotten you went there. When was it?"

"Four years ago next month. Billy had just started the university, and we left Charlie with his grandmother."

"George and I planned to go to Europe, but we never made it."

"Bea had been after me for years. It was great; Paris was so terrific neither of us wanted to leave. Oh, we saw Rome and London, too, but Paris was special."

"I want to travel," she said. Now that the girls are both on their own, there's nothing to hold me."

"If you get to Europe, be sure to visit Paris. You'll love it."

"When the time comes I'll consult you."

The waiter appeared, checked the champagne, found it not empty and stood nearby, waiting, saying nothing.

"Ready to order?" she asked.

"Hungry?"

"I don't mind enjoying the wine a little longer."

"We'll order later, Waiter," he said.

The waiter turned and walked away without speaking.

"What about a movie after dinner?" she said.

"I haven't been to a movie in . . . sure."

Later That Evening:

Leaning on her balcony railing he said, "The city lights are spectacular. I've lived in this city all my life, and I've never seen it this way."

"I imagine flying over it, looking into windows, learning people's secrets," she said.

"I never took you for a peeping tom."

She smiled, "I mean how they manage their lives. Wouldn't it be wonderful? We'd be like gods."

"Funny, but I feel like I'm seeing you for the first time."

"Because you're learning my secrets. Tell me one of yours."

"I'm too much of an introvert."

"Even to Bea?"

"She had lots of time, and she was pretty sharp."

"I know one of your secrets."

"Tell me."

"You're enjoying your loneliness, and you're afraid to part with it."

He looked out over the city. "That's not very flattering."

"Am I wrong?"

"I don't know . . . think I'm torturing myself?"

"Yes. It's normal for a while, unless you get to like it."

"Could I tell you something?" "Please."

"Last night when I went to bed and closed my eyes I couldn't remember her face. I tried; I got desperate and still couldn't. I saw only crazy, nondescript figures, like random numbers, flashing in the darkness. I pushed off the covers and turned on the bed lamp and pulled the top drawer so hard it fell dangling in my hand. There it was: her picture, smiling, eyes dancing, happy. How could I forget after so short a time, and with her picture in every room in the house?"

"You haven't forgotten."

"Remember the first time we met? I didn't call for over a week."

"Ten days."

"It was strange."

"How so?"

"The first morning especially. I felt bad and good and completely confused. Lately I've only felt bad. Anyway, I walked out to the back porch and before I could sit down, the slamming screen door scared hell out of me, and I jumped. I had finished off a whole pot of coffee over the newspaper."

"That might explain it."

"I don't know why I read the paper; it only ruins my day."

She nodded.

"Standing with my hands on the wooden railing, I wasn't even aware of the drizzle. I felt trapped where I always felt free."

She nodded.

"I retired early so we could travel and enjoy life . . . then she was gone, and I felt trapped." He smiled meekly, "I'm talking too much." She shook her head and he continued, "I sat on the rocker watching the rain. Suddenly it stopped and the sun appeared. A few minutes later a cardinal swooped down to drink at a puddle under the big oak. Brilliant red; I could see him clearly. Soon its mate flew down beside him. I leaned over to get a better look, but they flew off to a low limb on the grapefruit tree.

"By midmorning the sky turned blue. I sat in one of the oak rockers and let my head fall back with my eyes closed to soak up the sun and I wondered what I would do that day. My mind wandered all over and finally came to rest. I had never thought about love before bea died, what it means, what it is. But it had driven me crazy all those months and I still didn't get it. I knew I had lost it,

I still loved her, but how can I love someone who doesn't exist? Am I in love with a ghost?" He stopped and shook his head. "I couldn't navigate it. I felt lost. I felt alone even when I wasn't alone." He stopped as if he had said something horrible.

"I know."

"Wait, I'm not finished." Hesitating a moment he continued, "Anyway, as I wondered what I would do that day I realized I had not pondered that question lately."

She smiled. "Why not?"

"I think you had something to do with it."

She went to him and put her arm around his waist and said, "That's the nicest thing I've heard in a long time."

Gently he turned her and kissed her lips. He withdrew saying, "I hope you didn't mind."

She embraced and kissed him deep in the city lights of her balcony.

As they stood looking into each other's eyes, nervousness began to tighten his stomach and he said, "It's been a long day."

"I've enjoyed it. What about tomorrow?"

"Like to try the beach?"

"Great! I'll pack a picnic lunch."

"I'll pick you up around ten."

She walked him to the door, took his hand and said, "It has been lovely. Are you all right?"

"I think so. Why?"

"No reason. See you tomorrow."

Two Days Later:

She was clearly angry: "Was it something I did?" The phone trembled in her hand.

"What? Oh, hi! I meant to call, but I've been busy like you wouldn't believe."

"You didn't answer my question."

"I had a great time. The beach was perfect."

"Then why haven't you called?"

"I told you, this consulting job is really taking a lot of time."

"Surely you've taken time to eat and read the paper."

"Why are you doing this? It was only a day."

"Well I've been sitting here like a fool waiting for a call. It's embarrassing. I thought we had a good time and you'd want to talk about it."

"How about lunch?"

"You really don't have to."

"Please, I want to. Be a good girl. We'll have lunch and forget about the whole thing. It'll be as if nothing happened."

"I don't know . . ."

"I don't like being badgered. I'd like to see you for lunch. What about it?" After a long pause he said, "Well?"

"I don't want to pressure you."

"Don't spoil it, for heaven sake."

"OK."

"That Italian restaurant where we met the first time?"

"I'll meet you there."

"If you wish; a little before noon?"

Two Hours Later:

The restaurant was more crowded than usual and she did not see him through the restaurant window. When she did she went in, sat down. "I'm sorry. I've been a little overwrought."

"We've both got a lot to get used to," he said. "This is all new."

"Those two days seemed like a month; like you'd left me. I know it's silly. You have no obligation, but I just . . ."

"I should be perfectly honest," he said. "Part of me was urging me to call; another part was saying, 'Hold it. Not so fast.' I'm still afraid, I guess."

"Of what?"

"That I want to see you more than . . . more than I should."

"Well, that makes sense," she said, looking away, anger building.

"Please, try to understand. I want to see you, be with you, but I feel I'm being disloyal."

The waiter stopped at their table and smiled. "Ready to order?"

Without prompting she said, "A martini."

"Same for me."

"Would you like to order now or wait a while?" the waiter said.

Sharply, Bill said, "We'll wait if you don't mind."

The waiter turned with no show of emotion.

"What are we trying to prove?" he said.

"I think coming here was a mistake," she said. "Let's cancel our drinks and leave. We'll try again another time."

He put his face in his hands. "I'm sorry, really. I know I've acted like a screwball, but I just don't know what I'm doing."

"I do," she said. She stood and walked out.

He followed her out and on the way told the waiter to cancel the drinks. Outside he caught up with her and took her arm.

"What are you doing?"

"Your place or mine?"

She stopped and looked at him in astonishment, then her face relaxed into a smile. He turned and walked to his car and opened the door for her.

"My car is just down the street."

"I'll drive you back."

The noon traffic was backed up as they inched their way in silence.

"I like the view from your terrace," he said. "Do you have martini makings?"

"Of course."

He drove anxiously, constantly braking and accelerating as if late to an appointment. He did not understand his behavior and concluded he was not acting on reason, but panic. He parked in guest parking and opened the door for her. Together they walked, not anxiously now, but deliberately to the elevator where she pushed the twelfth floor button. They rode up in silence. She opened her door and walked in ahead of him. Turning to him she saw his face as serious as she had ever seen it. He stood silent, no longer driven, but now questioning. He knew what he had been thinking and planning, but how would he? He had not seduced a woman in years. With Bea it had become a pleasantly relaxed routine—a drink or two, put on a disk, dance sometimes, and soon she would lead him to bed.

Wanda walked to the kitchen and opened the liquor cabinet and took out a bottle of gin and one of vermouth.

She removed an ice tray and dropped a few cubes into the silver mixer. Without measuring she poured some gin and then vermouth, stirred, and poured the mixture into martini glasses, turned and handed him one. He took it, looked at it, and set it down on the counter and turned to her. Expecting him to retreat into his usual behavior, she set her drink down too. He walked to her, put his arm around her waist, and pulled her to him. Still frowning anxiously, he kissed her. She did not draw back, but held him closer. With his fingers in her hair, he felt warmth running through his chest. Still struggling with himself, he kissed her again. She pushed him away, took his hand and led him to the bedroom. He followed like a puppy on a leash. Inside the bedroom she noticed the closet door was slightly ajar and imagined something moved inside. She knew it was impossible, but her heartbeat spiked and she shuddered. She stood frozen and looked down at the bed then at the closet.

"What's wrong?"

Without taking her eyes off the closet door she said, "No! I mean I don't know." He felt her hand cold and trembling. Withdrawing her hand from his she shook her head and sat on the side of the bed and looked down at the floor. He sat beside her and reached over to embrace her. She stood and turned away. "I'm sorry."

"After all this you're sorry?"

"I know I owe you an explanation, but I just can't; I just can't. Please go now."

A mixture of relief and anger rose in his chest. He looked out the window feeling he was in a crazy movie with characters behaving irrationally. He recalled such a Pedro Almodóvar movie in which all the people acted out of character. He could not imagine what he would do in the next second; the world seemed to be spinning out of control into ever widening circles of absurdity.

He walked into the kitchen and picked up the martini he had left and took a deep swig, walked dumbly to the living room and sat in the plush sofa to finish it. She did not appear. He finished his drink, set down the glass, and walked to the front door, stopped, and walked back to the bedroom, where she was still sitting on the bed looking down at the floor.

"I'm leaving."

Without speaking or looking back she heard him walk out. She heard the door close, and then she wept.

One Year Later

As always the slamming screen door startles him. After four cups of coffee Bill has read the newspaper as if each page would reveal a magic salve to soothe the inarticulate void within. The morning paper ritual provides neither reality nor truth, but merely insures his day would begin sizzling in anger. Standing on the back porch with his hands on the wooden railing, he barely notices the drizzle. The only drizzle he feels is in his breast. As his eyes clamps onto a large ripe grapefruit hanging from a tall limb, it falls. He smiles recalling a movie in which an ape pounds his chest in victory.

The pale sky is more blindingly white than blue. His back yard is an island compound guarded from the rest of the world by overgrown fruit trees. He leans his head on the vertical post and sees a clump of mistletoe near the top of the turkey oak. Memories flutter like bird wings around the day he and Beatrice bought this land.

The rain falls harder now, like spikes into the ground. Thunder rumbles through opaque skies.

"Ah, clear at last." A cardinal swoops down near Bill and begins to forage under the turkey oak. He has found an insect when his mate swoops down beside him; the male, crested and brilliant red; the female, a dull, inconspicuous brown. Odd how that the male of most animals is more beautiful than the female. Bea always shook out the tablecloth for the cardinals after meals.

"Birds don't appreciate it; probably not even aware of it."

"Don't be so sure," she had said. "Creatures that pretty must feel gratitude."

There are still a few oranges. Maybe I'll have one later, after my nap; then a cup of tea. Bea loved afternoon tea—orange-flavored herb tea with toast and jelly.

The cardinals, sensing danger, fly off together entwining their paths like two strands of ribbon until they reach a low grapefruit limb.

Wonder if it's true that birds mate for life. He looked at his watch. It's early for lunch, but I could go on campus. Maybe I'll find someone to join me like in the old days. None of those guys are left, though, and the new people are too busy. They eat lunches out of a paper bag in their offices. Ugh! . . . I did it the first few years, but those were different times. We didn't make much money, and Bea didn't work. Nowadays everybody works—wife, children, everybody. And still they complain . . . I couldn't have made it without Bea. She organized our income like a financial planner. We always had enough; never plenty, just enough.

According to Bea squirrels never have enough. Said they'd steal an orange, take it up the oak tree, eat it, and throw the peels at her and laugh. No, she didn't like them at all, but she wouldn't let the boys shoot them with their slingshots.

A lame squirrel wobbles down the oak. Inexplicably, Bill's eyes well. He wants to help it, but knows it would scurry off. Bill looks at the cardinals on their safe perch in the grapefruit tree and down at the lame squirrel trying to pick up an orange with its teeth. *He'll never make it.*

The sun nears its zenith; the sky is blue now. Bill sits in one of the oak rockers and lets his head fall back, eyes closed, absorbing the sun's energy.

The creaking screen door startles him. "Watching the birds again?"

"Uh . . . I guess so."

"Want some company?"

"How about going out for lunch?"

"We can stop somewhere on our way back to the condo. Or, if you like, I have some nice leftovers."

Bill took Wanda's arm in his and opened the door into the house. With a slight bow, a smile, and a formal gesture, he escorted her in.

Counting The Days

The mood was clammy. The occasion drew weak handshakes and bland smiles. Charlie Tyke, the manager, had locked the front door of his Jewelry story and his wife had brought out the cake bearing forty flickering candles. In his formal, priggish way, Charlie said, "Thank you all for staying to help us say goodbye to our long-time friend and fellow employee, Stretch Longo." Then, turning to Stretch, "We all wish you a very happy and prosperous retirement. You have been a stalwart member of this business and have added much to our prosperity and wellbeing. You have earned a rest from the daily grind. You are the best watchmaker I've known. I'm sure we all wish you the best. My last advice is, 'Go fishing.'"

Though flattered by the group's genuine offers of congratulations, Stretch, never one to make speeches, merely smiled and said, "Thanks, everyone."

Gathering his colleagues' presents and his toolbox, he shook their hands. Finally Charlie embraced Stretch warmly and slipped an envelope into his jacket pocket. "A little bonus for the years you served Tyke Jewelry, Stretch. Please drop in whenever you're in the neighborhood. We'll always be happy to see you."

Stretch Longo's longish limp hair bounced gently as he walked. His new, unwelcome reality conspiring with his tendency to frown etched deep gashes into his lean, chalky cheeks. Round shoulders and a habitual forward curvature made him appear to be racing to keep from falling forward.

"Sixty-five is not old," he thought, "but it's no age to start something new."

Within minutes the sun had spread a blood-red glow over the sky, and Stretch found himself walking the route he had followed most of his forty years at Tyke Jewelry: Crossing the Kennedy Avenue Bridge west to South Boulevard and then the three blocks south to the small, one-hundred-year-old house he and his wife Patty had bought and remodeled two years after they were married. The twice-daily walk was short except during summer's heat, which had temporarily subsided. The walk would have been pleasant enough if Stretch had been aware of his surroundings. He did not see the sparkling stars heralding nightfall like tiny trumpets. Rambling thoughts moved in time with his heels' metronomic tapping against the sidewalk to conjure the sound of a heavy clock meting out niggling seconds. An impromptu breeze transformed large oaks into gentlemen bowing and turning away as he passed. The shroud of dusk that enveloped him and his tapping heels amplified the sensation of marching into dark, uncertain future.

Stretch Longo walked through his front door, set his toolbox on the floor with a loud clatter, dropped into his reclining chair, and picked up the book he had left the previous night. He flipped it closed to review the cover: "A Brief History of Time by Stephen Hawking." Smiling sardonically, he shook his head slowly and returned the open book to his lap.

Hearing the front door close Patty came down the stairs. Her sixty-four years were barely evident through her radiant smile and trim figure. Her auburn hair betrayed no signs of graying. "Tired, Honey? How about a beer?"

"I should have left these tools for somebody who could use them."

"It's a new start, Stretch. Now we can do what we want when we want and go where we want anytime we want. Sounds pretty good to me."

"How the hell do I know what I want to do or where I want to go?"

"Come on, Stretch. This is a new chapter in our lives."

Slamming the book closed and returning it to the table he said, "Feels more like the last page."

She sat beside him with her arm around his shoulder. "Kiss me, lover."

He pecked her cheek and gently eased her out of the recliner. "Not now, Patty. I'm feeling kind of low."

With a renewed smile she said, "There's a good movie on TV tonight—The Grapes of Wrath."

"Don't you think I'm depressed enough?" Seeing her smiling, he smiled. She was always able to make him smile.

After a few moments staring out the window at the few stars that had begun to flicker, he said, "I was just remembering the summer Dad drove us out west and looking out the window at the passing electric posts ticking off the miles. They passed by like seconds. And the phone lines waving down and up between the poles, like a conductor directing an orchestra. It seemed to be so periodic and even and constant, like the movement of the moon around the earth and the earth around the sun, like a great big clock, so regular and even and constant. I loved it."

After a moment he said, "There's nothing quite like a watch—wheels and gears clicking with determination, even enthusiasm. A watch is as mesmerizing as those telephone lines. Like waves lapping the beach—except that waves move at random; but their effects aren't random. Watches affect how we think about time, especially a good old windup watch that pours out time as a smooth, steady stream. Those damn digitals spit out seconds and minutes like bullets. It makes us live out our lives in chips of seconds, minutes, and hours. That kind of time ties us into knots. I've watched people fidget as I set and wiped clean their timepiece. Made me feel I was stealing their time. What is time anyway? We measure it in seconds, minutes, hours, days, weeks, months, years, decades, centuries, epochs like bookkeepers. Suppose these units didn't exist, how would we talk about the past or the future? Would we live only in the present? Would every event feel like part of the present? Would our entire lives be smeared out into a massive present?

"Don't say it: I don't know what I'm talking about; and this little book written by a genius tells me nothing. I know watches and how to fix them; I'm a technician. I wouldn't have the imagination to devise a better gadget for measuring time even if I wanted to; and I don't want to; Quartz watches are perfect.

"I've read and thought a lot about time, but I still don't get it. What's a millisecond? One one-thousandth of a second. Atomic events occur in picoseconds—one trillionth of a second. I can write all the zeros, but its meaning leaves me cold. Anyway, however I measure my life, what will it have meant, what will I leave when I'm gone? Lots of old watches happily ticking? Satisfied customers? But what have I added to the world? My father came here from Sicily with ten bucks, two changes of clothes, and the knowledge and tools of a master watchmaker. He left them to me with love and a vision of the future. Has my life fulfilled his dream? If he could look down on us what would he think?"

"Come now, Stretch. You've lived a good life; you've made me happy; we have a nice home and respect in the community."

"Patty, my string of ancestors stretches back to the beginning of humans a million years ago. But I'll be nobody's ancestor. That long line ends with me, and that's unbearably sad. I've lived my life between eternities, and I'll leave it without hope."

With tears welling she said, "Lots of people aren't able to have children. God gave us life and we should be grateful and not worry about what we can't control. We've lived well and we've helped those we could help. We've done our best. Our lives have turned out according to God's will."

"God must be a comedian, sprinkling lives all over the planet and then sitting back watching them bumble and stumble."

Seeing the tear stream down Patty's cheek, Stretch stood and embraced her. "I'm sorry, Patty. You're a wonderful wife. I shouldn't make you miserable with my stupidities. I'm sorry. You don't deserve that."

"It's all those books, Stretch. They're so deep—philosophy, history, science—They stir you up. Life is simple. You're born, live as best you can, help others, and thank God for the opportunity. Everything else is trivial."

As she turned away to look out the window, he said, "Let's eat out tonight. You know, to celebrate my retirement."

Stretch Longo sprang to a sitting position before he realized he was awake. The sudden jolt woke Patty: "What is it?"

He shuddered as if trying to shake something off, his eyes searching wildly. The clock read 6:13.

"What happened?" Patty said.

But he had bounded out of bed and was pacing the room. She stopped him and held his hands. "Come back to bed, Stretch. It's still dark."

"It was awful."

"It was just a nightmare."

He was still shaking.

"Tell me."

He shook his head.

"I'll make some coffee."

"Uh-huh."

A benevolent moonbeam through the small window above the sink bathed the stove and refrigerator; they appeared as porcelain islands. Patty flipped on the ceiling light and a small rectangular table with two chairs materialized. Stretch walked to the coffee maker, measured in the coffee and water, pushed the "on" button, and sat down. Patty dropped four slices of bread into the toaster, pushed down the lever, and sat across from him.

"I was standing in the middle of an enormous room with big boxes lining three walls; the other wall had floor to ceiling pegs that held every tool I had ever seen or heard of. It was dark, but I could see everything clearly. Nothing moved. I stood wondering how I got there, and then heard a soft, soothing, rumbling voice. I couldn't tell where it came from; sounded like Papa, accent and all. He spoke softly, but I could hear him clearly. Shivers went through me."

"And what did he say?"

"Your life will end in one hundred days.' Sounds silly I know, but it scared hell out of me coming in that calm, regretful, loving, Italian baritone. I think it was the tone that got me."

"Nightmares can be powerful. Everybody has them."

"It was a prophecy, Patty."

"Surely you're not taking it seriously. It was a dream. Probably means you're afraid to die. That's not surprising."

"I never think about dying."

"Maybe not, but you've given up a life's work you loved. That's an end, a kind of death, but you still have a lot to live for."

Looking away he said, "Maybe." He had never subscribed to Patty's psychological interpretations, but thought there might be something in what she was saying. At any rate he felt relieved and calmer.

"What would you like?"

"Just coffee and toast. I'm not hungry."

"How about an egg?"

With his fists in his cheeks he shook his head.

By the time they finished and he helped Patty with the dishes, he felt better. "I guess you're right, Patty."

Stretch was calm the remainder of the day, but the memory of the dream continued to needle in and out of his consciousness. Not wanting to watch TV or read or go out, he contented himself with sitting in his living room chair watching his neighborhood out the window as an observer, no longer a participant.

In late afternoon, as the sun dipped into the trees, he stepped out the kitchen door, surprised at the sudden warmth. Without the lightest stirring of a breeze, he imagined a blanket had fallen over the earth, squeezing all the air out leaving the trees jammed into dull, dead sky. The darkening tranquility felt stifling, frightening. Stretch had planned to water his flowers, but the crushing heat pushed him back inside.

Next morning Stretch again awoke in a sweat and breathing rapidly. Expecting it, Patty dialed 911. Stretch reached over and cancelled the call with a heavy finger. "Don't, Patty. It was the same dream. It's scary, but I'm not going to the emergency room to tell them my dream. They'd send me to the psycho ward."

"I'm worried, Stretch."

"I'm fine; a little shaken, but fine."

He had trouble falling asleep that night; two fitful hours passed before he finally succumbed.

The clock radio showed 8:10 when he opened his eyes. He lay quietly trying not to wake Patty, but she was already awake.

"The dream?"

Smiling, he said, "No; a different one and funny; I mean hilarious. I was at work repairing an enormous watch, so big I could barely lift it. The parts were so massive I could see them all without straining. I was using auto mechanic's tools, and when I wound it with a large wrench, its tick sounded like a sledgehammer pounding an anvil." He was laughing so hard he could barely finish.

To Patty's relief, Stretch spent the remainder of the morning in good cheer. He took a long walk through their neighborhood. Seeing his neighbor watering his flowers, Stretch stopped and commented on the heat.

"Not as bad as a hot engine," the neighbor said. I spend whole days with them."

"I guess I was lucky working in an air conditioned store," Stretch said.

"I'll say," the mechanic said. "Sometimes I feel like turning this hose on myself."

Stretch smiled and walked on.

That night, feeling confident, Stretch fell asleep in minutes. A little past midnight, he woke in a sweat, his heart racing. The dream and his father's voice were identical to the first two except for the number of days—now ninety-seven. Rubbing his eyes he thought, "God! Ninety-seven days." Careful not to wake Patty he walked to the kitchen and looked at the wall calendar. The moonlight was bright enough to see by. Moving his finger along the calendar he mumbled, "It's August 7th. Ninety-seven days takes me to November 12th, a little over three months. That's not long." He put a tiny pencil dot on that date.

Telling himself no one lives forever offered little comfort. That trivial eddy of crystal-pure logic could not obscure the solid, brittle reality that awaited him as the seconds ticked. And like those seconds, hours and days would click past with the grinding of the great clock. "Everybody has to die. Some of my healthy-looking friends could die before November 12th, so what's the big deal? Of course! The deal is they don't know when and I do . . . It's only a nightmare, but it feels so real, so solid."

By 1:15 he had settled into silent resignation and quietly walked back to bed, slipped in, and fell asleep within minutes.

Seeing Stretch asleep beside her, his feet exposed beyond the cover, Patty rose relieved. "How about eggs this morning, Stretch?"

"Sounds good. I'll get the coffee going."

Minutes later, finishing his coffee, Stretch said, "I had it again."

Patty put down her cup and looked at eyes that seemed calm. "No problem?" she said.

"No problem."

Patty smiled, "More coffee?"

"No thanks . . . OK, but just a little."

As she poured he said, "I've been a bore since my retirement."

"I wouldn't put it that way, just not yourself."

"I knew something was wrong the day I walked away from the jewelry store. Remember when we bought this house? It was so big. My parents never had such a house. Now it feels smaller. I seem to bump into you every time I turn around. It was a fine house for thirty-five years. Then it shrank. I don't know what to do with myself."

"Maybe you need to get out more."

"It's not that, Patty. A man's work means a lot to him."

"I guess if we had had a . . ."

"Please Patty. It wasn't your fault or mine; just nature, fate, whatever."

"You're a lot like your dad, Stretch. You worked hard and took it seriously. I remember how your customers would watch you with fascination, your tall frame hunched knot-like over your workbench, eyepiece jammed into your eye-socket, long thin dexterous fingers gently, deftly manipulating tiny tools with the skill of a surgeon. I loved to watch you. You were an artist like your dad.

What really did me in was those cheap, quartz, battery-powered watches. I felt trivial replacing batteries, adjusting wristbands, changing plastic covers. Remember that old watch I worked on last year?"

"The old railroad watch?"

"What a beauty."

"I remember how much you enjoyed it."

They sat silent a while before Stretch said, "Papa never lived long enough to retire. He was lucky, I guess."

"Oh, Stretch, it's not that bad. You've got your health. You were a star athlete in high school. Why don't you try golf? You'd make a great golfer."

"I had the dream again, Patty, and there's no doubt. I won't live past November 12th."

"Stop the superstition! You're too intelligent to believe such nonsense. So what if you can't fix watches anymore? It's not the end of Stretch Longo. You just need to feel useful again and feel good about yourself."

The following Monday morning he left without telling Patty where he was going. Four hours later he returned to find her almost in tears on the living room sofa. He sat beside her, took her hand, and said, "I've been taking care of some business I should have done long ago."

She sat up and looked at him with her fists in her sides.

"Please, Patty. It's not as bad as all that. I should've drawn up my will long ago, so I looked up Charlie Tate's lawyer friend. It was simple. You're my only beneficiary. Simple."

"Oh, Stretch."

"Everybody should have one. It's no big deal."

Failing to calm her he said, "I also took care of signing up for social security. I should have done it sooner. See: that's looking to the future." He smiled and moved into the living room and turned on the TV. His responses to Patty had become the understanding smile with no attempt to argue. Patty could not stand his resignation, but worse was his almost grateful acceptance.

"Also I left my toolbox with Charlie Tate. Their next watchmaker will appreciate them."

Filled with an incendiary mixture of anger and sorrow Patty went into the kitchen to fix lunch.

As the days and weeks ticked by he became more withdrawn. Patty tried cajoling him, ridiculing him, threatening him, but his response never went past a smile and a shrug.

At her wit's end, Patty visited their doctor, an old family friend and the son of Sicilian immigrants. After listening politely, Dr. Castellano said, "My dear, you'll never convince him. He truly believes it's a prophecy. When he wakes up alive and healthy on November 12th, he'll believe it was only a dream."

"But it's ruining his life and mine. Even if he's right, he'll have ruined his last days with his listless pessimism. He doesn't talk; just stares out the window, waiting for the end. He's counting the days, marked them off on the kitchen calendar with little pencil marks. I think he's gone a little crazy, and I don't know what to do."

"I can prescribe something to calm him if you think that will help."

With Exasperation she said, "He's too calm now. Can't you give him something to make him optimistic?"

Dr. Castellano shook his head, smiled, and took Patty's hand. "Patience, my dear. He'll be fine. Try to stop worrying and go on with your life as usual. That will help him more than worrying."

She left the doctor's office feeling no relief.

Stretch seemed pleasantly relaxed when she returned. "Missed me?" she said.

"I'll always miss you, Patty.

Sensing from his tone that his mind was still mired in his obsession, she did not respond and heeded the doctor's advice to wait patiently for that fateful day to pass. "How does baked chicken sound?"

"Fine."

The next morning Patty walked to the church where they were married. She could not remember when she last attended mass, but she had occasionally stopped to sit and admire the stained glass windows. It gave her an indefinable feeling of peace.

The church was nearly empty with only two elderly women in black kneeling at the front pew. She sat in the pew behind them remembering Stretch's mother dressed in black after her husband died. That was during their first year of marriage, and it was her first encounter with the old world custom that mandated that widows dress in mourning the rest of their lives. How backward, she thought. These must be recent arrivals. She had thought of going into the confessional, but decided instead to pray silently for Stretch to recover from the weird obsession that held his mind in its grip. To Patty it had become more than an obsession; an evil spirit had invaded his brain. But she had never believed in such things. Did she now? Surely, she thought, something in his mind has sprung.

As she tussled with these vague and troubling ideas, she finally relaxed and began to pray. At first she hesitated, thinking: we always pray for what we want. Shouldn't I pray for God's will to be fulfilled? But she was not ready to yield to such rationality. She did not care about God's will; all she wanted was for Stretch to live. In the end, with such ambivalence, she began to pray fervently, murmuring aloud, "Please, dear Lord, help Stretch; please." She repeated these words over and over as a child would, hoping that simple repetition would work the desired miracle.

She returned home to find Stretch sitting by the living room window looking out over the neighborhood. It was a bright sunny, cool day, and he was watching two boys tossing a football back and forth.

"How's it going, Stretch?"

"Fine. Just remembering how I liked to play football when I was their age."

"You're never too old to play, Stretch. Maybe not football, but . . . Say, would you like to take a walk?"

"No point, Patty. I'm fine here just looking."

"That's all you do these days—look at the outside world. But you've got a life beyond this window, Stretch. Why don't you get out in it? Look up some of your friends?"

"Maybe tomorrow."

"Today is November 11th, the day World War I ended. We used to celebrate it as Armistice Day; you're celebrating it as your last day. Don't think I haven't seen those sickening marks on the kitchen calendar."

He smiled back as his eyes filled.

"For heaven sake, how long can you keep this up?" She was almost yelling.

"Not long, dear."

She stalked out of the living room into their bedroom and slammed the door.

That night they watched an old movie on TV. At the end Stretch turned off the TV and walked to their bedroom, pulled back the cover, and slipped in saying nothing. Patty slipped into bed beside him and lay on her side facing him. Knowing what he was thinking, she felt helpless. He lay quietly and then turned toward her and kissed her with more feeling than she had felt in years. He looked for several moments into her watery eyes and finally lay back and turned on his side away from her. Knowing she could add nothing to what she had repeatedly said and knowing that Dr. Castellano was right, she faced the other direction as tears streamed down her cheek onto the pillow. Within minutes they were both asleep.

The next morning Patty awoke and turned to Stretch, who was still on his side. She watched for several minutes trying to detect his breathing, but saw none. Calmly she left the bed, put on her robe, and returned to see her husband still, his face relaxed and calm, smiling gently.

A Word From Our Sponsors

I didn't hear the clock radio come on that Sunday morning. Lying on the opposite side of the bed, Jean moved my head toward the clock so I could see the time: 7:55. Still trying to recall the dream she had interrupted, I lay there quietly as the announcer related the usual trivial, human-interest story they save for the end of the hour-long news session. She was saying something about signals from a star ten light years away. Still shrouded in my evanescent dream, I tried to estimate the distance: if it came from that star, the signal has traveled at the speed of light for ten years. Its message, if there is one, is ten years old.

One would have expected such news to come with shattering force, but it came instead as a footnote to the major news of the day. As I recall, it was a simple item on NPR's Morning Edition that ran something like, "Astronomers at the SETI observatory announced yesterday that they have for some time been receiving 'curious signals' from outer space. They warn that these signals may be no more than random interstellar noise." In the interview that followed, the director of the observatory related that SETI, which stands for "Search for Extraterrestrial Intelligence," has been listening for evidence of life beyond the solar system since the late nineteen fifties. The voice of the scientist continued: "We are not saying these signals carry meaning. They may be random noise. We are analyzing them to determine whether they carry any informational content."

The announcer broke in: "Is there a lot of random noise coming from outer space?"

"Of course. We've been hearing it for over fifty years. That's why we're so excited."

"How do you distinguish between random noise and a signal? In other words, how would you decode an actual signal? Obviously those beings would not speak English or any of earth's languages."

"Rather than language we look for mathematical relationships among the frequencies: some number or set of numbers that would be common everywhere in the universe, such as lines in the spectrum of hydrogen."

"Why hydrogen, Dr. Spangler?"

"Because hydrogen is the simplest element and the most plentiful element in the universe. We detect it everywhere."

"Thank you Dr. Spangler. And now a word from our sponsors."

The interview was far from moving, for the scientist spent most of the interview assuring listeners that static, meaning random noise, is commonly heard from many stars. "Occasionally the noises seem to have a pattern, but we have not yet deciphered any pattern. We must be careful to avoid the suggestion that we have made contact with extraterrestrial intelligence.

Though there was another mention of the SETI announcement several days later, it soon vanished from sight, and I thought little about it except to wonder how exciting it would be to contact intelligent beings from outer space. Adherents to the seductive idea of extraterrestrial life most often appear during late night radio talk programs, along with people who claim to be UFO abductees, fortune-tellers, and reincarnated characters from the past.

I immediately called the radio station to respond. When I said I was a physics professor at the local university, she asked if I would stay on the line to answer callers' questions.

"Of course."

She introduced me on the air giving my background and that I would be happy to expand or explain more about the announcement and to answer questions.

I started by giving some background on Project SETI, when it started, and how exciting their work could be if and when they receive unequivocal signals from intelligent beings elsewhere in our universe. The first caller suggested that we should not be trying to contact alien beings until we are sure they are not hostile. "They probably just want to move here and take over the earth."

"You're right in being wary, sir. The reality, however, is that any culture capable of making contact with us is probably more intelligent than we are and may want merely to expand their knowledge and improve life for us all."

"You're pretty gullible, professor. Why would they spend all that money to help us? Seems to me they expect to gain something if they're going to so much trouble and expense."

"I'm a scientist as I'm sure they are. Scientists strive to understand nature, not only on earth, but also everywhere in the universe. Making contact with another world would open them and us to a tremendous exchange of information, science, and technology, and probably art as well. We would all benefit."

"I don't agree, professor, but I'll drop it."

The second caller expressed similar feelings: "Hello, professor. I'm not a scientist like you and those aliens out there. I'm just a common man. I have a wife and three kids. I work two jobs just to pay our rent and put food on our table, and I can't barely make it. So the honchos in Washington are spending money trying to make friends with aliens, who may be after the little we have. I say we should close that there SETI, or whatever you call it. That's what I think. That's all."

The third caller had only a brief comment: "That fellow's your typical smart-ass professor. Thinks he knows what's right and what's good for everybody. I don't need no professor telling me what's right."

"Well, professor, we've run out of time, so I'll say thank you very much for helping us out. Now for a word from our sponsors."

The Outlander

Vivian Margin drove the long, black Buick into driveway and stopped with a screech. Edgar was lying face down in the middle of the front yard beside the azalea hedge he had planted the previous week. His jeans and khaki shirt were torn and frazzled. Her heart pounding, she threw open the car door, ran to him, and turned him over. His face and arms were covered with scratches; some still oozed blood through his clothes. She tried to revive him, but could not. Her heart racing, she ran to the door. It was locked. Fumbling the keys she muttered, "Go in, damn you!" Finally it did. She ran to the phone and dialed 911.

The next two minutes oozed like eternity. She tried vainly to revive him by mouth-to-mouth resuscitation. Within minutes the ambulance stopped in the driveway behind her car, lights flashing. Two men dressed in white rushed to Edgar. Vivian moved back. They listened for his heartbeat and then pounded his chest and listened again, but could find no sign of life. Finally one of the men turned to Vivian: "Are you OK?"

"Of course not. How's my husband?"

"Let me check your blood pressure."

"I'm all right."

The attendant led her to the ambulance and placed the sleeve around her arm as she continued to object. "One-seventy over ninety-five. That's pretty high, Mrs. Margin. Is it normally that high?"

"Damn it, don't just leave him there! Do something."

"I'm sorry, Mrs. Margin. He's gone. We'll have to take him."

"What do you mean he's gone?" she said through jerking sobs. "He was fine when I left a few hours ago."

"Looks like a massive heart attack."

"That's impossible. He was very healthy—jogged, dieted, did everything right. It can't be."

As the men rolled the stretcher into the ambulance she noticed the roll of papers in his left hand.

Prying his fingers loose she said, "Wait. What is this?" Noticing the patch of white skin she grabbed his wrist and said, "Where's his watch?"

The attendant shrugged. "Judging by the scratches, it may have been ripped off. Want to ride with us to the hospital?"

"He never made a move without his watch."

The men anchored the stretcher inside the ambulance. She was about to say something when another car arrived. The driver emerged and spoke quietly with the ambulance driver. Vivian watched dazed, the papers clutched in her hand.

"Excuse me, Mrs. Margin." The man, wearing a tee shirt, jeans, and a baseball cap, showed her his open wallet. "Detective Hopper, Tampa Police Department. I know how upset you must be, but would you mind answering a few questions?"

"You don't look like a detective," she said.

"I can't discuss that, Ma'am. Just a few questions if you don't mind." He walked to her car, turned off the ignition, and handed her the keys. "This where you found him?"

"Somebody took his watch. He never went anywhere without it. I think the ambulance people . . ."

"We'll look into it, Mrs. Margin. Please try to remember."

"I found him by the azaleas. It was a little past three when I drove up. I almost couldn't get in the house to call 911. Then I tried to revive him. These men say he's . . . gone."

"Yes, Mrs. Margin."

"He was clutching these."

Stretching out the ream of papers he said, "Larger than usual . . . U.S. Government watermark. Is this the paper he normally uses?"

"How the hell do I know? What's the difference?" she said, sobbing. "He's dead."

"I'm sorry, Mrs. Margin. It may not mean anything, but he looked a little battered. These papers might shed light on what happened. May I have them?"

"I don't . . . I suppose so . . . wait. Who are they addressed to?"

Finding the first page he said, "To whom it may concern."

"Well it concerns me and I want them."

"OK if I run down and make a copy? It won't take long. A few minutes at most."

She nodded through sobs. The ambulance driver asked again if she wanted to go to the hospital. She waved him on without answering.

Vivian Margin waited on the front porch tapping her foot, her hands shaking. Pretty for her age, she wore her long hair up in a bun that flattered her slim face and high cheeks. Tall and slender, Vivian refused to relinquish her image of the slim, curvaceous beauty. Her green eyes blazed with anxiety and anticipation. She wondered why she was waiting there in the cold, when she could as easily go inside and sit down. But she remained frozen to the spot, tapping her foot on the brick tile floor. She was not sure she was trembling from the shock or the cold, January day, mouthing to herself, "I'll call Laura when I know what happened. She'll be devastated."

Half an hour later Detective Hopper returned with the copy and found her still standing on the porch. He stepped up to the porch with the papers and said, "It's very interesting reading, Mrs. Margin. I think you'll be interested. Here, take a look."

"Now?"

"Just the first page, if you don't mind."

She frowned through teary eyes as she read and soon began shaking her head. "Poor thing . . . sounds like he was hallucinating."

"Possibly, but is it his writing?"

"Pretty erratic. Edgar was always extremely precise about everything. But yes, it's his."

"It's a strange story, Mrs. Margin, and you'll want to take your time. I'd like to send the original to Washington for an opinion."

"Opinion? About what? Why Washington?"

"It may not be important, Mrs. Margin. But if it's . . . well, I don't really know, but considering his story, it bears examination. You'll see why when you've read it. The folks in Washington may say there's nothing to it, but I'd prefer to tie up the loose ends."

"I guess so."

"I'll be back as soon as I hear something."

Vivian Margin walked into the house, sat in the living room sofa, and straightened out the pages of Edgar's manuscript. It read as follows:

*   *   *

To Whom It May Concern:

My name is Edgar Margin. Until I retired on June 30, 2000, six months ago, I taught chemistry in the University of South Florida. The chemistry building sits eight tenths of a mile due west of my house. I am 63 years and nine months of age and in good health. I am married and have a daughter named Laura. The last time I saw my wife . . . no, not yet. Laura is, was, a recent graduate of Harvard University and lives in Cambridge, Massachusetts with her husband, a physicist. I apologize for wandering so.

I have not yet grown accustomed to retirement. Having worked all my life in a profession I love, it is difficult to turn it off like a faucet. I must admit that I succeeded beyond expectations and have achieved considerable recognition from my peers in chemistry. I say this to discourage you from reading this testimony as the ranting of an ignoramus or lunatic, even though what follows will sound implausible. As anyone who knows me will attest, I am not given to flights of fancy.

I report the following not because of its devastation, but because it defies scientific reason. Devastation is neither unusual nor uncommon. But unnatural events are extremely unusual. Just days ago, I would have said they are impossible. Please understand: I do not mean miracles. I consider miracles mere flights of overactive imaginations. I am confident that some day science will explain what I have endured, but for now it strains all reason. However, beyond reason lies the indisputable fact too dreadful for words. Though this testament may be futile, I have no other alternative than to hope it will one day find its way into understanding hands.

Beginning makes me feel like a child trying to grasp a swimming fish and feeling it slip past.

I shall include every detail as it occurred so you will see that I have not concocted this unbelievable (absurd is probably the better word) story.

I begin with my first recollection of that morning four days ago: the clock radio went on at 7:27 and pushed a dream out of my mind. As Vivian pulled the covers over her ears, I lay still, my eyes closed, trying to recall the dream while the radio announcer, in a high-pitched, irritating voice frantically described the weather and the advantages of saving at the First Suburban Bank. I could not recall the dream. Taking my pulse for one minute by the digital clock radio as I often do, it was 126 beats per minute.

"Must I go first?" I said.

"Don't rush me, Edgar."

Vivian grudgingly threw back the cover leaving me partly uncovered. I scrambled to cover myself as she tiptoed on bare feet into the cold, tile brilliance of the bathroom. A few minutes later she pinched my toe through the covers to let me know she had finished and was going downstairs. I rose carefully out of a chronic backache that dissipates soon after I stand and move around.

The only thing I recall about the bathroom was that Vivian had moved my shaving gear from its normal place, which irritated me. When finished, I walked down stairs in my bathrobe. Breakfast was nearly ready, so I helped Vivian set the table. We each had an egg over light, toast, coffee, and a small glass of orange juice. The digital kitchen clock showed 7:55 when I sat down. "Where's your watch, Edgar?"

"I left it in the bathroom. You moved my things again."

She chuckled, "I like to keep you on your toes, Edgar."

I ignored her and mention this only to demonstrate that I am not the neurotic timekeeper some people claim I am. As usual, I read the paper during breakfast.

"There's a University Women's Club meeting today. I'll eat with them and then do some shopping. Will you need the car?"

Flipping the page of the newspaper I said, "I'll be at my desk most of the day. If I need to go on campus I'll take my bike."

"Shall I leave something for lunch?"

Each morning began like this—a series of nonsequiturs to interrupt my reading. "I don't care. Aren't we dining at the Buchners'?"

"Yes."

"Then I'll make a sandwich." Throughout the conversation I did not look out from behind the paper hoping she would leave me alone. Oh, how I wish I could hear her voice now. But I mustn't ramble.

I finished my coffee, folded the newspaper under my arm, and helped Vivian gather the dishes into the dishwasher. She spoke, but I don't recall her words. Something in the newspaper preoccupied me, but it, too, has slipped my mind. I moved into the living room to finish the newspaper. The next time I saw Vivian she was walking down the spiral stairs.

Jerking my bare wrist into view I said, "When will you be home?"

"It's a little past nine; I'll be back around two thirty. I may stop in on Karen. She called twice yesterday, and I didn't have time to talk."

"It's not a little past nine, Vivian; it's 9:33. And now that we're at it, what does 'around' two-thirty mean?"

"Damn it, Dr. Perfect; what the hell's the difference?

"Please, Vivian; you know I detest profanity! How can you possibly plan your day with such imprecision?"

Shaking her head as if she did not want to argue, she bent over, kissed my cheek, and left. Through the window I watched her back down the gentle slope of our driveway and glide down the tree-lined street and around the corner. I poured myself a second cup of lukewarm coffee and walked upstairs to my study to work on my new book.

My desk faces a large window that overlooks the front yard and down the hill to the bend in the road. Our house stands (stood?) at the highest elevation in the area, 113 feet above sea level. I can see all around and down to the Hillsborough River approximately half a mile east. In our front yard stands, or stood, a massive live oak. It was that tree that sold me on this property. Its eight-foot diameter near the base made it a landmark in our neighborhood. One of my first acts when we moved here was to plant azaleas around the foot of the tree. We designed our house to take advantage of its shade. One large limb stretched past my study window. Often a squirrel would perch on it and watch me work. The oak rose from the pinnacle of our hill and shaded most of our house.

Vivian had redecorated this room in blue for our son—cartoon character wallpaper, crib, changing table, everything she could think of. But we didn't need it. I thought it would help to change the room's appearance and find another use for it, so it would not remain a constant reminder. The room had become a tomb, and not seeing baby things made our loss even more complete. Vivian's eyes would tear each time she looked in. Perhaps . . . but that's behind us now.

Sitting at my desk staring at the pile of chapters, I tried to think about the book and not the little boy who never came. I wanted to devise a thread that could link concepts together into a new, different, rational whole. Yes, I had retired from the university, but not from chemistry. I would write a textbook that would revolutionize chemical education.

All general chemistry textbooks are essentially the same. As I looked at the pile of papers, a new approach gelled spontaneously like a flash of light in my mind. And with it came a strange and serene confidence—a revelation, you might say: Why not present the subject as it developed historically, giving experimental observations first and then explaining how theories evolved from them? It wasn't foolproof; a historical approach would repel some instructors, who, saying they want change, always adopt textbooks that follow the same old approach. But it could work, and it would be truer to the science as well as more interesting. Students would learn from the start how chemists know what they know and not just memorize facts and concepts to be used in subsequent courses. The idea lifted a massive weight from my shoulders. I fished out my tentative table of contents, turned on the computer, and began composing an introduction to lay out my new rationale. I've seen and used many texts in my career, but I've never seen this idea expressed or developed. I imagined this book spreading my name through the chemical world like magic dust and transforming the teaching of freshman chemistry. My research had not chiseled my name into stone for posterity. I had produced chips at most. My work had been solid, but pedantic; journeyman's work, with little brilliance. I had not explained any of the important mysteries of nature. My new textbook would show the world that I am an innovative scientist after all.

Time vanishes when I dig into my work; it is like entering a timeless cavity with no awareness of the world outside—a chronological vacuum. I've always enjoyed that state. I don't remember even once lifting my wrist to check the time. I got up once to relieve myself and took a page to proofread and forgot to retrieve my watch; such was my concentration. I don't know how much time I spent fleshing out the rough draft of that introduction, but the words poured out miraculously. At a stopping point I walked downstairs to the kitchen, turned the burner on under the pot of leftover coffee, and looked at the kitchen clock—10:06. I went outside and the cool January day raised goose flesh on my arms. The morning was still gray. A squirrel scurried across the top of the wooden back fence and jumped to the lower limb of a water oak. Trees sold me on this lot. This one dominates the rear of the property but not like the large live oak in front. The shade made summer gardening possible. The squirrel looked at me quizzically, darting his head and tail nervously. I sat on the back steps, and we watched each other.

Remembering the coffee, I stood, and the squirrel scurried away. The pot was still cold, and the digital clock still showed 10:06. Irritated, I jerked my wrist into view, but saw only blanched skin. I flipped the light switches and they were out too, so I went to the breaker box in the utility room, flipped each one off and on, and returned to the kitchen. Still no electricity! I picked up the telephone to dial my neighbor—no dial tone.

Wondering what had happened, I looked out the window. The neighbor's house was not there! Tall grass and scrubby oaks covered the area. With my forehead pressed against the window I saw only virgin forest. I dropped the telephone and ran out the front door, forgot about the large flowerpot, and knocked it over as I turned and ran down the steps. The lawn was intact. It had been trimmed the day before and ended on a precise line where the street had been. But there was no street, no power lines, no streetlights. Only forest. The driveway ended at a young pine. I ran to the back of the house, looked, and ran around the other side to the front again. The fence and all the shrubs and the four citrus trees I had planted years ago were still there. My property was a neat rectangle carved out of a dry, brown forest. I felt I had lost my mind, but reasoned that asking the question meant I hadn't. My house and yard were intact. My vision turned yellow-brown.

I could barely lift my head off the ground. Slowly, trying not to fall again, I walked to the house and leaned against the stucco wall. *Calm down and think*, I told myself. I went inside and sat in the living room sofa. My stomach felt queasy; I began to salivate copiously and tried to hold it as I ran to the bathroom, but it was no use; I vomited all over the floor. The total absence of a rational explanation gripped me by the throat; I was afraid to fall again. It was too much: like a sharp needle in my chest.

Maybe other parts of town still exist, but I can't telephone anyone. I found my wristwatch on the dresser—1:45. Vivian had been gone four hours and twelve minutes! I tried to think calmly about where she might be and how I would find her, but it was no use. I ran out of the house, pulled the bicycle out of the garage, and pedaled as fast as I could, failing to comprehend the new pine tree. I ran into it at the end of the driveway and picked myself up trying to separate the real from the unreal. Luckily only my right arm and face were scratched. What was I thinking?

Did I think I could maneuver a bicycle through a forest? Leaving it I ran over crunching grasses and under scraping branches trying to follow where the street had been. *Where was Vivian?* The silent, unfamiliar terrain held no trace of human life—no houses, streets, power lines, no roaring of the nearby interstate highway—only deep, silent wilderness. I wandered through the scrub and over the landscape of my mind for over an hour before I made my way back up the hill. That was when I began to understand that I would not find Vivian. I repeated her name and my daughter's over and over, trying to make them exist.

As I caught sight of my house and the backyard perimeter fence, the university popped into mind. The edge of campus lies only a hundred yards west of my house. I walked through silent woods at least half a mile before I allowed myself to believe that all I had known was gone.

With a pain in my throat I stood where I judged the chemistry building had been and began to cry violently. Finally I gave in to exhaustion and sat with my face in my hands under a large, moss-draped live oak that now dominates the landscape. I may have dozed off; I can't be sure. I hoped the campus would reappear when I opened my eyes. Instead, my watch's nonjudgmental face scowled the time—5:09. As the sun dropped behind the trees I made my way home, not knowing if it would still be there.

The sun was setting as I arrived. Though I hadn't eaten since breakfast, I was not hungry. I took ham and cheese out of the refrigerator and put together a sandwich, reminding myself not to open the refrigerator door unnecessarily so the food wouldn't spoil. As dusk approached I rounded up all the candles and matches I could find and spent the early part of the evening in the living room watching a candle burn. I thought of the ancient Greek philosopher Heraclitus: *the flame changes but it doesn't change.* Just like me. I imagined the holocaust of activity in that flame—a hurricane at the atomic level. The candle burned calmly, the wax yielded gently, and I derived more rational comfort than physical warmth. I had spent my life looking for order in nature. Where's the order here? I knew there had to be a rational explanation. And I knew I was not crazy! This was real and I had to understand it. In my lifelong search for order, I had ignored the chaos. The sum of disorder may be order after all, like the candle flame.

I struck a match to light a second candle, but decided that watching candles burn would lead only to running out of candles, so I blew it out and sat a while in semidarkness. The moonlight entering through the large window lighted my way upstairs. I sat on the edge of the bed. Cool blue light bathed the Singer sewing machine and the picture of our beautiful daughter. I began to weep again, but this time no sobbing, only the ache in my throat. After a while fatigue overcame me and I lay down. Within a few minutes I began to feel calm for the first time. I slept lightly and felt awake much of the time, but I have learned that when I am not sure whether I've been asleep or not, I've slept.

The Second Day:

As the sun lifted past the treetops it was difficult to visualize yesterday's view out this window—roofs of neighbors' houses, driveways, cars, palms Midwesterners had planted to remake the rough, natural beauty into their image of Florida. All I saw was forest—moss-draped scrub oaks and pines shading brown weeds and an occasional wild flower. A squirrel flicked its tail on the great live oak branch near my window.

Surveying the backyard I suddenly realized it wasn't the same! Everything seemed so natural that I'd barely noticed—the backyard fence was gone! Yesterday it limited my property and held back the forest that had spread over the rest of the world. Now the fence was gone, but the grass and fruit trees were still there. My stomach again began to roil. I ran outside and found the shrubs I had planted against the fence had also disappeared: all forty-two of them. The four citrus trees seemed younger, smaller, but they still had fruit. The house, its shrubs and flowers were still intact. I tried not to think about tomorrow, knowing that if this process, whatever it was, continued, my house and I would soon disappear. Not only was the organized world disappearing and leaving only chaos; the chaotic forest was tightening like a noose. Out my study window I saw the great live oak in the front yard. It was smaller! No more than four feet in diameter. It had grown younger. The full disk of the sun clarified the scene, but offered no other clarity. Long shadows of dread spread across the lawn. After gulping down some milk, stale bread, and jam, I stood out back listening to the birds and squirrels chatter. My book manuscript flashed across my mind. Total nonsense now! I went inside with a stride of determination, though I had no clear idea, no plan.

Out loud I said, "I'm a scientist. I study natural phenomena. That's it!" I found my 100-foot, metal tape measure in the utility room, ran up to my study, picked up a clipboard, a pen, and a magic marker and ran to the back yard. First I noted down the positions of the citrus trees—two navel oranges, a Duncan grapefruit, and a Meyers lemon: all were there. Then I numbered each fruit on each tree with the magic marker and jotted down how many each tree held. In the next hour I measured the entire yard: back, sides, and front. The forest was indeed closing in. The width of my yard had contracted from 100 to 89 feet; the depth from 150 to 127.5 feet, approximately. I then measured the circumference of the great oak in front:

thirteen feet, which equals a diameter of 4.138 feet. I had spent my scientific life measuring rates of chemical reactions to learn how molecules interact with one another. Perhaps the rate of disappearance of my yard would shed some light on whatever was happening. The width had shrunk eleven feet and the depth 12.5 feet. I'd have to wait until tomorrow to determine whether the rate of shrinkage was accelerating or constant.

Immersed in these measurements and calculations, thoughts of my family receded. Having measured everything, I sat on the back porch. Suddenly my mind drifted to Vivian and our daughter. The horror of having lost them to some unknown process was unbearable. I tried to think of something else—anything—but I couldn't. I spent the rest of what may have been the longest day of my life on the porch trying visibly to observe the forest move in. I couldn't.

The Third Day:

Looking out the window at the sooty cavern of morning, I began to feel a loneliness I had never known before. Alone in prison or stranded on a deserted island, you can at least take comfort in the knowledge that you are separated by walls or a vast ocean. My situation was nothing like that. For all I knew the entire human race had disappeared leaving me stranded on a deserted planet. It was too much. I had to shake loose from these thoughts of isolation and try to comprehend what nature was telling me. Reading nature is the work of science. I would resume my measurements. But the thought of encountering a wild animal stopped me.

A candle lighted my way to the kitchen, where I ate two oranges. As I stood at the back door, violet-red had begun to stretch its fingers into the sky, and I became aware of the scent of wet grass. Persistent insomnia had offered many sunrises in recent years, but this one was to be different. As the red disk silently pierced the sky I was able finally to see that my citrus trees had vanished! Near where the water oak had stood, a young pine rose. My suspicion was right: the change was definitely accelerating. Further measurements were unnecessary.

Though I had steeled myself for the inevitable, a surge of panic nearly overcame me. Except for electrical and water failure, the house was still intact as far as I could tell. At this rate the house would soon be gone. As to what would happen to me, I could not imagine nor did I wish to. I might disappear along with everything else. Perhaps that wouldn't be so bad if it happened quickly. I might not even perceive it. As the world closed in on me I felt at its center or at least at the center of a tightening circle of being. But I ran through the forest that first day, so I knew I could exist outside. Also the mirror verified that the change did not include me. I had not changed.

The change had been strange in another way: it had left no uprooted plants or fence boards, only pristine land with no evidence of previous civilization. But whatever was happening, I would soon have to find another shelter, for our house would not stand much longer. That word, *our*, struck a sharp chord in my chest. Where are they? I had to force myself not to think about them, for doing so would certainly inhibit my ability to carry on, as I knew I must.

The Fourth Day:

That night I slept downstairs, reasoning that if the house disappeared, it would do so as the yard had: at its extremities. I awoke wet and trembling on the living room sofa beneath a starry sky. The second floor walls were still up, but the second floor and roof were gone. Not knocked down or battered, the house looked as if it had been abandoned in mid-construction. Was it being carefully disassembled? Watching the sunlight up the eastern sky, I knew time was still moving forward and at approximately the same rate. The moisture I thought was perspiration turned out to be dew; I was trembling from the cold. The kitchen was gone too, along with my meager food supply. The archway leading to the kitchen now dropped off to the dense forest that had now devoured the entire yard. My house looked like an interrupted construction. A pine branch reached into the living room. At that moment I knew that would be my last day there.

It took less than half an hour to gather what I needed—knife, pliers, fish hooks, fishing line, extra set of underwear, two oranges, candles, matches, first-aid kit, compass, sweater, raincoat, and a water-repellent hat. Before leaving I saw my old Boy Scout hatchet in its carrying case on a shelf and strapped it on. I have never been a religious man, but I slipped Vivian's small bible into my coat pocket. I felt ready to face the irrational world and the irrational in myself. Finally, I stopped at the live oak in my front yard. I did not measure it, but it was no more than a foot in diameter. Assuming it would grow to the great tree I knew, I hacked my initials, EM, big and deep into it using the hatchet with a vengeance I neither recognized nor understood. Then I looked around guiltily to see if anyone had seen me. Stupid! I calmed down and stood back to survey my crude handiwork, so unlike my research papers on which I had slaved to insure clarity and precision. Those initials did not represent me. Stiffening my back and throwing my head back, I carefully carved away the rough places with the knife to make the letters clear and presentable. This mark, after all, may be the last tangible trace of my presence in this world. My wristwatch showed 8:52 AM.

Having decided that the river would offer my best chance for survival, I headed east. I had seen it daily from my second floor study, but not from ground level where trees obscured it. At least the river would provide fish and water. I walked about a hundred yards and turned for a last look at my house. The walls were gone, and a thin pine rose where the living room had stood. Nothing I had known remained. I felt an urge to go back, took a few steps, and stopped. Confusion, remorse, and fear filled my brain. Bracing myself, I looked around to get my geographical bearing, took out my compass, and continued east to the river.

Though the day was cool, the sun pounded mercilessly, and I soon felt my scalp burning. I put on the hat I had rolled up in my pocket. By that time I was approaching a swampy area I recognized as the edge of the north campus. The university kept that large area as a wild life preserve. Where I stood, four lanes of Fletcher Avenue had bordered the swamp just three days ago. I always detested the roar of traffic; how I wanted to hear it again! With no evidence of civilization, the breeze filtering through trees broke the eerie silence. I wondered if the earth itself was alive. It was, of course, except for human life: tall cypresses with their bulging bottoms, sparse leaves and "knees" popping out of the water, and grasses and all kinds of smaller plants. I had never noticed how many different kinds of plants there were. A frog croaked. I recalled hearing that alligators make a croaking sound. I sped my pace east around the swamp along the high ground that had been Fletcher Avenue until I spotted the river through a thick stand of cypress trees. Speckling sunlight through a canopy of branches seemed inviting. Increasing my pace I reached the water's edge at 9:16 AM. The trek had taken only twenty-four minutes. Though I knew where it was, I was surprised to find it. Nothing these days made sense. Perhaps I could control, or at least understand, some things. For all I knew the terrain and the path of the river could also have changed. My hands were bloody from scraping branches. I wiped my face with my handkerchief and it was bloody too. Walking through this dense forest I felt engulfed in the earth. I had always felt I walked on it, but now I was in it. Enveloped in green and brown I recalled the movie, "Snow White" and how the trees in the forest grabbed at the frightened girl with gnarled, knotty fingers. The earth is a silent force greater than the roaring of any wild animal. Across the river an otter sauntered lazily. To my left under a tree a cottonmouth moccasin lay with its blazing white mouth open wide waiting for someone or something curious enough to inquire.

The river, quite broad at that point and curving sharply, had been the University Park. Oak limbs hung over to shade large patches of water, whose movement was imperceptible. A fish jumped; a fat alligator lay calmly on the opposite shore. After making sure there were none nearby, I looked for a place to dig worms. I had not done that since childhood in Alabama. They were not hard to find, and in a few minutes I was sitting under an oak, my line rippling the water, and, for the first time in days, I felt calm.

A guttural moan woke me out of my reverie like a lightning bolt through my chest. Horrified, I turned toward the sound. On the bank leaning on a tree stood a man holding a rifle in his left hand. His right sleeve was wet with blood, his stance unsteady. As I stood he whipped his rifle in my direction using only his left hand. I raised my hands, oscillating between fear and joy at finding a fellow human being. The man's faded gray trousers had a pale stripe down each side and looked vaguely familiar. His large-brimmed, crumpled, gray hat shaded a deeply grooved face. Black whiskers grew high up his cheeks. The hat had holes that could have been bullet holes. His apparent weakness caused his rifle to quiver in his hands.

I asked if he was all right. His right arm hanging, he pointed his rifle at my chest and said, "Reb or Yankee?"

"What?"

"I asked you a question, mister."

Sensing he had lost his mind, I forced a smile and tried to humor him: "Please put down the rifle. I'm not armed. Let me treat your wound."

"I won't say it again."

Slowly, with clear, deliberate movements, I slipped my first aid kit out of my backpack and sat him down, which was not difficult considering his weakness. I lifted his arm; he winced, and his rifle butt hit the dirt. I carefully rolled up his sleeve. The source of the bleeding was a gash just above his elbow. He probably needed stitches, but I could not provide them, so I reached for the alcohol. He must have realized I wanted to help, because he did not resist, always holding the rifle in his grip. Before applying the alcohol I said, "This will hurt, but the wound has to be cleaned."

He gritted his teeth as I cleaned around the gash with an alcohol-soaked cotton swab and spread antibacterial ointment over the cut. Then I laid a piece of gauze over the wound, and bandaged it tightly to close it as best I could. All the while I distracted him with chit-chat about my experience of the past four days.

"I used to live about half a mile west of here, but . . ."

"You talk like a Reb."

When I finished he said, "Stand over there, against that there tree."

"How did you get such a nasty cut?"

"Indians."

"Please! There are no Indians here."

"Maybe you'd like to go upriver and tell them."

This man did not sound crazy. When I asked what day it was he stared at me dumbly. I repeated the question and he said, "Mid-January. I don't know. I've lost track."

"And the year?"

"1866."

"At that moment I was convinced that he was indeed crazy and wondered if a crazy man with a gun would finally end this chaos for me. His musket looked new, but old-fashioned. My grandfather kept one like it hanging over his mantle in Alabama.

"Where did you get the rifle?"

"Thomasville, Georgia . . . when I joined up."

"Joined?"

"Enough questions! You going to answer me or not, mister?

"You're not making sense."

"And you are not being forthright," he said, squinting and leveling the muzzle at my chest. "What are you concealing?"

"Nothing! I'm from Alabama, but I've lived in Connecticut and Michigan."

"So, a Reb by birth and a Yankee by sentiment?"

Looking deep into the barrel I said, "Hear me out, and please believe me. The Civil War ended a hundred and thirty-six years ago. The year is 2001."

"I don't know what you're up to, stranger, but I don't have time to put up with a crazy man, so I'll explain it once: Lee surrendered last April, and I've been shot at by half a dozen murderous Yankees since then. That's why I'm in this mosquito-infested country. Maybe you ought to tell those damned Yankees the war has ended."

"It's not 1866; it's 2001."

He stood and dug his feet into the ground to steady himself.

"It really is 2001," I said, lifting the antibiotic tube from the first aid kit and pointing to the label. "See: December 2000."

"12/23/00? What does that mean?"

"That's shorthand for December 23, 2000. And look here: University pharmacy, Tampa, Florida."

Seeing him staring at my wristwatch I held up my wrist for him to see.

"What is that?"

"A wrist watch."

He held my arm and studied it. "It has no hands. Just numbers flashing. How do you do that?"

I slipped it off and handed it to him saying, "It's a digital watch. It gives the time in hours, minutes, seconds."

He looked at it closely and held it to his ear. "It isn't ticking."

"Believe me," I said. "You're wrong about the date."

"What are you doing out here without a weapon?"

"I'm a chemistry professor in the university just a mile west of here."

"They ain't nothing but scrub and swamp in these parts. Down river there's a town of white folks. That's where I'm headed. The war may have ended, but that hasn't kept rabble and carpetbaggers from taking shots at me."

"You're a Confederate soldier?"

"Don't you recognize the uniform, man? Of course! I'm Sergeant Rudolph Alexander, Georgia Seventeenth Patriots."

"Please, let's sit and talk. My back is killing me." Apparently he needed rest, so we sat beneath the oak facing each other.

I reasoned that, unless one of us is crazy, I've moved back in time. The only way to prove the year was by showing him my house and the university, but they're both gone.

I tried to explain as much to myself as to him: "If you really are a Confederate soldier, then I've moved back in time. And spontaneously! I have no idea how. I've always considered time travel to be wishful thinking. On the other hand, I read recently that one could move out of the flow of time by tunneling through the boundary of the space-time continuum. Problem is that I don't understand exactly what that means.

"Now, to analyze this logically I propose two hypotheses: First, one of us is insane. I think we can rule that out. Back in Alabama as a child, I knew an old man who thought he was still fighting the Civil War. Of course, no one took him seriously. That's why I questioned you, Sergeant. Second, moving back in time explains the disappearance of my house and family and the university and the city and everything. All signs of 2001 have disappeared, and where I lived looks as it might have in 1866! This second hypothesis is also consistent with the gradual disappearance of my home and yard without leaving debris, as if time had moved in reverse. This second hypothesis is also consistent with finding you, a Civil War soldier, who has fought Indians and carries an antique rifle. What it doesn't explain is why I didn't grow younger and disappear along with everything else and why the sun's movement didn't go in the reverse direction. That last question will have to wait; I have no ideas about it."

Rudolph Alexander was looking at me as if I were raving. I suppose I couldn't blame him. The story was indeed bizarre.

Squinting suspiciously as if not to rile me, he said in a patronizing manner, "Appreciate your help, mister. I never heard of nobody going back in time, but who can say? Strange things do happen. The Lord stopped the sun." Then he stood. "I'm feeling fine now; I'd best be going if I'm to reach the village before nightfall. Thanks for the bandage. It feels much better."

"Wait; I know it sounds crazy, but . . . listen, my name is Edgar Margin. I'm sixty-three and three-quarters years old. I retired from my university position six months ago." I held up my wristwatch and said, "Anyway, it's only 10:07 AM. You've got plenty of time, and I'd like to go with you. But let's rest a little longer. Tell me about yourself. Please try to understand: if I have indeed moved back in time, it could be the most scientifically significant event in history!"

The look on his face told me he didn't believe me. Perhaps he felt sorry for me because he sat again saying, "I estimate eight to ten miles to the town. I don't want to get there after dark, but I am obliged to you for bandaging my arm. I was born in Thomasville, Georgia. Alexanders been in Thomasville since before the Revolution. I remember Granddaddy talking about fighting Indians not far from our farm."

"Amazing! We all read about the Indian Wars, of course, but to hear about it from you, well . . ."

"We Alexanders have always owned our land. Not big farms, but we grew lots of cotton before the war. Mother taught me to read after supper when the day's work was done. We'd read the Bible. It was the only book we had. Poppa owned a hundred and twenty acres two miles south of Thomasville. Five years ago he came down with bad rheumatism. I was the elder son, so he asked me to take over the farm. My younger brother Alvin stayed on to help. He was fifteen and wasn't married. My sisters, Ruth and Virginia, stayed too. We owned fourteen slaves when the war started. And we cultivated over sixty acres of cotton. As soon as South Carolina seceded, almost every young man in Thomasville joined the Georgia Seventeenth Patriots. We fought in South Carolina, Tennessee, even Mississippi. But the worst was Chickamauga. Half our boys died, but we won. Then we lost Chattanooga just days later. Anyway, when word came down about Lee surrendering, well, I walked home. On the way I stopped at a cousin's farm north of town. They were packing up to leave. Said they'd been ransacked; then Yankees bought them out because they were three years behind in their taxes. Carpetbaggers took my farm too, after killing my wife, my parents, and my sister, Virginia."

At this point his voice began to crack.

"Alvin and Ruth ran off and waited for me at a cousin's house near Tallahassee."

"So you didn't return to the farm?"

"Not right away. Alvin and I went there by night to look around. From the barn we could see them in the house, moving around, eating, like it was theirs. Everything my cousins said was true. I wanted to break down the door and kill the damned carpetbaggers, but Alvin wouldn't let me. Said the authorities would get me sure. He was right. Nothing's sacred no more.

"Alvin said there weren't many folks living south of Lake City, and I ought to be able to find land there. He was sharecropping for another carpetbagger and said he'd join me later. Alvin's a good boy. Knowing what I would do if I met any of them, he got me out of Thomasville. Kept saying, 'Georgia ain't ours no more.'

"I walked south till I found a spot south of Tallahassee. Good soil, a river, lots of water, and nobody around—so I thought. But it'd already been claimed. A stranger I met a little ways south of there told me about a town at the mouth of the Hillsborough River called Tampa. That's where I was headed when I ran into the Indians and then you."

I had begun to feel comfortable with this man, so obviously uneducated and rough-hewn, but honest and forthright. I recounted my background: raised in a little town near Birmingham, then studied at Yale and the University of Michigan, then my first job at the university nearby. He listened politely, nodding occasionally.

"What do chemists do?"

"With your background you wouldn't understand."

His face hardened. After a few seconds he stood and said, "Thanks for the help, Professor, but I'd best be going."

"Wait. I wasn't expecting to find another human out here. I'm really glad we met."

"I may not be educated, Professor, but I'm not stupid. I was taught that education is important, but respect, honor, and duty are more important. Good day, Professor."

I picked up my pack and followed until I caught up with him. "I apologize, Mr. Alexander. That was rude of me. May I walk along?"

He nodded.

I told him about my university work, the academic battles over what I now consider trivial matters—scrounging for research money, fighting to reduce my teaching load.

He smiled throughout. When I paused he said, "I guess the difference between us is your problems are complicated; I've got only one, and it's simple: staying alive."

He was right. For the first time I saw how difficult staying alive can be. We kept within sight of the river. As a result, we walked farther than necessary. Tired as I was, I enjoyed talking. When I ran out of topics I told him about the past few days and the disappearance of my home and family.

"I'll admit: it doesn't seem real."

He nodded.

The walking and talking seemed to calm him. Finally he said, "You an inventor?"

I thought long before answering, not wanting to insult his intelligence again. "We scientists strive to understand nature, hoping that one day some smart inventor will use what we discovered in the service of mankind. We never know if our work will be useful. But I'll say this: when Michael Faraday discovered the laws of electricity and applied for a patent they asked what it was good for. He said he didn't know, but he was sure the government would one day tax it."

He smiled and said, "Somebody must think your work is important, or they wouldn't pay you to do it."

"In the long run research pays off. It's brought us air travel, radio, television, automobiles, telephones, computers, x-rays, cat scans, MRI, and lots of other advances, and, of course, nuclear energy."

He shook his head. "I never heard of none of them things."

I spent the next hour explaining twentieth century innovations. I enjoyed the lecture more than any I ever gave at the university, for he was interested; unlettered, but intelligent; and he drank in my words with a thirst I saw rarely in the classroom.

We reached a large open area where I asked to sit a few minutes and rest my back. Treating me as if I were an old man, he helped me down and sat beside me. He stared when I opened my backpack zipper. "That one of your new inventions?"

"No. I don't know when it came along."

"Sure is nice—easier than buttons."

"Have an orange; from my trees."

"It's been years since I saw an orange."

After the orange he stood, reached down, and helped me up. I thanked him and we walked on.

"I don't understand all this business about moving in time, Professor, but it is interesting. Sounds true the way you tell it."

"I'm not sure what's true anymore."

"Tell me more about the year 2001."

"Last week this area was a city park. They had picnic tables all around where people could come out on weekends. There was—I should say, will be—a dam across the river to control water flow. Tampa is—will be—a city of three-hundred-thousand people. The bay area has over a million. You must see the beautiful beaches twenty miles west of Tampa. People from all over the United States take their vacations there. That is, they will."

"Hard to believe. What about the Yankees? Will they get out of the South?"

"People from all over the country have moved to Florida. Native Floridians are a minority."

"What about the Darkies?"

"They're citizens like you and me."

"I reckon I'm not a citizen anymore."

"You will be. But there are still strong feelings about Blacks."

"What about slavery?"

"It's gone, but race still bothers some people."

"I reckon."

We passed an area where tall oaks hung over the river. It was too beautiful to pass up.

"What's wrong?"

"Look at that, Rudolph. It looks like we're floating in the air. The water is so calm you almost can't see it. It reflects the trees above it to make it look like a cavern. I'd love to be out there on a boat. It would feel as if I were flying."

"It certainly would, Professor. I don't know when I've seen a more enthralling sight. Would you like to stop a while?"

"I'd love to, Rudolph."

we sat at the edge of the river to look at the vision of vanishing, weightless water. We were both speechless. The silence was absolute with not a bird or insect stirring. All I could hear was my breathing. After a few minutes our reverie was broken by a strange rattling sound. Rudolph looked around carefully and then stood slowly and reached for my hand to help me up. "Don't make any sudden moves, Professor. It's a rattler. He's beyond striking distance, but we don't want to rile him. See him up ahead?"

I nodded.

"Just back up slowly and we'll be fine. If we don't threaten him he won't strike."

In less than a minute we had evacuated our blissful spot and were again walking toward our destination.

"It seems you are never safe out here," I said. "But it was beautiful."

"That water back there reminded me of our battles," Rudolph said. "Sometimes we would spend an hour waiting for the command. During those times it was so quiet you could hear a leaf fall to the ground. I remember one battle in particular, when the silence was finally broken. It was Armageddon with all the yelling and shooting and cannons blasting the air. I ran with the others, rifle in hand, not knowing where we were going or even seeing the enemy. They exploded in our faces when they started firing. The forest was blazing. It's a time in your life you can never forget, but while it's happening, you have no idea what you're thinking. It's as if an invisible will drives you. When it's over, you try to think about it, what you did and why, but it all seems a blur."

I was breathing fast listening to Rudolph's recital. "What battle was that, Rudolph?"

"They were all pretty much like that; the one I was thinking of was Chickamauga. For a time I thought we had gone to hell. We could barely see the enemy with all the trees, the thickest forest we ever had to fight in. We lost a host of good Georgia boys there. I remember my closest friend, Matthew Gay. We signed up together in Thomasville. A Yankee bullet got him in the chest. He just slumped over. I couldn't do anything during the fighting or even go to him until it calmed down. How much later I don't know. It was as if time had stood still. He lived ten days in terrible pain, delirious much of the time, before he finally died. We won that battle. I suppose that means we kept the position and the Yankees retreated. Matthew lost the battle, though, along with hundreds of others.

"Trouble was, not long after that, we engaged them again at Chattanooga, and they beat us bad. I sometimes wonder why so many good, honorable men had to die. What did it accomplish?"

"Rudolph, all I know about your war is what I've read in history books, but the Union survived. Most people thought the war was over slavery, but the real result was that the United States remained one nation."

"So you're glad we lost?"

"That's a hard question, Rudolph. I wish you hadn't had to fight the war in the first place. But if you insist on an answer, I'd have to say I'm glad the United States remained intact. In the next century we became the most powerful nation in the world."

"Being from the next century, Professor, you can see our war more calmly than I can. I've been up to my ankles in the blood of boyhood friends; it's hard to be calm about that."

We walked along a few minutes before either of us spoke. "But you may be right, Professor. If we had won, the South would be a separate country. But I'm not sure why that would be bad. What's wrong with having two nations instead of one?"

"I never thought about it, Rudolph. We could not be as strong, but I really don't know."

"You seem to be an intelligent and kind man, Professor. The war's over. We've got to move on. There's nothing else we can do."

"Moving on has a different meaning to me, Rudolph. How can I go on? My life is in another time. Am I to become part of this time, this world? What of my wife and daughter?"

"I have no answer, Professor."

Not really wanting an answer, I hesitated. Something had changed. Afraid time was once again changing,

I looked up to see great, black clouds rolling up on us. "Those clouds look ominous, Rudolph."

"Never fear. They're not the Lord's wrath, but only water."

"We'd better hurry."

"Rain is nothing new to me, Professor. I have lived in the rain for days at a time. I reckon we'll manage.

Our journey took into a different hue as the sky darkened. It was only 3:16 PM, but it seemed like dusk. Without consulting Rudolph, I hurried my pace. He smiled and kept up. Intensifying the daylight darkness was the forest that had swallowed us. Tall, arching oaks and cypresses at the water's edge seemed to be closing in on us. It is strange how menacing nature can feel. I had rarely noticed that before, probably because I had never been so deeply embraced by it. I felt as if I were treading on new ground, earth that had never before known the feet of humans. Of course, Indians had lived in the vicinity for centuries, but somehow, that was different. I was treading virgin earth much as our earliest ancestors had done. How could they have survived to create, in just thirty centuries, such a vast, complex world as mine in the year 2001? It truly was a miracle. I detest that word. I have already said what I think of miracles, but truly it is difficult to imagine such advancement. Now, here, in this dense, primeval forest, I can feel the gap between that early ancestor and me. Was it genius, or did something else push him along? I suppose that kind of question drove early man to create gods: to answer questions he could not answer. I suppose even early man had questions. And they undoubtedly needed answers as we do. Today, we seek answers in experiment and observation; the earliest man had not yet conceived science. He merely observed and created answers that seemed reasonable. We know today that the reasonable is not necessarily true, though it might be quite satisfying.

It grew so dark I was sure we would perish in a celestial deluge. As if the great rain god was waiting for the right moment to bring us to our knees. We raced, as Rudolph smiled at my fear of rain. Within a very short time—ten minutes at most—the sky had cleared away useless fears. I felt strangely happy and relieved. Then I realized that weather comes and goes, but my situation, whether under clouds or clear skies, had not changed.

Spotting a man in the distance, Rudolph said, "Look over there. That fellow's plowing a field. We must be getting close."

We walked to the man, who stopped his mule and stood waiting. The look on his face was not welcoming, but neither was it threatening. As we approached, Rudolph said, "Good afternoon, sir. We're headed for Tampa. How far is it?"

The man looked us over before he spoke. "Two or three miles along the river. But if you take the path over there, it's a little shorter, and the going'll be a little easier. A little ways down you'll find a footbridge. Cross it or you'll be on the wrong side of the town."

"I don't see a path, sir," Rudolph said.

"It starts just past my house over there. In fact, it's my path . . . I see you're a soldier."

"Yes, sir. Georgia Seventeenth Patriots."

"I fought with Sherman in Georgia."

Seeing the two men staring menacingly at each other, I said, "My name is Edgar Margin. I'm from a little north of here. Gentlemen, the war is over. Do we need more hostilities?"

"You're right, Professor," Rudolph said, and turned to the man, "Thanks for your help, sir. Maybe we'll see each other before long. I plan to settle here. Know of any farm land available?"

The man's face uncurled and a smile broke out. "There's plenty if you're willing to work. Find the land office in town. It's on Ashley Street along the river. They'll help you."

Rudolph thanked him graciously.

"By the way, my name's Clarence Knapp. I was born in upstate New York, but I lived most of my life in Michigan.

I got my fill of war and decided to settle down here. The weather's too good to pass up. Good luck."

Rudolph put out his hand and said, "Good meeting you, Mr. Knapp. Reckon we'll be seeing each other again."

As we walked away, Rudolph said, "Another carpetbagger."

"Perhaps not. Land must be plentiful if all you have to do is claim it."

"I reckon."

As we walked onto Knapp's path, two ruts in the grassy land, I felt we were traveling finally on a paved road. The storm clouds had completely disappeared, and the path to our destination looked inviting and clear. Soon we found the bridge and crossed it."

We reached Tampa at 6:26 PM. The sun was setting. We walked west into town on an unpaved, path marked Whiting Street. Whiting seemed to end at the river several blocks farther west. To our left stood a high wall with an entrance marked "Fort Brooke, U.S. Army." At Morgan Street we passed a gate to the installation. The gate was set back fifty feet or so from the outside wall. I suppose it was designed to stop intruders before they could get inside the fort. Inside, there were wagons and lots of horses. We walked past a sergeant who looked at us, smiled sardonically, and tipped his hat. Rudolph kept his gaze straight ahead and picked up the pace to Ashley Street five blocks ahead. Beyond Ashley flowed the river.

Tampa is little more than a scattering of houses radiating out from the eastern edge of the river at Whiting and Ashley Streets. Ashley Street is lined with frame houses and a few businesses, including a post office, a barbershop and dentist's office, a doctor's office, a general store, and a blacksmith's forge. At the point nearest the mouth of the river a fish market sells the catch of the day. Rudolph wanted to stop at the Land Office to inquire about farmland and found that it was part of the general store, so I browsed as Rudolph talked with the clerk. Judging by the goods for sale, the major occupations seemed to be farming and fishing.

"Lockwood's the name," the clerk said, extending his hand. After shaking our hands he turned to Rudolph: "All you got to do is find a parcel to your liking and let us know where it is. Then you can start farming. We'll register your claim right here. Try up river about half a mile, beyond the last farm, the Collins place. The land's better near the water. When you're ready to buy seed, tools, or anything else, come by. I'm the only supplier around, and I'm here to help my fellow man."

Mr. Lockwood stood tall, lean, and strong. A broad black hat covered a thick head of sandy hair. He was about forty and smiled as he spoke. Rudolph's now familiar squint told me he was not impressed.

"Alexander's my name. Where can I put up for the night?"

"Right here," Lockwood said, pointing up. "A clean room upstairs with a bed. You gentlemen can share it."

Repelled by the thought of sharing a bed with a man, I asked for a private room.

"Sure, if you're willing to pay."

I hadn't thought about money. It wouldn't have mattered; my money would be as alien as I am. "I'll find a place outside somewhere."

"I'll stake you, Professor," Rudolph said.

I was inclined to refuse politely, until I imagined sleeping outdoors. I followed Lockwood and Rudolph upstairs. The bed barely fit in the tiny room with a small table with pitcher and pan, a ladder-back chair on either side of a window that opened to the unpaved main street. Between the chairs stood a spittoon. Beyond the street and across the river a forest of sable palms rippled in the breeze and, beneath them, mangrove. The elegant Hyde Park neighborhood would one day dominate that area, where mangroves now line the river's edge. Nothing is familiar; I'm sure none of these buildings will remain standing in 2001. I had spent my entire working life in the university. Seeing the pristine river pour languidly into the bay, I wished I had spent more time enjoying the beautiful Florida landscape. But that was the price of a career.

After sharing Rudolph's provisions, I went to bed. We faced opposite directions, but I still felt uneasy about the arrangement. After a while I quietly got out of bed.

"What's the matter, Professor?"

"Can't sleep. Hope you find good land tomorrow."

"And I wish you well too."

I sat in one of the ladder-back chairs by the window. I could not bear any more thinking. "I'm afraid my future's evaporated, Rudolph."

"It's been hard on us too, Professor, but we have to have faith in better times ahead."

"Time . . . I've dribbled out my life in minutes and seconds, and now I'm one-hundred-and-thirty-five years from home with no way back."

"God is leading us. He'll pull us through."

"You don't understand, Rudolph: I've been yanked out of my life. I don't belong here. My family exists somewhere several lifetimes in the future. Sure, you've lived through a war, but that's nothing compared to what I face. You still have family who know you and need you. I have no one. I'm an alien."

For several seconds Rudolph said nothing. Then, "We each have our crosses to bear, Professor. You might think of the string of your forefathers that stretches all the way back to the first day. You must have family in Alabama. Why don't you look for them? You're not an alien; this is not a foreign land. It is your past. You might not get back to your time, but you're here now and you're alive, and you have the chance to see where you came from."

I was weeping when he paused. "I can't. I just can't. It's unreasonable. I can't reason my way out. I can't."

He raised himself on one elbow. "Stop whining! Of course you've trouble; that's what it means to be alive. I've watched men die, their legs and arms and eyes blown away. That's trouble. You're so used to your petty life you think every setback is a disaster. Lay aside reason! Reason won't help; what you need is courage. Face the day like a man. If you can't you're not worth saving. Now go to sleep. I've got to get up in a few hours."

No one had ever talked that way to me, and it shook me. After a while I said, "You're right, Rudolph. You're a very wise man, maybe the wisest man I've ever known."

"It's not my wisdom, Professor. It's the Bible's. Read Ecclesiastes sometime."

As he lay back on the pillow, I lifted Vivian's Bible out of my coat pocket and looked through the table of contents. "Here it is: Ecclesiastes." I turned to the page and read. When I came to the end I looked at Rudolph. His eyes were still open. My wristwatch showed 9:55. I wondered if he had ever heard of daylight saving time. I stared at the face of the mute timepiece waiting for the minute to drop into the next minute, as I had done countless times. *I've spent my life tracking time!* With determination I slipped off the watch, held it a few moments, and then handed it to him.

"What . . . ?"

"I saw how you admired it this morning. I want you to have it."

"I can't accept this, Professor."

"Please, Rudolph. By the way, you don't wind it. The battery will one day run out and then it will be useless. As of today it's useless to me. Rudolph, you staked me and fed me common sense. You've been very generous. As Ecclesiastes said, *"To everything there is a season, and a time to every purpose under the heaven."* I have been given two seasons. When you've lost more than a century, minutes and hours lose their importance. For the first time in my life I can truthfully say time has unraveled and no longer has meaning for me."

He accepted the watch graciously and thanked me. I read a while longer and finally got into bed. I must have fallen asleep within minutes because I don't remember anything after that.

I expected to sleep poorly, but I don't think I moved until the sun lit the room. Rudolph was gone. On the chair I found a note:

I am gone to look for land.
Let us talk again this afternoon.
Keep faith.

Rudolph.

I washed my face, put on my shoes, and went downstairs.

"Reckon your friend headed up river; seemed anxious to get going."

When I told him he was a Confederate soldier, Lockwood smiled. "Can't miss him in that uniform. But that don't bother me. War's over, and I hold no grudges. Every man's got to find his way through these awful times. I came down from Ohio; had enough of no work and hard winters. Where you from, Mr. Margin?"

A strange feeling overcame me. As a courtesy I was about to explain my predicament, but I couldn't bring myself to repeat it. Rudolph was fulfilling his future, and I was facing my past. I may never understand what happened, but Rudolph was right: what would it matter if I did? I could head for Alabama to look for ancestors. It might be worth a try. I don't know.

Instinctively I jerked my wrist into view and saw the blanched skin that had tried for years to breathe under the ever-present digital watch.

I looked up to see Lockwood staring at me. "Something wrong, Mr. Margin?"

"Oh . . . no. I'm from Alabama. Say, where can I get some writing paper?

"Seeing as how you don't have any money, I don't know. Maybe the post office next door. Sam's a nice fellow. Want me to ask him?"

"I'd appreciate it."

He went out the door and in a minute called me out. "Meet Sam Stephens; Sam, Mr. Margin."

"Shaking my hand and handing me a stack of writing paper, Sam Stephens said, "You're welcome to this, Mr. Margin, compliments of the Union Government. Got anything to write with?"

"No, sir."

"Well, there's a bottle of Union ink and a Union pen on that table. Sit down and help yourself and stay as long as you like. I don't watch the clock. Writing home?"

"Yes."

"Where you from?"

"Alabama."

"Well, good luck to you, sir."

The post office is nothing more than a small store with a counter half way back, a desk and a safe behind the counter, and a simple table in front of the counter by the window. I'm sitting at the table with a bottle of ink at the upper right corner, a pen in an indentation beside it. Outside the window a woman is tending flowers in her front yard. Jerking my wrist into view and seeing pale skin I wondered when I would stop repeating that useless act.

One thing has never left my mind: returning home. It's irrational, I know; irrationality seems to be infectious, but I want to; no, I *must*. That lonely forest is the only home I have.

Nature wins! Rationality loses! And I feel fine! The more I think about that piece of land, the heavier irrationality presses on me—not a pain exactly, but a pressure, a drive to move, to do something.

It is mid-morning as I write these last lines. The sun is high above the horizon. I don't know the time, and it doesn't matter. I will return as we came: along Knapp's path and then the river.

Edgar Margin

*   *   *

The following week Detective Hopper knocked on Vivian's door.

"Hello, Lieutenant. Won't you come in?"

"Just for a moment."

"Care for some coffee?"

"No thanks; I have to be across town in a few minutes. I saw you at the funeral, but I didn't want to intrude."

"You've been very kind, Lieutenant. But I still can't believe he's gone."

Hesitating, he said, "About the stationery he used: it could've corroborated his story, but the FBI said it's quite ordinary. I still wonder about the pen and ink, but they didn't seem interested in that either; just said I should drop it."

"Edgar was meticulous; you might even say picky, but frankly he had little imagination. I can't see him making up a tale like that; yet, the watch bothers me. He lived by it. He wouldn't have lost it. Giving it to that man, Rudolph Alexander, makes sense."

"I guess we'll never know for sure. Anyway, I didn't mean to stir you up."

"Not at all, Lieutenant. Oddly, his story has helped me through the ordeal. It makes a strange kind of sense. Anyway, I appreciate your interest and your help. Sure you won't have some coffee?"

Extending his hand he said, "Thanks, but I really can't."

"By the way, what about the original document?"

"They kept it and returned a photocopy."

"But it's mine. I want it back."

"I don't understand why they'd keep it if it's nothing, so I called Washington. All they'd say was it was routine to keep original evidence.'"

"Evidence of what? I thought they didn't believe his story."

"They say they don't, but they wouldn't budge. I'll have to let it drop, Mrs. Margin. Sorry."

As Vivian walked him to the driveway she said, "It's mine and I'm going to get it back.

He shook her hand again and wished her luck. Her eyes followed his car until it turned the corner. Halfway back to the front door she stopped, turned, and went to the great oak in the front yard. She moved around it passing her hands over the bark. She saw no semblance of carved initials until she stood back and looked again. "My God!" she said aloud." Bark had overgrown the marks, but the broad, gentle indentations were clear enough: "EM."

Mulberry Darkness
A Memoir

Uncle Mario's house was a typical 1920's bungalow
built on a fifty-foot-wide lot. Its front porch spanned the
width of the house. The large living room led, through
an archway, to the dining room and kitchen, where most
of the living occurred. Alongside those rooms were two
bedrooms separated by a bathroom. Behind the kitchen a
house-wide screened-in porch had been partially closed in
for Uncle Mario's father-in-law, Pablo, after he became a
widower. Though I found it warm and inviting, my parents
felt that a mysterious tragic force held that house in its
grip. My cousin Serafina was the direst victim. She had
struggled with rheumatoid arthritis that invaded her body
at age ten and held her in its fist until her early forties,
when she finally succumbed, a shriveled sack of bones in a
corner of her hospital bed. In spite of her plight, Sera could
laugh; her main merriment was a collection of jokes and
tricks that included a whoopee cushion and a drinking glass

that dribbled beverage down the drinker's chin and shirt. Yes, Sera found her fun; you might even say she learned to enjoy life. Her sister Gloria, who later came down with the same disease, managed to live a relatively normal life into her seventies.

One of the attractions of that house was a gigantic mulberry tree that formed a dome over their entire back yard and the neighbor's. That regal tree's shroud allowed very little earth to feel the sun's warmth even on the brightest day. To me that hard, gray dirt shouted out for an impromptu game of marbles.

Aunt Cucha did not share my love of that tree, and not merely because it repressed the grass. She hated the dark stains it yielded. She tolerated no stained floors or clothes. Knowing how she felt I carefully cleaned my shoes when I entered the house. But Cucha's feelings never prevented me from enjoying my fill of fruit or throwing those purple bullets at my cousins to inflict bloody wounds. They, of course, fought back valiantly as we ran, dodged and laughed. Within a few years I stopped throwing them, but I always ate a few in memory of carefree times with my dearest cousins.

That tree witnessed a different darkness, for in its shade unfolded a bleak day for a family who knew dark days. My cousin Sera and I, both teenagers, were sitting in the kitchen talking as I cracked walnuts for Sera and me. We stopped when we heard Aunt Cucha pick up the ringing phone. Her words were, "My brother, Evelio, has been arrested and I have to tell Papá . . . It will break his heart. He has to be told, but Mario won't be home for hours. What if someone else tells him first?"

The news shocked our conversation. Cucha finally hung up and returned to scrubbing the last of the black beans out of a large pot, as Sera and I watched silently. Suddenly she dropped the pot and stepped out to the back stoop, wiping her hands on her apron. Pablo was sitting on the steps smoking a cigar, his large blank eyes focused on the long ash. He liked to see how long he could grow it. As he studied the ash, long deep lines in his face carved a semblance of the cadaver he would one day become. Frowning at the red-purple splotches on the back stoop, Cucha found a clean spot and sat down, put her arm around her father's shoulder and said, "Papá, Evelio's in trouble again."

Pablo turned to her and the ash fell. "*Ese hijo mío!*"

"It is bad this time, Papá. He was with that new friend of his . . . a man was killed."

Pablo dropped his cigar; it rolled off the porch onto the hard dirt. With lips trembling he stood raising his fists as if beating the sky and stepped down to the deep-splotched, leaf-covered, gray earth and began to stomp across and back crying and pulling his hair and moaning, "Why? Why my son?" His crying seemed to erupt from his soul.

Now in his early thirties, Evelio had long been a *chulo*, a gigolo who lived off women, drink and marijuana. He dressed ostentatiously, his oily hair plastered down in the style Rudolf Valentino sported in the nineteen-twenties. But this was the nineteen-forties; the war had ended; good times beamed ahead. And Evelio, still mired in his past, seemed to be rushing headlong into a brutal future of his own creation. With the end of the war and the rebirth of optimism, men were back to work, and the future signaled a brilliance no one could have imagined a few years earlier.

Transfixed by the specter of her father's ranting, Cucha ran to him and led him back to the steps.

"Who did he kill? No, my son could not kill a man. No . . . no. But why?

"He was with that no-good bum he's been hanging around. I knew he would bring trouble. They tried to force their way into Las Novedades Restaurant. When the waiter opened the door to tell them they were closed, Evelio's friend pulled out a knife and stabbed him." She waited for that to sink in and continued, "The waiter died early this morning. Evelio and his friend are both in jail. It doesn't look good, Papá."

Trying to make out details in the mulberry darkness, Pablo lunged out again, crying loudly, tears dripping from his chin. I watched paralyzed as he stomped to the back of the yard and back, pulling his hair like a mad man. The Uncle Pablo I knew was a humorous, docile, quiet man who, though born in Florida, never learned to speak English and who mesmerized us children with his wonderful tales in his quaint way of speaking. This cigar maker had found time to write poems and songs and to create several beautiful oil paintings, including an almost photographic pencil sketch of his stepson, Miguel. I cannot rip from memory the scene of that quiet, loving, funny old man ranting, stomping, and weeping, moaning and pleading for answers to questions that roiled his soul.

Years earlier Pablo had urged my father and his brother Mario, prosperous shoe repairmen, to teach Evelio the trade. It had not been easy because the younger man did not want to damage his beautiful hands or dirty his clothes. Now he would fix prisoners' shoes. When my father heard the news, he was neither surprised nor concerned. He knew Evelio would end like this. Dad had come close to the same end in Denver twenty years earlier. Only with luck had he managed to extricate himself from the dark element that had drawn him in during his late teen years.

I attended with fascination the trial of Evelio's accomplice. For three days I sat in the courtroom. The prosecutor kept the crowd entertained as witness after witness testified to the cold-blooded killing. I especially remember one witness, a waiter in Las Novedades, who claimed not to speak English.

When asked to tell what he had seen, the waiter told of the defendant knocking on the door and the other waiter telling the two men they were closed.

"Then what?" the prosecutor said.

"*Sacó una navaja y se la metió en la barriga.*"

The translator said, "He took out a razor and stuck it into the man's belly."

Seeing confusion ripple through the jury, the prosecutor said, "Did you mean razor or knife?"

"*Navaja, cuchillo, la misma cosa.*" the witness said.

"Razor, knife, the same thing," the translator said.

Hoping to avoid ambiguity, the Spanish-speaking prosecutor asked, "What do you shave with in the morning?"

The witness replied, "*Yo uso maquinita.*"

Needing no translator, the audience burst into laughter. Trying to keep a straight face the translator said, "He uses an electric shaver."

Though it was a serious crime, a sense of dark comedy seemed to waft over the trial. Throughout the process I remained amazed by the defendant's white face and neck. My father said that was evidence of time spent in prison.

After a brief deliberation the jury returned a guilty verdict. The judge sentenced the man to twenty years in the state prison in Raiford.

Evelio's case was settled a few weeks later in a plea bargain in which Evelio pled guilty to being an accessory and received a five-year suspended sentence. He and his wife moved to Jacksonville and opened a shoe repair shop, where he worked until he died years later.

When he saw his son after the trial, Pablo embraced him with flowing tears. Evelio smiled victorious.

A later memory of Pablo was seeing Uncle Mario, a normally sweet and quiet man, helping his father-in-law out of the car. He had to hold the old man upright to walk him haltingly toward the rear of the house. Reaching the curb just inside the shade of the mulberry tree, Pablo seemed unable to raise his foot to the sidewalk; perhaps he couldn't see the curb or lacked the strength to lift his leg, for he kept bumping the tip of his shoe against it. At this, Mario began to yell at him using surprisingly strong language. In Spanish he spit out vile names that dripped with hatred. I wondered how Mario could blame the old man for his misfortunes. Perhaps this useless old man's longevity had rubbed too often against Mario's daughters's illnesses.

Pablo lived out his last years with his daughter and Uncle Mario. His bedroom continued to occupy that part of the screened porch directly under the massive mulberry tree. Pablo's room never felt the sun's benevolence and remained as dark as his thoughts must have become in his later years. I never went into that room, but I saw it many times on my visits to the mulberry tree.

Pablo never again wrote poems or songs, and he never again put brush to canvas. His productive life (most of his family believed he had never had a productive life) seems to have ended when his son moved to Jacksonville.

My last memory of Pablo was at a dinner gathering at my parents' home just a short while before the old man died. Seemingly oblivious to surrounding conversations, he had said little that evening. Finding him alone in a folding chair in the back yard, I walked over and said, "Pablo, I've always heard about your poems, but I never heard any. Could you recite one for me?"

He smiled and asked me to sit by his side. Looking out into the darkness he began to recite from memory. The deep, crackly voice spoke mesmerizingly as from another century. His Spanish was more cultured and classic than I was used to hearing in Tampa. My cousin Gloria helped her sister Sera walk toward us, and they sat down to listen to their grandfather. After another touching recitation about unrequited love, the shriveled old man said, "Want to hear a song?"

"Of course."

In a scratchy, poorly intoned voice he sang quietly but with great feeling about life in Cuba amid palms and mangos and sandy beaches. Knowing he had never been to Cuba, I was stunned by his depth of feeling. Pablo always considered himself Cuban. I never quite understood it, but accepted it as common among his contemporaries.

He continued to rhapsodize until Aunt Cucha stomped toward us. "Stop that, Papá. Nobody wants to hear your nonsense."

Pablo stopped in mid-stanza, looked up, and shrugged.

I told her how much I was enjoying his poems, that I had never heard them, but she ignored me as she pulled him out of his chair and walked him into the house.

That was the last time I saw Pablo.

Haunted

People swore that the house was haunted, which probably explained its low price. Of course, neither Jane nor I believed such nonsense, so we were happy to get the wonderful old two-storey house for half what we expected to pay. Although we had been married for nearly twenty-five years, we had always rented. Jane giggled throughout the closing. As we left the realtor's office she burst into joyous laughter.

We moved in our belongings the following week. There was only one other house left on the block. The remaining houses were cleared after the terrible hurricane four years earlier.

As the movers worked we noticed an old man come out of the house across the street and set up a folding chair under the only tree left standing in his front yard. He walked with a cane and seemed to be in pain, but curiosity, I suppose, brought him out. Every time Jane looked over at him he shook his head ponderously. Finally, overcome with curiosity, she walked over and introduced herself. "I'm Jane Clark, your new neighbor. That's my husband helping the movers. He's the skinny fellow in the green tee-shirt."

"My name's Homer Whipple. Glad to see y'all move in," the old man said. "It's been lonely since they took the other houses down."

"It's a beautiful house," Jane said. "I'm looking forward to sprucing it up a bit."

"Well, Mrs. Clark, I'm glad you and Mr. Clark aren't superstitious."

"Why is that, Mr. Whipple?"

"I've heard the old stories, but never believed them. It's all imaginings."

Smiling, Jane said, "Well, I'd better get back. Good to meet you."

Our first two weeks in our new old house could not have been happier. Jane quit her job as she planned and devoted all her time to unpacking boxes, setting out knick-knacks, and arranging the furniture. She already knew where each piece was to go and was determined to keep a neat and beautiful house. She became irritated when she found one sock I left on the floor. And she nearly became unhinged the morning she found that I had left the front door unlocked. I had never seen her so angry.

We never perceived any evidence of a haunting. Not that we expected to, but no one's exempt from doubt, I suppose. We celebrated our twenty-sixth anniversary just before the end of our first year in the house. Having observed nothing out of the ordinary, we relaxed into happy comfort in our lovely home.

Shortly after our first anniversary in the new house Jane came down with a strange ailment. She became weak to the point of barely being able to walk more than a few steps at a time. The doctor could find no problem, except a mild anemia, which, he said, could not account for her ailment. A month later she died. The shock was incomprehensible. Of all people, Mr. Whipple helped me with the funeral arrangements. His only reaction was to shake his head knowingly. We had had no children and had concentrated all our energies on our jobs; I'm a hair stylist; Jane worked most of our married life in a used bookstore.

Needless to say, I was devastated and wondered how I could continue without her. One morning a week after her funeral I got out of bed and saw one of Jane's blouses lying on the floor by my side and the closet door, which I had left closed, was open. The following day I awoke to the same—blouse on floor, closet door open. Unable to explain these strange occurrences, I began to imagine she was still present. I could not describe in what form she might exist, but she apparently did somehow. After I accepted that conclusion the stray clothes and open doors stopped. Desperate for an explanation I embraced the only possibility: she really was present. That should have been a comforting thought, but it was not; I was horrified. That also puzzled me, for I loved Jane and would have given anything to have her with me again. But to have her as a ghost or spirit or whatever she had become was far from comforting. It was strange; no, frightening. Was she watching me throughout the day? Could she know my thoughts?

I finally decided to sell the house and move elsewhere, anywhere away from that old house. It no longer felt like home. But I felt guilty leaving her. Would she follow me to a new house? I would never know until I moved, which I did the following month. I made the decision when I started seeing her stray actions at unexpected times: never regular or expected, but random, as if she didn't want me to forget.

The new house was brand new and quite different. I was the first to live in it; it had no history and no skeletons, so to speak.

A year later I still feel her presence. She no longer leaves clothes on the floor or doors open, but she fills my every waking and sleeping hour. I have not figured out what I'll do except keep living and waiting.

World War II Whistle
A Memoir

In the heat of World War II, Dad's shoe repair shop thrived on Franklin Street between Cass and Tyler. My father and his brother worked ten hours each day six days a week. Still living under the cloud of the Great Depression they determined to take advantage of their wartime business bonanza, for many believed another depression would follow.

I was twelve and loved working in the shop. I never went through an actual apprenticeship, but I could do nearly all the operations, including using the Landis finisher, the series of wheels and pulleys that ran sanders, scrapers, and brushes.

On this particular Saturday the work had not let up since morning, and Dad and Uncle Mario knew they would not get free for supper, so Dad sent me to the restaurant on the corner of Tampa and Cass Streets for two roast beef dinners. I took two dollars out of the cash register and worked my way through streets of khaki screaming with traffic and car horns. At the Cass and Franklin intersection a policeman in dark uniform directed traffic standing directly under the traffic light. He was a marvel to watch. As far as I could tell he could not see the traffic light, but he knew when it changed. As it turned yellow, he would blow his whistle and hold up his hand to oncoming cars. If a car ran a red light, I imagined he would draw his pistol and shoot it dead. I watched the policeman for several minutes before I remembered my mission and hurried on.

A few minutes later, I found every table taken, and half a dozen people waiting near the cashier. I wormed my way to the cashier and asked for two roast beef dinners to go. She took down my order and gave it to one of the waiters. I paid; she punched the cash register and returned my change.

Self-conscious, I withdrew from the cashier and the waiting customers and looked out over a sea of khaki. Sitting at a table near the back, a soldier motioned me over. I looked around thinking he was calling someone else. He nodded at me, and I walked over.

"You can sit here, son."

"I'm waiting for a take-out order."

The sergeant appeared to be in his late twenties—a tough old man in my eyes—broad, lean, strong, with a blonde, GI cut. You could cut yourself on the creases in his uniform. I must have been staring at the thin gold rope around his collar whose end was tucked into his shirt pocket. Without breaking the silence between us, he lifted the rope over his head and handed it to me with its brass whistle dangling. Tempted to blow it, I held it and the rope in both hands wondering what to do with it.

"Take it," he said. "I won't be needing it anymore."

"Thanks." Seeing my order at the counter, I stood, put the necklace around my neck, and walked to the cashier. I don't remember the walk back.

I have tried many times to recall details of those few minutes. It must have been summer judging by my khaki-tinted memory. That day has been a source of uneasy pleasure, uneasy for what I didn't do. I didn't ask why he would no longer need it. He wouldn't have told me, I'm sure, but he would have known I understood. I could have asked where he was from, but all that came out was, "Thanks." I have gone over it countless times. Was he worried, dejected, angry, or merely nostalgic? Was he going to Europe or the Pacific? Did he simply want to leave something of himself to someone who would survive?

That day broke nearly seventy years ago, and the whistle and its rope still hang on the wall over my desk. The whistle is dark now and lusterless; the rope has frazzled, but no matter. They connect me to an unknown soldier I knew for a fleeting moment, but whom I remember well.

He would be well into his nineties now if he made it. I hope he did.

Entropy

Professor Noah Verlassen's eyes snap open. Without hesitating he gently pushes back the covers, slides into his slippers, moves silently into his study, pushes the computer "on" button, and fidgets as it boots up. Desperate to urinate and fidgeting nervously, he opens his "OPUS—New Version" file and reads his last four pages. Smiling with satisfaction, he rereads his use of the Second Law of Thermodynamics and quantum mechanics to explain how life began on earth as a random miracle in which order rose out of chaos. He replaces the word *miracle* with *event* muttering, "Miracle is for magicians, theologians, and other phonies."

He continues reading: "A spontaneous change from chaos to order contradicts the Second Law of Thermodynamics, which states that spontaneous changes always involve an increase in entropy (entropy is a measure of the degree of disorder). For example, water flows downhill, never uphill." About to burst he dashes to the bathroom, urinates, and returns. "Where was I? Oh, yes, 'Apples fall to earth. Pool balls will not group themselves spontaneously into an equilateral triangular pattern when thrown onto a pool table. For any system to change spontaneously from disorder to order, the overall system *including its surroundings* must undergo an overall increase in disorder. In other words the local increase in order must be offset by a greater overall increase in entropy (disorder).'"

Fingering his stringy gray hair off his eyes he discovers his mouse battery is dead. Irritated, he opens a desk drawer, pushes aside random items—screwdriver, wrench, tweezers, pliers, letter opener, paper clips, stapler. He plucks out the last two new batteries, inserts them into the mouse, and resumes reading: "The theory of quantum mechanics is also consistent with this description of the origin of life. I shall not present a solution of the Schrodinger equation for this problem, however, for it lies beyond the understanding of lay readers. (See, however, Appendix I.)"

Professor Noah Verlassen smiles at his clear description of a complex concept.

*   *   *

Heavy clouds greedily guzzle every sliver of morning sunlight. It is still dark at six-thirty, and the temperature reads 101° F as Professor Noah Verlassen backs his ten-year-old electric auto down the driveway. Bent over the steering wheel, he feels the black, low clouds breathing down on him. His headlights drag the white brick, front porch columns into view, as the rear-view image of the shiny-wet brick street slides underneath. Madelyn chatters while redrawing her lips. During his curving retreat the wheels rattle over the brick pavement. Shifting into forward, he releases the steering wheel, and the auto, as if sensing his plan, straightens itself. He glances at his smiling wife and steels himself for the thirty-minute ride to the airport and the hour-long return through morning rush hour.

Professor Noah Verlassen's thoughts hover over Madelyn's verbal avalanche. He smiles recalling how well his book is developing. "She thinks I spend too much time at my computer, but it's what I enjoy. She says I'm just stuffing words into files. But overwhelming problems threaten our twenty-first century society. Science can explain life and death and war and the chasm into which the world has plunged and mankind's love of conflict and our unrelenting consumption of natural resources and allowing the warming climate to raise sea levels."

Sighing through her rapid-fire monolog, Professor Noah Verlassen drifts back to his post-doctoral year in London, where they met. Madelyn has not seen her mother in ten years and rattles on about their reunion. She recalls London's weather as sunny and bright. She has brightened her husband's life for forty years, but dark practicalities dangle behind his fond memories—house payments, meager bank balance, thin pension. Madelyn chatters on. Professor Noah Verlassen squirms through thick traffic. Dense asphyxiating clouds trap humid air. Streetlights scream as eastern sky squeezes slivers of pink through thinning clouds. The silent electric auto vibrates against rough pavement.

*   *   *

Sitting at his computer planning a new argument in his manuscript, Professor Noah Verlassen looks down at his V-phone: 10:36 AM, 09/11/53, temp. 102°, predicted high 110°. "It's been two hours since her plane took off!" He skims the news on his V-phone, growing impatient with opinions passing for facts. Last Thursday's announcement of the end of the nearly seventy-year-long Mideast War, the longest war in American history, has sparked less a celebration than a national sigh of relief. Now, less than one week later, commentary has trickled to zero.

Professor Noah Verlassen saves his computer file and, V-phone in hand, paces in and out of every room. In the kitchen he stops to refill his coffee cup and fingers his long, gray-brown, shoulder-length hair off his face. His wife's flight should have landed half an hour ago. He conjures several delaying scenarios—midair explosion, bad weather, terrorist with bomb on board. He would know by now, but agitation dispels logic. He surveys the kitchen shaking his head at the expensive, unused electronic kitchen equipment.

The ringing V-phone abruptly shatters his musings. He clicks it on to Madelyn's cheerful, red-lipped smile, "Hello, dear. What a wonderful flight—New York to London in just over two hours. It's beautiful and sunny. London sparkles. Mother met me. She wants to say hello . . ."

"Wait, I . . ."

Her mother's voice: "Hello, Noah . . ."

Sound dies. Screen goes blank.

"Hello . . . hello." He closes the connection and clicks the operator. "I was just talking to my wife in London and my V-phone went dead."

The operator looks harried: "Sorry, Sir. Our lines to Europe have gone dead."

"What?"

"Please retry later." Picture and sound die.

Professor Noah Verlassen lays the V-phone on the kitchen table and walks to the front door, sandals flopping. In old jeans and T-shirt the tall, thin man stands on the front porch a few moments, his pale blue eyes dashing side to side seeking focus. Returning to the kitchen he presses his wife's V-phone number. The screen blinks *No*

Service. He calls the overseas operator again and watches a woman comb her fingers through her cropped hair. "This is the Tampa operator; we've lost all out-of-state communications."

"Why? What's happened?"

"Please try later, Sir."

"Damn it!" Dropping the V-phone in his pocket Professor Noah Verlassen returns to the kitchen mumbling, "Damn . . . damn . . ." He lifts the V-phone out and presses "TV mode." No picture appears; he presses a local radio frequency, where a high-pitched female voice reports: " . . . a series of explosions have destroyed many European and Asian capitals and several American cities including New York, Washington, Philadelphia, Atlanta, Chicago, Denver, Austin, and Los Angeles." The shaky voice continues, "We're unable to confirm it, but these may have been nuclear explosions. We have lost communication with Washington, but it . . . it seems to be . . . a concerted terrorist attack." Long silence with muffled voices in the background, ending with, "I'm sorry, Bill, but what else can it be?" Another brief pause with muffled voices in the background. The shaky woman's cracking voice continues, "I'll try to recap: One week after the end of the seventy-year-long World War, representatives from all the major nations had converged on London to discuss peace terms. With the end of the longest world war in history have come warnings that the most fanatical groups would never accept defeat, and have been planning . . ." Voice muffled, as if speaking with the microphone covered, "I am remaining objective, but this is just too . . . I'm sorry, Bill . . ." The radio reverts to static, then silence.

Professor Noah Verlassen falls into a ladder-back chair. In a stupor and feeling the chaos expanding around him, he punches Evan's V-phone number.

"You look tired, Dad. Have you heard from Mother? Was London bombed?"

"Why is that cloth over your face?"

"It's awfully warm; the wet cloth helps. Anyway, what about Mother?"

Noah nods. "She called, but the connection broke off. All out-of state connections are dead. Big cities have been bombed. Have you heard any details?"

"No, Dad. But try not to imagine . . ."

"If they bombed London she's . . ."

"Please, Dad . . . The boys are sick, sores all over, Susan too. Can't reach the doctor."

"I'll be right over."

"No, please! It's contagious. I have it too. Wait a few days."

"May I see them?"

The phone goes dead.

Standing by the kitchen table, Professor Noah Verlassen turns the V-phone back to radio mode. Over his pounding heart he hears an agitated male voice, " . . . the following announcement: Savannah is reporting a smallpox epidemic through the city and nearby communities. We are trying to connect with other parts of the country and will report further developments." Silence with mumbling in the background, then: "Dallas, Kansas City, and St. Louis also report smallpox. This pandemic may be connected with the bombing, but that is as yet unconfirmed. Smallpox was eradicated worldwide over a century ago. Large-scale inoculations ceased soon thereafter, so most Americans are susceptible."

A loud voice erupts: "That's speculation."

"People need to protect themselves."

The sound of Debussy's Clair de Lune abruptly replaces the voices. A few seconds later all sound dies. Noah Verlassen sets his V-phone on the table and returns to his chair and lays his head on his hands. He tries vainly to phone his son the rest of that day.

*   *   *

On his front porch, Professor Noah Verlassen watches night crawl across the city. In bed sleep refuses him. Moonlight is a cloudy smear. He moves to his computer.

The screen is blank. Unable to recall turning it off, he presses the "on" button. No reaction. "Of course: power grid's gone. My files, will I ever retrieve them?"

He walks down towards the bay. Dense clouds obliterate starlight. Only a hazy bright area suggests the moon's presence. In that faint light he can barely make out the land across the water. The hot evening is still, as though every air molecule had stopped dead in its path. The bay bears a glassy calm. "Has the moon's motion around Earth and Earth's motion around the sun changed?"

He walks home, drops into bed, and falls asleep. Typically he wakes often during the night to urinate, but when he opens his eyes sunlight fills the room. His first thought: "Must see Evan today."

*   *   *

Professor Noah Verlassen sits looking at his bookcase that now houses only nine of his most prized books: An ancient *Handbook of Chemistry And Physics* he used as a student, a single-volume *Complete works of Shakespeare*, *Goethe's Faust* (in German), The *Oxford Unabridged English Dictionary*, *Don Quixote de La Mancha* (in Castilian), two out-of-print chemistry reference books, a bound collections of his research papers, and a general chemistry textbook he wrote years earlier. Hundreds more reside in his computer as e-books. "Those electronic arrangements may never resurface." Turning to his bookshelf, "Those will survive as long as there are eyes and the will to learn. This wispy, elusive electronic world floats in the ether. With no thoughts or aspirations, it is a vacuous world of electrons written in number duality—ones and zeros—a world without feeling capable of holding the entirety of human knowledge in a language of 0's and 1's. To build a world of information from two digits is truly marvelous, but now it resides in a tangle of wires, plastics, and semiconductors, its existence balancing on the knife-edge of belief in what can never be seen. And such belief eventually becomes deified. True belief is the pit of chaotic doom."

Still staring at his dead computer, Professor Noah Verlassen sees a tiny icon appear on the otherwise dead screen. Not believing, he moves closer. It is a plume trimmed to use with ink and beneath it the word *Cursive*.

The plume juts from the screen. Professor Noah Verlassen takes it with his fingers, dips the tip in a small, open bottle of dark blue ink that has appeared near the computer, and begins to write on a piece of scrap paper. With nervous hand he writes, "Now is the time for all good men to come to the aid of their party."

"Where did that come from? Suddenly the pen slips from his fingers and begins to write as if held by an invisible hand. In a florid, early American script it writes, *"When in the Course of human events, it becomes necessary for one people to dissolve the political bands which have connected them with another, and to assume among the powers of the earth..."* Shutting his eyes, Professor Noah Verlassen asks, "Maybe there really are parallel universes. Is that where I am, trapped between them?" He throws the feather against the computer screen and runs out of the room.

*   *   *

The strong odor of decomposing flesh strikes Professor Noah Verlassen as he walks towards the deserted city center. Eerie silence hangs like a shroud over the city. Most window blinds are open; many front doors remain ajar. A lone man walks towards him. Seeing Noah, the man immediately disappears into an abandoned building. A few blocks later a woman across the street walking ahead of Noah and in the same direction glances back, sees Noah, and vanishes around a corner. In the distance a young man dozes on the sidewalk with his back against a storefront. Obeying the second law of thermodynamics, Professor Noah Verlassen ignores him.

In the scorching late morning Professor Noah Verlassen is soaked in perspiration as he knocks on the door. Hearing no response, he punches the code into the door lock and lets himself in. The living room looks normal except for a magazine and a single woman's shoe on the floor. The rancid odor of death nearly overwhelms him. Slowly, trembling, his heart racing, he enters the bedrooms. Both boys lie bloated and motionless in their beds. Swollen and covered with the terrible scabby pox, they look barely human. He walks into his son's bedroom where Susan lies under a thin cover. Evan's upper body lies on the bed, his legs on the floor. A shovel leans against the wall. Professor Noah Verlassen surmises that Susan and their sons were already dead when he spoke with Evan, and that Evan died before he could bury them.

Standing over them, staring into their eyes, he realizes he must bury them—lay his family like animals to rot in the damp earth, where their atoms will randomize and disperse into the chaos of death. Returning to the back yard with the shovel he looks into the blazing sky. He sinks the shovel into the shaded earth close behind the house. Each shovel-full is heavier than the last. He doubts he will finish digging without plan, aiming only downward towards the center of the earth. Piles of dirt riddled with dangling roots reveal the dark of eternal night. In the grandsons' room, he wraps the two boys in a blanket, carries them out, and lays them into one of the holes. In his son's room he wraps Susan's petite body and Evan's in separate blankets, carries them out one at a time, and lays them side-by-side in the larger hole.

He speaks timidly, apologetically: "If there is a God, please . . ." He cannot continue. Looking down at the remains of his family, death becomes a fond hope.

He sinks his shovel into the dirt pile and reveals a wiggling worm. Raising the shovel he pounds the worm repeatedly as hard as he can. He falls to his knees and throws up.

Finally, with both holes covered, he tamps down the mounds and then walks through the house leaving the door ajar.

*   *   *

Professor Noah Verlassen sits on his front porch mesmerized by a gentle rain. He walks up to his study and sits at his desk. The computer screen is blank. It begins to vibrate, then to shake and throb, as if sobbing. His chest heaves; his body shakes uncontrollably. He tries again to start the computer, a futile gesture, he knows. Finally he plows through the tools and random objects in his desk drawer until he finds a wrench and smashes it into the screen yelling, "There! I, too, can expand entropy. Now it's truly, finally and forever gone." He lifts the computer and throws it against the wall. Pieces of metal and plastic fly in every direction as the second law of thermodynamics demands.

Frightened by his uncharacteristic violence he sits down. "How could I have accepted the permanence of binary data stored on electronic chips? It's been my religion. Handwritten manuscripts have survived thousands of years. My thoughts are lost forever."

*   *   *

Eyes click open. With moonlight illuminating his bedroom, Professor Noah Verlassen stands and begins his trek through every room like an animal re-staking his territory. In his study he opens Don Quixote, his favorite book, reads a few lines, slams it shut, and shoves it back into the bookshelf. "Such a long novel about a lunatic; no, not a lunatic; they're all crazy. We're all crazy. Is that the message?"

He has no idea of the time when he returns to bed. Tired as death itself, he reclines and instantly falls asleep.

Suddenly he sits up perspired and breathing violently thinking he is having a heart attack. There is no pain, but his breathing feels constricted. A large dark hole in the earth has opened before him. He enters groping his way into the darkness. Passing his hand over bare rock walls he feels moist roots. Water streams up the rock wall into an opening overhead. He urinates to see if it will also flow upwards. It does. He cannot find his path out. Hearing a sound behind him, he turns straining to see. Through warm humid air Evan waves and whispers, "This way, Dad." Professor Noah Verlassen turns and runs away into even deeper darkness. Lifting his legs high to keep from stumbling he trips on a loose rock and slides head first into the wall. Reaching desperately for something to grab, he opens his eyes with his arm around the bedpost. Not sure if he is still in the cavern, he sits up, jumps out of bed, slides into his slippers, throws his robe over his shoulders. Nervous and unstable on his feet, he stumbles to the porch.

Surrounded by darkness deeper than he has ever known, Professor Noah Verlassen wanders towards the bay. Without the usual halo of city lights and the unusual absence of clouds, the clear sky explodes with stars. Calmer now, he pushes aside thoughts of the cavern and forces himself to think about Madelyn and their son's family. But the cavern still lures him: "Evan called; I should have gone." He walks barefoot towards the water embracing the glorious Milky Way. Through earthly silence under his stellar canopy Professor Noah Verlassen hears echoes of past footsteps: Evan's first steps away from his playpen, sounds of the baseball game with parents cheering as Evan stumbles toward first base, dashing up an endless staircase to the maternity ward to hear his first grandson's cry for life, stepping into his first chemistry lecture, thirty-five years later strolling through the neighborhood on his first day of retirement.

A breeze revives him. He looks up at the Milky Way, that calm sash that wraps around the cavernous sky's belly. Professor Noah Verlassen loves these clear, dark nights when glittering stars evoke the grandeur of the universe: the flickering light specks that testify to the life-giving stellar energy that fills the universe. And the non-flickering light specks that encourage the hope of life reigniting.

Through the years he has spent countless evenings peering through his small telescope at the cosmos, relishing the peaceful darkness alone with the silent, reassuring thoughts that buoy him on his sea of scientific contemplation. On those dark nights he becomes a child of benevolent Earth, feeling he might drift away on the next breeze.

On this night Professor Noah Verlassen, rationalist, dedicated scientist, feels overwhelmingly powerful. Exhilarated, he steps into the water. It recedes. He takes another step, and the water recedes further. Angered, he leaps forward and finds himself balancing triumphantly upon the undulating surface. Looking down and around at the dark water beneath him he mutters, "I've done it; I've violated entropy, thermodynamics, and common sense." Then he yells into the sky, "For the first time in the history of the universe I have stood entropy on its head! I have finally done something important!"

Leaping towards dry land he sinks into the warm, womblike liquid. His toes dig into the mucky bottom's glop as he slogs his way back and falls panting on hard earth.

Leaving a trail of muddy tracks all the way home, Professor Noah Verlassen, exhilarated and barely aware of the cooling relief of his wet clothes, wonders, "Have I truly upended entropy? Have I undone this disastrous world? No, that's not possible. The world's not a computer you can reboot . . . But wouldn't it be wonderful!"

Back home he walks upstairs, drapes his wet robe on a chair, drops into bed, and falls asleep almost instantly.

Professor Noah Verlassen rises to urinate and stops to look out his window at the shroud of purple clouds sliding silently across the birthing eastern sky. Large raindrops splatter loudly against windows as they often do before a heavy downpour. A rain of biblical magnitude mutes all other sounds. Abruptly it stops. A grand luminosity spreads across the sky.

*   *   *

After the most restful sleep Professor Noah Verlassen can remember, he wakes to the odor of brewing coffee. Soon the odor of frying bacon mingles with the coffee's aroma. The pillow next to his is indented as if someone has slept on it. The covers on that side of the bed are neatly smoothed out. "Yes—entropy." Sitting up he looks around wondering if this is his room, although the orange tree out the window is familiar enough. A loud clattering sound startles him. Rising, he slides into his slippers, and wraps himself in his robe. On his way downstairs he hears the crackle of bacon frying.

"Hello, darling," Madelyn's voice rattles cheerfully. "I tried to be quiet. You were sleeping so soundly I didn't want to wake you. Sorry about the clatter. Evan and Susan and the boys will be here any minute. The boys have a ball game in late morning, but we'll have plenty of time for a nice brunch. Oh, my hair's a mess. I'll have to go up and fix it before they get here. You'll watch the bacon for me won't you? Don't you love the smell of bacon frying? . . . What's wrong, darling? You look startled."

Professor Noah Verlassen turns and, taking the stairs two at a time, dashes to his study and finds his intact computer on his desk. He depresses the "on" button. The screen brightens. Still standing he opens his "OPUS—New Version" file and marks "print." As the clicking begins he runs downstairs laughing loudly. Unable to say anything sensible or relevant, he wildly scoops her off the floor in a wild bear hug.

Out Of The Blue

In a clipped, measured accent Major V-119 said, "Hark, general; the crew grows restive. How long must we remain in orbit? Verily Sir. I beseech you to make contact."

With similar clipped accent General W-355 replied, "Anxiety dulls lucidity, major. Be brief, for I am presently restudying the 'Old Report' and 'Recent Addendum.' Upon completion I shall seek the crew's mind; thence will the decision follow."

"I know no other choice but to land," The major said. "So long have we hid in this orbit and durst not peep out, and all the while our planet expires."

"That we must find a new home planet lies beyond dispute. Whether it be Earth remains the question."

"Shall the crew's opinion carry weight?"

"Please, Major: *will*, not *shall*. Let us not trample the hallowed language of Shakespeare."

The major cringed.

A smile cutting across his silvery-white face, the general said, "According to our commandments for planetary exploration, the decision falls upon the commanding general; however, the crew's opinion will weigh heavily." Then in a more conciliatory tone, "I share thy feelings, Major. We all grasp the gravity of our plight. And so, with thanks and pardon, I do dismiss thee to thy station, that I may complete my task."

"I do entreat thee to decide favorably and with haste, Sir."

"Duly noted, Major."

Turning away from Major V-119 the general turned to the summary page of the "Old Report," dated 400 Zyzytia years earlier (ca. 1,000,000 Earth years). Translated into current English it read:

"Earth thus appears to be the best candidate of the planets thus far explored. Though none seems entirely satisfactory, Earth's salubrious atmosphere and temperature will require few adjustments. The most troubling issue with Planet Earth is its inhabitants. Only a few species of ants, bees, and other insects exhibit sufficient complexity, intelligence and social ability to interact cooperatively with Zyzytian settlers. The crude and hostile primate species we encountered demonstrate little potential for positive interaction."

The "Recent Addendum" describes a more recent orbital scan taken 410 Earth years ago):

"Species evolution has occurred more rapidly on Earth than on Zyzytia, probably due to the higher revolution rate about its sun. Accordingly, one of the primates described in the "Old Report" has evolved into a relatively intelligent species that now dominates the planet. Called *Homo sapiens*, that species is extremely competitive and belligerent. Furthermore, their devotion to intellect-stifling religious beliefs has led to relentless wars of conquest over most of the planet. In fact, warfare became the driving force on Planet Earth when *Homo sapiens* appeared, which was after the "Old Report" was issued.

"Given these findings we urge extreme caution. Careful contact by an exploratory delegation is recommended before making a final determination to land."

As he read, General W-355 made notes for the forthcoming meeting.

*   *   *

"Seeing all ten crew members present, I pronounce this meeting convened," General W-355 said. Though the quarter was cramped, all seemed relieved finally to be addressing their urgent mission. Major V-119 sat in the first row between two of the females. The remaining three females and three males occupied the remaining chairs. Still troubled by the general's apparent uncertainty, Major V-119's jaw twitched. Obeying standard military rules of comportment, he had not revealed to anyone his discussion with the general.

"We have all read both the 'Old Report' and the 'Recent Addendum' and are thus conversant with the facts. I remind you that the duty of deciding our fate rests upon my shoulders. Yet methinks the crew must freely express their opinions."

"What alternative remains to landing, General?" Y-119 said. "We left a planet in its death throes, and no other planet affords us the least possible future."

"We shall consider that question during discussion," the general said. "But as to protocol: I shall adopt the Planetary Government's commandment that requires a majority of 75 percent for any action; that is to say, eight of our number.

V-119 raised his hand for recognition.

"Yes, Major?"

"Why thus, Sir? Seventy-five percent of ten is 7.5. Wherefore eight?"

"I grasp the arithmetic, Major. I interpret the rule to mean '*at least* 75 percent,' ergo eight."

"I request my objection be recorded," Major V-119 said with trembling jaw.

Nodding, the General continued calmly, "In summary I offer the following:

(1) The Zyzytian year lasts 2,500 Earth years. Our average life span of 80 Zyzytia years equals 200,000 Earth years. Earthers' life span is ca. 80 Earth years.

(2) Our longer live spans will afford us a great advantage and will certainly propel us into leadership roles. That possibility could breed disdain among the natives.

(3) Nearly all Earthers' technologies focus on warfare, which suggests that their means of solving political problems, including our presence, is fraught with peril.

(4) With propagation in mind, our crew includes both sexes. However, we shall succeed only if mating with Earthers is physically and biologically possible.

(5) Not having seen Earthers, we assume they resemble the primates described in the 'Old Report' and that they are physically stronger than we. On the other hand, they are intellectually inferior.

(6) From the 'Recent Addendum' we know little of the role of art, music, history, and philosophy in Earthers' lives. They have developed rudimentary

mathematics and a simplistic science. We sampled their literature, mostly the poems and plays of their major writer, Shakespeare, via electronic image scanning of their libraries. Those literary works reveal insights into their character, behavior and motivations as well as provide a means to learn their major language.

(7) It is essential that we find a new home planet; however, we must first be assured that Earthers will allow us to flourish and integrate productively into their culture. We have much to add to theirs, including a much needed, ready source of non-polluting energy.

(8) As an aid to gaining acceptance we shall adopt familiar Earth names. I shall call myself Hamlet and suggest Major V-119 call himself Macbeth. Handing out a list of names he said, "I suggest this list of acceptable names for our crew:

Males: Lysander, Othello, Shylock, Julius, Richard, Henry, Edward.

Females: Ophelia, Juliet, Jessica, Olivia, Portia, Desdemona, Lady Macbeth.

Please choose a name from this list. I shall approve others only if they are common Earth names."

"I now open the discussion."

Major V-119 winced at being called Macbeth, a Shakespearian villain, but remained silent, then smiled at the general's choice of Hamlet, an indecisive weakling.

Raising his hand for recognition, Major V-119 said, "Macbeth moves to establish immediate contact with Planet Earth and land as soon as we receive their approval."

"Thank you, Macbeth, for accepting your new name with grace. Do I hear a second?"

Two hands rose. The General recognized Lieutenant V-120, Macbeth's sister. "Ophelia seconds Macbeth's motion."

"The motion has been made and seconded, Ophelia." The General said. "Before we begin discussion, please announce in order of decreasing rank your choice of name. Yes, Lieutenant Y-123."

"Glancing longingly at Macbeth beside her, Y-123 said, "I wish to be called Lady Macbeth."

The remaining officers and enlisted personnel made their choices from the general's suggestions.

Hamlet began the discussion by summarizing their plight: "To land or not to land. That is the question. Whether 'tis nobler in the mind to suffer the flaming tongues and tortures of solar cremation, or to gamble upon a sea of hostility . . ."

To Ophelia Macbeth whispered, "He taketh his new name seriously."

"Do not distrust him, brother. His kindness and intelligence have raised him to an exalted role. I happily trust him with our future."

"I also, nor do I question his desire to know our feelings. My concern lies upon the demise of our beloved Zyzytia and the thought of the last of our species abandoned to orbit perpetually around a hostile planet."

*   *   *

The message was marked TOP SECRET, FOR THE PRESIDENT'S SCIENCE ADVISOR'S EYES ONLY. Following the required security protocols, which took several anxious minutes, the Science Advisor finally unscrambled the code. The message from the National Science Foundation's Green Bank Telescope (GBT) read:

(1) We have evidence that a spacecraft has been orbiting Earth for several days. New Mexico's Apache Point Observatory initially sighted the alien object in a stable orbit five days ago. We have since received confirmation of the sighting from six other observatories. When first noting its stationary orbit, the NMAPO did not assume it was an alien spacecraft. However, the National Radio Astronomy Observatory (NRAO) at Green Bank,

West Virginia and five other observatories now confirm the presence of the powered spacecraft in Earth's orbit. We have not been able to determine their power source.

(2) Of possible relevance: Several observatories have reported a massive star with several planets in a distant galaxy. At least one of those planets has the temperature range, water, and other features necessary for life. That galaxy is 2.6 million light-years from Earth. We do not claim or suggest that the orbiting spacecraft is from that galaxy.

(3) Most reports of UFO sightings over the past sixty years have been unsubstantiated and unsupported. However, the present observations by competent scientists in several observatories must be taken seriously. Accordingly, we request permission to make contact with this craft to determine its purpose.

(4) Having made a trip of such distance these individuals clearly possess a highly developed space technology.

(5) We urge extreme caution whether or not contact is approved.

*   *   *

"Hello, if thou hast received this signal, please respond . . ."

The repetitive recording was in a high-pitched voice in strangely accented, antiquated English.

The electronic technician at the National Observatory had summoned the colonel who stood over the technician's shoulder. Both men stood rapt at the monotonous voice repeating the same phrases over and over.

"That guy is definitely neither an American nor a Brit," the colonel said. "I'd guess he's not from Earth. You are recording it, Lieutenant?"

"Yes, Sir. I've had it on since it started. Should I respond?"

"No. Our orders are to listen *only*." The colonel stressed *only*.

The colonel abruptly left the room, went to his office, and sent this message to the White House:

"We're receiving the following recorded message: 'Hello, if thou hast received this signal, please respond.' Request permission to respond."

After several minutes the colonel resent his message, adding, "Urgent: please reply to my request."

A moment later a cryptic answer appeared on his screen: "Received. Do not respond. Orders follow."

The colonel shook his head in disbelief muttering, "What the hell are they waiting for? You know damn well the Middle East Axis is also listening. If they respond first, they could sink us!"

*   *   *

Macbeth knocked on the General's compartment, and the tinny voice said, "Enter."

"Hast thou received a response, General?"

"Macbeth, during this period of contact you and the rest of the crew will call me Hamlet, not General. No, there has been no response."

"Might their language have changed?"

"That is possible, Macbeth, however we shall continue until we know. Remember that even if the language has evolved, the strong cadences of Shakespeare would surely live on. Our message has been received, I am certain. Whether they respond remains in doubt."

"Sir . . . Hamlet . . . we should we not have heard by now?"

"Patience, Macbeth." Then he thought further and said, "I shall send a more friendly message explaining who we are and our purpose. For sooth, Macbeth! I shall prepare the statement and ask you to read it before I transmit it. Please remain." Hamlet then proceeded to compose the following statement on his computer:

"Dear People of Earth, I am called Hamlet, Commanding General of the Space Exploration Unit of Planet Zyzytia. Our sun will soon explode into a Red Giant that will devour our planet and eradicate our species. Upon our honor, we seek only a planetary home that will welcome our crew.

The steadily rising planetary temperature caused by our expanding sun has already devoured most if not all Zyzytians. Our crew numbers ten individuals—five females and five males.

I offer data on our planet and its inhabitants:

Planet Zyzytia is much larger than Earth and much less dense. Our revolution around our sun is slower than yours—our solar year is 2,500 Earth years long.

Zyzytian life spans are ca. 80 of our solar years, which is equivalent to 200,000 Earth years. Though this may seem incompatible with your species, we are a peaceful, loving species that knows not war.

Zyzytians have quite uniform features. We are thin by Earth standards. We are uniformly eight feet tall (in your units) with long arms and legs composed of flexible bones. Our heads are also elongated consistent with our bone structure. Both males and females weigh uniformly fifty Earth pounds.

Because of our long year and strong solar radiation, Zyzytians have evolved silvery protective skin and silvery hair. Though we have not seen your species, we have concluded that your planetary properties and solar conditions have led Earth people to evolve along quite different directions.

I restate that we are a docile and peaceful species. We have no desire to interfere with your planet, your species, or your government. We simply seek a hospitable home.

As a peace offering we bring considerable scientific knowledge. The major technical innovation we offer will allow you to generate highly efficient, large amounts of electrical energy directly from cosmic rays. Our invariant method is independent of your sun's radiation. We know you are still heavily dependent on a diminishing supply of fossil carbon fuels. Our technology will satisfy all your energy needs and will thus liberate you from unnecessary and destructive wars.

We look forward to sharing our culture and living together in peace on Planet Earth. We send heartiest regards.

* * *

Excited by the possibility of making contact, the colonel relayed the new message to the White House and waited. After several minutes he sent another note stating, "Please! If the M.E. Axis responds first, we'll lose the advantage."

The answer was almost instant: "The White House is preparing the response. Stand by."

After several minutes the colonel could not contain himself. He phoned Dr. Will Ostwald, Head Scientist of the National Observatory, to ask if he could drop in. The answer was: "Of course."

Aware of the spacecraft's messages, Dr. Ostwald was standing at the window looking into the sunny sky when the colonel knocked.

"Come in."

"Thank you, Sir. The White House is delaying. I've urged them to respond or let us do it, but they've ignored my request. How could it hurt to send a brief note saying we received their message?"

"Drop it, Colonel. The White House is running this show."

"But what if the other side responds first?"

"The White House is in charge, Colonel, and they know more than we do."

"I'm not so sure about that, but . . . I guess it is their call."

"And when they decide, Colonel, you'll be informed."

Seeing Dr. Ostwald's eyes dart toward the sky, the Colonel moved to the window for a closer look. The sudden white flash ballooned over the horizon and gradually yielded to a long trail of white smoke.

"Oh, no!" the colonel said.

Dr. Ostwald nodded knowingly and plopped into his chair.

His arms hanging limply, The Colonel slowly walked back to his office.

"Did you see it, Colonel?" The technician said.

The colonel nodded, "From Dr. Ostwald's window. That was the White House's response . . ."

"Yes, Colonel," the technician said, tears welling.

Seeing Is Believing

Transcriber's Foreword

Rare is the event that cannot be explained. It might even be said that all events are explicable and that an inexplicable event is impossible. The episode described in the following manuscript is such a case. Whether it is true or not is beside the point, for clearly the author of the attached manuscript believed it to be true. Whether he was in his right mind or merely a tormented delusional soul is also irrelevant. The reader alone must plumb these questions to reach his own conclusions.

Lest you suspect that I concocted this flight of fancy out of my own imagination, please know that what follows is a faithful rendering of the original as I discovered it at a library book sale. I have no idea how it got there, nor do any of the librarians I asked. The spiral-bound, handwritten manuscript was battered, but the pages were quite legible. A few pages had been torn out. I know this because of the page numbers.

I assume I am the first person who read it. I had it typed and reproduced in the present form because it is curious and strangely charming, if bizarre and possibly wacky. Besides, there is an outside chance that it may serve as the only surviving testament of a forgotten event.

*   *   *

It was early when I left home, 6:49 AM, to be exact; I recall everything that happened that day. Having refused to obey all my attempts at combing, my thick mop of brown hair felt electrified flopping atop my thin frame as I walked across the athletic field. I liked it that way, long and thick; it gave me a professorial, scholarly look. My students say I bounce when I walk, like a wig on a bone. That's fine. Being eccentric is all part of being a professor. I don't attempt to be eccentric, but if I am, I won't apologize. Anyway, I don't care what people say. I walk fast even when I'm not in a hurry. I enjoy being busy; motion is the spark of life.

My father really was eccentric: an astronomer who wore long hair before it was stylish and topped off with a beret. I don't think he was aware of being eccentric or anything else; he just did and thought whatever he wanted. Dad was a happy man. I tried to be like him, engaged in work and carefree. But I could not handle astronomy. Math kept me at a distance. Organic chemistry felt more hospitable.

The dew was especially heavy that morning, so I wore my overshoes. Because they slowed me down I walked even faster. Soon after my wife and I moved to the house just beyond the edge of campus at the end of my first year here, I measured the distance to the chemistry building on my bicycle odometer—exactly eight-tenths of a mile across the intramural playing fields and then along a row of buildings that provided shade in summer and shelter when it rained.

I barely noticed the sun on my back, for my mind raced. Those morning walks provided welcome solitude to think. That morning's internal conversation began with academic politics, but I angrily pushed that aside in favor of my eleven o'clock lecture and the impossibility of covering a whole semester of general chemistry in six hot, summer weeks. Every time I used that phrase, covering the subject, I imagined myself pulling a sheet over a cadaver and folding my hands in prayer. With luck I'd soon have a research grant that would pay my summer salary.

Barely aware of the wet grass and buildings, I found my way to the chemistry building like a horse, bouncing along the path to my stable. Even through the haze of time I remember feeling good, strong and alive.

My wristwatch showed 7:03 when I entered the chemistry building. I had made good time. My skin tingled from the exertion, moist spots had formed under my arms, and I felt good. I met no one as I walked down the narrow hall to the stairs and up the two flights to my laboratory. Even after all these years the details of that day are still vivid.

After less than a year I had made a good start on my conducting polymer research. No one had yet succeeded in making plastic electrical conductors, and the possibility dangled like a carrot just beyond my reach. According to theory all that was needed were long molecules through which electrons could move freely, but that was easier to say than to accomplish. Pulling off my overshoes, I flipped the light switch and brought the dark, windowless laboratory to life. Everything was as I had left it—glassware laid out on the lab bench ready to assemble, lab notebook open to the quantities I would weigh out. I moved around the lab completely consumed by a passion that had burned since childhood. I had no way of knowing if it was sunny or storming outside, for windowless walls and a sharp focus on scientific questions insulated me from the world. I refused a telephone. Of course there was one in my office next door, but I could not hear it from the lab.

Preparing to distill a new compound I felt like a stone-age savage stalking a wildebeest. Only the prize, the joy of the hunt, the eventual adulation of my scientific villagers could have kept me isolated in that dungeon of a lab all those months. But I controlled that tiny part of the world from which would emanate wondrous discoveries that would reach far beyond its walls. Ah! Youthful dreams.

After starting the distillation I glanced at my wristwatch. It showed 7:33. It had taken slightly less than half an hour to set up the apparatus.

The distillation was complete in about an hour. I turned off the heater and looked at my watch. It still showed 7:33. I tried to wind it, but it was fully wound. I stepped into the hall to check the wall clock. It also showed 7:33. It seemed odd that an electric clock would have stopped at the same time. Then I returned to the lab, removed the distilled sample from the receiving flask and poured it into a clean sample bottle, and stuck a label on it. I smiled with satisfaction at the beautiful, clear, colorless liquid—hunt completed; prey in its cage. After putting the sample aside I disassembled the still, washed it, and hung it to dry on the rack above the sink. Though I was not sure of the exact time, I always had a good instinct for time and estimated it was approaching the hour for my lecture, so I washed my hands and stopped at my office to pick up lecture notes, colored chalk, molecular models and books. The wall clock still read 7:33.

The moist, cool air braced me on the fifty-yard covered walk to the lecture hall. Again I had begun to grumble at the stupidity of covering a subject like gas laws and kinetic molecular theory in a two-hour lecture. Fifteen weeks crammed into six weeks is inhumane, no, immoral. As if you could cram a big blob of time into a tiny vial. How could I allow myself to participate in such a travesty?

A student ran past me, but I barely noticed, though the way he ran added to the vague feeling of abnormality. It seemed too early for class. Later, I could not recall exactly how I felt at that moment. I decided the memory had been lost in the tumble and confusion of what followed. As I walked into the vacant lecture hall a spider of doubt lurked on the edge of my consciousness. The rows of seats lining the funnel-like amphitheater were all empty. The clock above the chalkboard read 7:33. Puzzled, I walked back out and looked across the quadrangle. As I stepped onto the sidewalk, a bicyclist swerved around me and knocked the books from my grip; a young woman lay under a tree, smoking. I called out to her and asked for the time. No answer. Across the quadrangle, a group clustered around a two-car wreck. The random movements of people and bicycles struck me as chaotic, as if entropy were somehow reaching an explosive maximum.

I walked back to the chemistry department office and found portly Mrs. Kantley standing and shaking with her hands over her ears. Her long, limp, amber hair, normally draped over her chubby shoulders like a silk shawl, now looked stringy and tangled. Sobbing, she managed to blurt out something about people coming in, asking the time, and shouting.

Several desk drawers were open; papers were strewn over the floor; strange for the meticulous Mrs. Kantley. "What time is it, Mrs. Kantley?"

"Not you too, Dr. Adams!" she said through sudden sobbing. "All the clocks stopped at 7:33."

"Calm down, Mrs. Kantley. What happened?"

"Look at the sky," she said. "The sun . . ."

I sat her down and turned on her small desk radio and heard: " . . . and there should be tremendous wind and tides . . . . To summarize, the sun has not moved since 7:33 A.M., E.D.S.T. All clocks seem to have stopped at exactly that moment.

"Now we take you to Cambridge, Massachusetts, where our correspondent Matthew Hardy is talking with Professor John Needlehouse at the Harvard Observatory:"

"Dr. Needlehouse, we're hoping you can tell us exactly what has happened?"

"Something very strange indeed. Not only have all the clocks stopped functioning simultaneously this morning, but also the motion of the sun across the sky stopped at the same precise time, 12:33 Greenwich Meridian Time, 7:33 A.M. local time."

"But isn't it true, sir; that the sun doesn't actually move around the earth; it's the earth that rotates around its axis?"

"Yes, that is true, young man," the professor said curtly. "Thank you for correcting me."

"Then does this mean that the earth has stopped rotating?"

"That would be the obvious hypothesis, young man, but such a sudden stop is inconceivable. Nothing I know of could stop the earth's rotation. But if it did, the abrupt change in momentum would result in wind turbulence and monstrous tides that would unleash tsunamis and other forces of inconceivable destruction. It's equivalent to stopping a speeding car instantaneously without slowing down and, instead of flying through the windshield, feeling no change in velocity. That is absurd; it defies all laws of physics. It's as far-fetched as saying that hot water in the Pacific Ocean could cause floods and snow in New England."

"What about the clocks, professor?"

"We have no explanation for that either, though the two events do appear to be connected."

"With all the clocks out of order and the sun immobile how will we know the time, professor?"

"I have set up an hourglass and instructed an assistant to turn it as it empties and to keep track of the number of times he turns it. That'll give us a rough estimate."

"What next, professor?"

"The President has called an emergency meeting of members of the NAS in Washington at 5:00 this afternoon. I am leaving shortly for that meeting. He has asked us to make recommendations to the National Security Council as soon as possible."

"NAS is the National Academy of Sciences, right, sir?"

"Of course."

Seeing Mrs. Kantley sitting and seeming more relaxed I asked, "Where is Dr. Buchner?"

"The dean called him for a chairs' meeting."

I went up to the third floor and ran into Charlie Hollowell. "What's happened, Charlie?"

"You know as much as I do."

I recounted the radio interview with the astronomer, as Charlie Hollowell shook his head. "Beats me."

Charlie's perennial smile had disappeared leaving a blank, red face. For a moment I thought he was going to cry. "Take it easy, Charlie. It can't be what it seems. Everything looks normal."

Charlie said, "Think there's a connection between the sun and the clocks?"

"If I were a religious man I'd say we're witnessing a miracle."

"I just called my wife; she's pretty upset," Charlie said. "I'm going home."

I ran into my office and picked up the phone. Ruth's voice sounded shaky. "The radio is reporting strange things about the sun. What's going on, Joe?"

"Don't worry. I'll call Dad to see if he knows anything; then I'll come home."

The phone rang five times at Dad's office, so I hung up and dialed my mother at home.

"Hello, Mom? I'm trying to get hold of Dad."

"So am I. His secretary said he was at a departmental meeting."

"How are things in Gainesville?"

"Same as everywhere else. You're calling about the sun, right?"

"Yes."

"I don't know anything. When I hear from Dad, I'll call you. Better go; I'm waiting for his call."

I hung up, left my books on the desk, and ran down the stairs and out the door and across campus until I ran out of breath and then walked the rest of the way. Though I was distracted by random thoughts, I noticed the ground was still wet with dew. "It must be near noon," I thought, "and it's still cool and wet."

My clothes were drenched in perspiration when I stumbled into the kitchen and found Ruth rolling out piecrust. She wore an apron over a flowered pink dress and a kerchief over her short black hair. With a broad smile, said, "I'm covered with flour; you'll get your welcome-home kiss in a minute."

"An apple pie? That's pretty cavalier."

"Apple's your favorite."

"Why aren't you panicking like everybody else?"

"Pangloss said to tend your garden just in case the world doesn't end." Then, with her blue eyes wide, she said, "Really, dear, what's going on?"

"All we know about nature tells us it can't happen. It's definitely unnatural."

She continued to roll out the dough, laid it in the pie pan, and ladled the cut apples over the crust, poured sugar over it, laid the top crust on that, and slid the pan into the oven. She looked at me and said, "What do you think?"

"How can I think about it? If the earth stopped rotating, there'd be chaos. Look outside; it's a beautiful day."

"What did your dad say?"

"He was tied up. I'll bet the whole astronomy department is going nuts."

"Could it be an optical illusion?"

"It's real. The confusing thing's the time."

"OK; you relax while I finish dinner."

"Relax? How?"

She took off the apron, washed her hands and then walked to me and put her arms around me and kissed me. "Welcome home, dear."

I went into the living room and turned on the television. Most channels were rehashing earlier reports and scenes of the paralyzed sun in the sky. The most engaging had the sun seemingly half submerged in the Indian Ocean. One channel showed a series of world leaders attempting to calm the masses. Another had a TV evangelist screaming, "Repent, the end is at hand!"

I turned it off and returned to the kitchen.

"Why are religious fanatics always assume the end of the world?"

"How about a glass of champagne?"

"Great. We'll tuck the truth into the bubbles." I sat at the table.

"Take it easy, Joe."

"Just look at that sky. Even you have to admit something's wrong."

"Couldn't ask for a prettier day."

"Suppose it stays like this?"

"Then we'll have a beautiful forever."

"That's silly, Ruth."

She put her arms around my neck and said, "We're together, it's a beautiful day, and I have a beautiful meal planned. The supermarket had live Maine lobsters, and I've got an apple pie in the oven."

"What'll I do with you?"

"Want a hint?"

"This could be the end," I said, dramatically. I couldn't stand her optimism in the face of such possible doom.

"If it is, we'll end it together."

Then she sat across the table, took my hands and said, "Are you going to open the wine or do you plan to grump all evening?"

"Evening?"

"Let's pretend."

I worked on that bottle several minutes before I could pop the cork. She held out two long stem glasses and I filled them.

"To a wonderful, long day," she said, holding up her glass.

"And tomorrow, if it comes."

After a sip of wine she said, "I have candles for this evening."

An hour later we were still talking and enjoying the wine on the back terrace under a large live oak tree. I was calmer now. The sun was still glued to the same spot in the sky, clocks remained stilled, and dew still clung to the ground.

"Tomorrow will come," she said.

"Tomorrow as a concept is now in serious question. We may not be able to depend on anything anymore. Everything's up in the air."

Lifting her glass she said, "Right."

"You always joke when I get serious."

"One of us has to face reality."

"Reality is a joke to you?"

"Tell me, Joe. How will your worry help?"

"It's a serious problem."

"What problem?"

"Understanding nature. That's my job."

"Living a happy life is mine, Joe."

"I want to be happy too, for Heaven sake."

"Then let's open another bottle. What do you say?"

I stared at her.

"They were on sale, so I bought four."

I finally smiled.

*   *   *

After drowning my worries in champagne, we went inside, where Ruth closed the shades and said, "See? The sun just set." Then she lit candles, and we toasted each other again and sat down to a beautiful dinner.

When she mentioned having a baby I reminded her of our plan to wait a little longer, until my career gelled.

"It's as gelled as it's going to get, and the time is right."

"Really?"

She walked into the bedroom and slipped off her dress.

I said, "How about one more look?"

She caressed me and led me out to see the bright orb still hanging over the trees like a gloating giant reigning over endless morning. The source of life on earth had cast a shadow over the world. All I could think to say was, "I feel like it's time to go to work."

"No way!"

Lifting the telephone I said, "Dad never called. I'll try Mom again before it gets too late."

After three rings Mom answered.

"Any news from Dad?"

"Nothing. The astronomy department met and adjourned, but your father wouldn't leave. He's been in his office since morning. I spoke to him briefly a few hours ago. Said the others had given up, but not him. Said he would call when he found something."

"Thanks, Mom. You OK?"

"Hard to believe anything's wrong."

"I'll keep in touch."

When I hung up I looked over at Ruth. She was under the covers.

*　　*　　*

I awoke and looked at my clock radio. It still showed 7:33. I turned on the radio at low volume so as not to disturb Ruth's sleep and waited for the hourly news, but nothing newsworthy had occurred. The sun was still stationary and so were the clocks. At the end of the news summary the announcer said a special interview would follow, so I left the radio on:

"We have with us this morning a man who has asked to speak to us about the sun. He has told us very little, and we're all excited to hear what he has to say. He is Professor Jonathan Wells. Welcome, Professor Wells. Would you explain your theory on the stationary sun for us?"

"Thank you for inviting me to appear on your program. But first, let me correct your request. The sun is not stationary, and neither is the earth."

"But Professor Wells, everyone can see it hasn't moved in many hours."

"The only way the sun could stand still in the sky is for the earth's rotation to stop, and we all know that is impossible; the reasons have been amply aired."

"Well then, how do you describe what's happened?"

"If you will allow me . . ."

"Sorry, please go on."

"It's quite simple, actually. A substance has spread across the earth that alters people's perceptions. What we see is an illusion."

"But, Professor Wells . . ."

"Please, young man, if you will just allow me to continue."

"Of course."

"An alien invasion is in progress. These aliens have managed to spread a gaseous chemical containing a previously unknown, very light, chemical element so light that it can penetrate the human brain and cause changes in its response to stimuli. I have not yet determined how they have spread this agent so completely. I'm guessing they did it from outer space."

"But Professor, no one has seen any aliens."

"Of course not. We cannot perceive their presence. These aliens are crafty. They have rendered themselves invisible. They are apparently plotting to subdue our planet. That, actually, is why I volunteered to appear here. We must make preparations to repulse them before they completely take over our brains and our civilization."

By this time my heart was pounding. Listening to this lunatic's ranting had completely awakened me. I wondered if it was somebody's idea of a joke.

"Professor, how have your colleagues responded to your, uh, rather unorthodox theory?"

After a pause, "As a matter of fact, they have been completely duped by the aliens and have ignored my suggestion."

"Where do you teach, Professor Wells? What university, I mean?"

"I'm not actually in a university. I'm a free-lance scientist."

"I see. Is your doctorate in astronomy?"

"I have not bothered with a doctorate, but my fields of research are astronomy, physics, chemistry and biology. I am qualified in all those fields. My major research for many years has been in unidentified flying objects, UFOs. I have recorded countless sightings of alien spaceships. Perhaps I could appear again to discuss those findings."

"Thank you, Professor Wells. We appreciate very much your taking time out of your busy schedule to enlighten us."

"But I . . ."

Pop music cut Professor Wells off. I got up as quietly as I could, walked to the living room, looked up the phone number of the station, and dialed it.

"Station WZYX."

"I just heard that crackpot on your station. I'm Doctor Adams at the State University. I'm a member of the chemistry faculty, and I can tell you that man is no scientist. There is no unknown light element. Such an element is inconceivable. The man is an impostor, and you should apologize to your listeners for allowing him on the air."

"Thank you, Professor Adams. As soon as he started with the aliens I began to worry. But he had such a convincing story about his background that we thought it would be a public service to put him on the air. We should have investigated him a little more, I suppose, but . . . he seemed so cultured and professorial . . . anyway, I'll clarify the error right away. Thanks for calling."

I went back to bed and continued to listen to the radio, waiting for the apology. After an hour of obnoxious rock music, I got up and again dialed the station number.

"This is Dr. Adams again. I called in a complaint an hour ago, and the person who answered assured me that the station would apologize for airing that crackpot who passed himself off as a scientist. I'm still waiting."

"We've had literally hundreds of calls; yours was the only unfavorable one. They want us to bring him on again, so we're arranging to have him for another interview."

"If that's your audience, then we're doomed. But in any case, you have no right to spread misinformation and lies."

"Thanks for your interest, Dr. Adams."

I stewed the rest of the night, or whatever it was, about Wells and the radio station. Adding to my discomfort were the shafts of sunlight that penetrated the shifting drapes as the non-stop air conditioner blew across them. When I could stand it no longer, I got up and peeked between the curtains. The bright light shocked me, and I drew the curtains shut again.

Ruth slipped out of bed and walked over, put her arms around me, and said, "I had a nice evening, dear."

"Nothing's changed. Look outside."

"I don't care. I'm happy," she said. "How about some eggs?"

"Wait till I tell you about the nut I just heard on the radio."

*   *   *

As I dressed, a radio announcer interrupted the morning news program with a special announcement: "The Naval Observatory in Washington has just announced that the sun resumed its movement at 7:33, and so have clocks everywhere. Whatever it was, it's over, thank God!"

"Did you hear that?" I said walking into the kitchen. I looked at my watch; it showed 7:45. "Look at the wall clock."

"Did he give any explanation?"

"No. It's incredible! That moment, 7:33, lasted exactly twenty-four hours, and from all appearances nothing's changed. I've got to get to the department and see what's going on. I'll just grab some coffee and run."

"Take time for breakfast. I had a wonderful time last night, and I'm not ready for it to end."

I embraced her. "Me too."

*　　*　　*

A party atmosphere had spread like laughing gas through the chemistry department. As I walked into the departmental office Mrs. Kantley smiled, "The sun took a day off. I don't know whether to bill it as sick leave or annual leave."

I had never seen her toothy grin so broad.

Charlie Hollowell extended his hand. "Congratulations! The world goes on. Wasn't it biblical? I waited all afternoon for a voice to boom down from the sky."

Harvey Baron, another new member of the faculty, was at work in his lab. I poked my head in and asked why he wasn't celebrating.

"Too busy."

"Haven't you heard? The sun's moved on."

"Fine, fine."

"Come on, Harvey. This is big."

"Got a lot more data to collect for my proposal; deadline's breathing down on me."

"Yesterday looked like the ultimate deadline."

"Please, Joe, I'm busy."

"You really ought to come up for air, Harvey."

Charlie pulled me out and led me to the coffee shop in the basement. "By the way, what day is this?" he said.

"It was July 2nd yesterday. But you raise a good point, Charlie. Time passed whether the clocks show it or not. I'd say it's the 3rd."

"But time is determined by star positions. Suppose they didn't move either. It might still be the 2nd."

"Somebody from on high will have to decide."

"Maybe it was a miracle."

"Strange word from an agnostic."

"What is a miracle, Charlie?"

"As a matter of fact I looked up the dictionary definition. It's an event in the physical world that deviates from the known laws of nature."

"Uh-huh."

"I think the Devil's hiding in the word *known*. If someone comes up with an explanation that fits into the known laws of nature, then it wasn't a miracle."

"We'll just have to wait and see."

"That's the NAS committee's job, Joe. Wonder what they're up to?"

"Haven't heard. They're pretty smart boys, but if they don't find an explanation, it'll be declared a miracle. And that'll really get the nut fringe going."

We finally parted and went to our labs, but I couldn't concentrate. Thoughts darting through my mind pushed everything else out. I walked to the library and checked out two astronomy books and spent the rest of the morning reading.

At about 11:30 Ruth called to say that my father had had a heart attack and was in the intensive care unit. I called the hospital from my office.

"What is it Mom? Ruth said you called. How is he?"

"Not good, Joe. He had just come home after more than twenty-four hours working on his calculations. He walked in the door and collapsed. I called the rescue squad; they came right away, and brought him to the emergency room."

"We'll be there in three hours or less."

"Drive carefully, Joe."

I tried my best, but my foot kept getting heavier. It took two hours and fifteen minutes from the time I picked up Ruth to the minute we drove into the hospital parking lot.

Before I got to the information desk I saw my mother waiting in the lobby.

"How is he?"

"It's too late, Joe. He died an hour ago."

Ruth put her arm around her and sat her down. I stood petrified.

"It was so fast," I said. "He was only sixty-two."

Mom was too shaken to talk. She sobbed as Ruth sat by her side, holding her as she would a baby.

"May I see him?" I said.

Mom shrugged.

I found him still on a bed in the ICU. He looked peaceful, but I could not bear to look at him. His face was chalky-gray, cold, and still. I walked back to the lobby.

"Did he say anything?"

"Yes, but it didn't mean anything."

"What?"

"I knew it would happen . . . son . . . stop . . . son . . ."

"What did he want?"

"I don't know. I just don't know."

"He always called me Joe. Why would he call me son?"

"Yes, that was strange. I'm sorry. I guess we'll never know."

"Could he have meant s-u-n?"

"I don't know, Joe."

"Did he say what he was working on?"

"Same as always: astrophysics, celestial mechanics, things I don't understand. It was all he thought about."

At that moment I knew I was right. He must have figured out why the sun stopped. "Where are his research notes?"

"In his campus office, I guess. Wait; a few days ago he brought a stack of notebooks home. I asked him why, and he said he planned to work at home for a while."

"May I have them?"

"I don't see why not."

*   *   *

Ruth and I spent the next few days in Gainesville, helping with funeral arrangements and trying to get Mom back to something approaching a normal routine. Eventually, to ease my worry, Mom agreed to stay with my sister in Gainesville for a while. That same evening Mom gave me Dad's research notebooks. I spent several hours fighting through the mathematics and cryptic language with negligible success. I could find nothing that seemed related to the long day.

The next morning we left Mom at my sister's house and made her promise to spend some time with us too. I walked to the car cradling Dad's notes in both arms, a treasure to savor later.

Most of the way home I could think and talk of nothing but the long day and the possibility that Dad had uncovered something. Ruth indulged me, though I knew she had little interest.

*　　*　　*

Because no change in the positions of the other heavenly bodies could be detected during the long day, the Director of the U.S. Naval Observatory announced that no time had passed; he tentatively declared that, astronomically at least, July 2 simply appeared to be abnormally long.

When I read the announcement in the next morning's newspaper, I could not take my eyes off the words, "appeared to be." Holding the newspaper I went to Charlie's lab and held it under Charlie's eyes and said, "There it is! The weasel word! It didn't *appear* to be a long day, damn it; it *was* long."

"I've got a class in a few minutes. Let's talk later."

"They've started the cover-up."

"Later, Joe. OK?"

"OK, OK."

*　　*　　*

By July 7 foreign news stories and sports had pushed the long day off the front pages. The twenty-member commission of the National Academy of Sciences had settled down to preparing a comprehensive report, and the earth continued to turn. As days passed the dire feeling eased, and the long day began to dissolve into a harmless curiosity. With no explanation, talk of a miracle began to sink roots, as church attendance rose. In time the long day melted into a brew of murky ideas and omens stirred by charlatans predicting God's retribution, alien invasions, and communist plots until, confused by all the fanciful claims, people began to let the question ease into nonsense. Not me. Not only did my interest not wane; it had needled deep to create an exquisite ache in my consciousness. Much of the ache was worry that the event would eventually be ignored, forgotten, and impossible to study. To me the cause of the earth's inexplicable behavior on that July 2nd had become a grail that dangled in space, clearly visible, but beyond reach. Even after studying several books on astronomy and cosmology, I still couldn't understand my father's notebooks, much less create a hypothesis. The errant sun had left only one mark: a fracture in man's faith in predictable, understandable nature. And with each passing day, that fracture was generating scar tissue that could preclude examination. The greatest unanswered question in history would remain unanswered, as it became an obsession, no, an abscess that would not stop throbbing.

After two months I could stand the suspense no longer. Ruth was pregnant, apparently having conceived on that memorable day. As thrilled as I was at becoming a father, a baby could not shove that nagging question out of view.

On the fourth of September I telephoned the Washington office of the National Academy of Sciences. After holding on as they shuffled me from one secretary to another, I finally reached someone who was willing to provide a list of commission members. One of the names jumped out as I jotted them down: Rudolf Lazar, my major graduate professor. I telephoned Dr. Lazar's office to get his phone number in Washington, and Dr. Lazar answered.

"What's going on with the commission? I can't stand the silence."

"I read about your father, Joe. My condolences. He was a good man and a good scientist."

"Thanks, Rudy. But what about the Commission?"

"I resigned last week."

"Why? What happened?"

"Nothing."

"You didn't quit for nothing."

"Nothing is exactly what we were doing. We weren't accomplishing a damned thing, and my research was languishing."

"But Rudy, this is important."

"That's what I thought, but there have been no effects, no evidence that anything happened. And with no data, no evidence, no facts, we got mired in a hopeless swamp of arcane speculations about ultimate causes and effects. Reminded me of an undergraduate philosophy course I took years ago."

"I don't understand."

"There were no observable disruptions, no scars, so to speak. With no tangible effects, how can you conclude or hypothesize? It's impossible. Maybe it never happened." He sounded tired.

"But Rudy, this is the greatest question nature has ever posed."

"So great that we have no choice but to ignore it."

"But the lunatics will steal the day with alien invasions and Heavenly wrath. People eat that stuff up."

"I know."

"We've got to stop it." I could think of no more persuasive words.

"Someone else will have to do it, Joe. Sorry."

I hung up feeling limp and hollow.

The following week the chairman of the National Academy Commission announced that he had resigned also because his research was suffering. There was no announcement in the press. I discovered it in a brief note in *Science Magazine,* which said that several members had resigned after Dr. Lazar, and they had been replaced. I recognized none of the new names. By the time their work was done, the Commission consisted completely of unknown and undistinguished scientists.

The Commission finally submitted its report on March 29 of the following year, nine months after the long day. I found that date ironic because that was the day my daughter, Esther, was born. None of the original Commission members signed the final report. The report attracted little attention. Most newspapers ignored it. A brief article in The New York Times explained that the commission failed to find an explanation because the long day produced no physical effects. "In fact," the article said, "strange as it might seem, the commission found no conclusive evidence that there was actually a long day or if there was, how long it lasted." Furious, I threw the newspaper into the waste bin and then retrieved it, cut out the article, and filed it. I immediately telephoned the Washington office of the National Academy of Sciences.

"I just read the New York Times article on your report of the long day. I find it ludicrous that competent scientists have reached that conclusion. I'd like a copy of the full report."

"Of course, Dr. Adams. I'll put it in the mail right away."

Two weeks later the letter came from the National Academy of Sciences with the seventy-five-page report. I ripped open the package, sat at my desk and read it from beginning to end. When I had turned the last page I knew the New York Times article had been accurate. The Commission had crafted the painfully long, excruciatingly detailed report to satisfy every political, religious and scientific persuasion. I walked down the hall to Charlie's lab.

"You won't believe this."
"Huh?"

"The Times article was right. The report actually concluded that nothing happened."

Tapping a manometer without looking at me, he said, "Yeah, I know. I don't get it."

"Lack of evidence."

"But the whole world saw it.

"Like the eye witness account of Moses parting the Red Sea?"

"What evidence did they want?"

"Scars, like the bombed-out buildings and cemeteries of World War II."

"And there aren't any."

"Right. Doesn't add up; the expected weather, nothing; not even astronomical evidence that time passed. That's why they denied it happened. Hard as it is to swallow, they figured their conclusion would go down easier than declaring it a miracle and stirring up the loonies. Unless there's a repetition, people will soon forget it."

"OK. Except for getting you a baby daughter, it hasn't made any difference that I can see."

"Come on, Charlie. You know it happened! We can't let them sweep it under the rug. Can't you see what this means?"

"I see that I need research results to get tenure, and so do you."

"How can you ignore this fantastic research opportunity, Charlie?"

For the first time since I walked in, Charlie looked at me. "What do you have in mind?"

"I don't know yet."

Returning to his experiment he said, "You'll be working out of your expertise, Joe, and you'll be taking on the whole scientific establishment."

"We'll see."

*   *   *

That afternoon I got home a little before four o'clock.

"I'm glad you're home early," Ruth said. "Esther's been asking for you."

With my mind still racing, her words made no impression.

"Don't you want to see your daughter?"

"I got that NAS report today. The newspaper had it right."

"How could they?"

I shrugged.

Ruth picked up Esther from the bassinet. "Here, Daddy; take your daughter."

I took the baby and smiled at her momentarily, then abruptly said, "I can't take this lying down."

"You just got home, Joe. Let it rest. You'll do better tomorrow after you've slept on it."

"Got to do it now, Ruth. It's driving me crazy."

"Joe, this wonderful little baby needs her father even more than I do."

"I'm sorry, Ruth, but I've just got to. I can't think about anything else. I'll be back as soon as I can."

"Try to get back by suppertime. I'm getting tired of eating alone."

Unable to respond, I said nothing and walked out.

Ruth turned and took the baby back to her room. She was so rarely angry with me that I almost stayed, but I couldn't.

*   *   *

After throwing away three drafts of a letter I sat back and reread the toned-down fourth draft:

"Thank you for sending me the report of the Special Commission. I must express my dismay over their conclusion that nothing occurred on July 2 of last year. I respectfully request permission to appear before the commission to testify to what I observed and what I have learned. If that is not possible, then I demand the right to append a statement to the report."

For the next five weeks I heard nothing. Finally I found a letter from the NAS:

"Dear Professor Adams:

"The commission disbanded on the day it submitted its report. While the NAS sympathizes with your feelings, we bear the burden of facing public reaction. We feel that the commission's conclusion, though scientifically unsatisfying, is technically sound, intellectually honest, and expedient. It will enhance public order and calm.

"The issue is closed. We thank you for your interest."

I immediately sat down and wrote another letter. It wasn't easy to remain calm; I was approaching my boiling point. My letter read:

"I just received your letter denying me permission to address the commission about the long day. By precluding further investigation you have assured that the most important phenomenon that nature has ever posed will remain unexplained. I cannot accept the commission's judgment, and I insist on testifying or at least adding my own statement to the report."

Until I dropped the letter in the mail slot, I had not thought about the testimony I would give. With no theory or tentative hypothesis to explain the long day I could think of nothing constructive except its importance, but I did not care. I could not allow this question to drown in the murky prose of political posturing. I even imagined myself testifying in a Senate committee room like those I had seen on television, sitting alone with long, hostile faces staring down at me. I'd face them down. Yes, I'd testify, and I'd be prepared.

Two months passed before I convinced myself that there would be no answer and decided on another approach: write articles and letters to scientific journals and newsmagazines warning that if such an event went unexamined, it would remain a mystery, and the world would never know if and when it would happen again. But most importantly, we would miss a chance to understand a deeply significant wrinkle of nature. The few responses came from those who saw that day as a sign of doom. I felt I was hanging on a cliff of loose gravel wondering whether nature could suspend its laws: Would water boil the next time I heated it? Would a baseball return to earth at the next home run? A cavern of chaos and unpredictability had opened its door onto darkness.

After a few months even newspapers began to reject my articles, so I took a different approach, one that could help me professionally as well as satisfy my curiosity. I phoned the new astronomer on the faculty.

"Hello, Stanley Starr?"

"Yes."

"I'm Joe Adams from chemistry. I'd like to discuss something with you."

"Sure. How's one-thirty this afternoon?"

"I'll be here."

At 1:25 I knocked on Dr. Starr's door.

After introducing myself, I said, "I have a research idea I'd like to talk over. It deals with the day the sun didn't move. I think it's terrible the way the scientific world has ignored this phenomenon, and I want to do something about it. What do you think about taking it on as a joint project?"

"That was quite a day!"

"Got any ideas?"

"Wish I did. Apparently nothing in the heavens moved, not even the stars. But the most interesting part was that clocks stopped too, as if time itself stopped."

"Has the astronomical community shown any interest in it?"

"At first, but no more."

"Astronomers should be jumping in with both feet."

"I know."

"Well, how about it?"

Stan looked dubious."

"I'd like us to submit a joint proposal to NSF. First thing would be a complete literature search."

"You'd have to start with the Bible. That's the only known reference. But seriously, Joe, I wouldn't know where to begin."

"Good enough. I'll get something together. In the meantime, these are my father's notebooks. My mother gave them to me when he died."

"J. P. Adams was your father? I didn't make the connection."

"Yes. His last words were pretty cryptic. He might have known it in advance. I can't follow his notes. Would you mind looking them over?"

"Wow! I'd be honored. He did great work in astrophysics."

"Thanks. See you soon."

*   *   *

In my inquiry to the National Science Foundation I explored the possibility of funding an interdisciplinary group of scientists to study the long day and outline a method of attack. The project would involve faculty and graduate students from all over the country and overseas.

Within a week I received the answer. Apparently they took me for a troublemaker, for the NSF offered no hope of funding and didn't even ask for a formal proposal. When other governmental agencies followed suit, I took the responses to Stan Starr's office. I must have looked dejected because he could barely look me in the face.

"As bad as all that?"

"Here they are: all rejections. Any ideas?"

"For a while I thought I had something."

"What?"

"It doesn't hold water, Joe, but it was nice for a while."

"Tell me."

"If we accept the expanding universe, there are two opinions of what will eventually happen: If the total mass of the universe is great enough there will eventually come a point where the force of gravitation will overcome the centrifugal force of the big bang, and the universe will begin to contract. If the total mass of the universe is not great enough, then the expansion will continue forever."

"And?"

Stan smiled sheepishly. "What if the universe reached its outer limit of expansion and started to contract. At that crucial moment everything would begin to run in reverse.

But for an instant, which could be pretty long in universe time, time and everything in the universe would stand still as it stopped expanding and started to shrink. I have no way to test that idea or even to know if it makes sense. Nobody knows what would happen at that point."

I sat amazed at the simplicity.

"But after thinking about it, I realized it doesn't make sense. To account for the observed immobility of the sun, we'd have to show that the earth's rotation stopped. Nothing about the idea would account for that."

I heard none of his objections; only the possibility. I was frozen to my chair. Finally, I said, "Do you realize, Stan, that's the first sensible idea I've heard from anybody. And that would explain how my father could have predicted it."

"Actually, that's where I got the idea. His notes contain calculations of the expanding universe. He didn't relate it to the sun's motion, though."

I stood to leave and said, "I've got to think about this."

"We'd better forget it, Joe. I discussed your plan with my department chair. Without blinking an eye he told me to drop it."

"Another ineffectual academic with no imagination."

"I wouldn't say that. Smith is a respected astronomer."

"Uh-huh."

"Your father was doing some interesting work, but it wasn't related. I'll be blunt, Joe. My chair has heard of your interest in this problem."

"And?"

"He thinks I should stay as far as I can from it and you."

"What do you think?"

"I don't know. He's smart, and he is the chairman."

"You mean he's got you by your tenure."

He grimaced and nodded.

Standing, I said, "Thanks for nothing."

"Don't take it personally, Joe. Only the real scientists ask the tough questions, and I respect you for that. Most people take on sure-fire projects that yield lots of papers that few people ever read. I mean it, Joe. But the thing is, well, frankly nobody I know has any ideas on how to tackle this one. Working alone as a chemist you'd have no chance. I wish I could help. Honest. If I had a good idea I would, irrespective of my chair. But I don't. And neither has anybody else."

I stood through Stan's speech and when he finished I opened the door and turned. "Thanks anyway, Stan. Maybe we can have lunch together sometime."

"I'd like that, Joe. Anytime."

*   *   *

The phone was ringing as I opened my office door.

"Dr. Adams? My name is Professor Jonathan Wells. I understand you're interested in pursuing the long day phenomenon."

"Are you the person who was on the radio that night claiming it was an alien invasion?"

"That's right, Dr. Adams. The station gave me your name. I want to have a televised seminar on the long day. The station has agreed to host it. I'm inviting several scientists and others to discuss that highly provocative phenomenon, and with your interest and credentials you would be a good person to have."

"Not interested."

"Sorry to hear that, Dr. Adams. It would be good to have representation from an academic scientist like you."

"Who else is participating?"

"I'm hoping to get men and women of excellent credentials from industry, science, the clergy, and a philosopher."

"I'm not interested in associating with charlatans."

"Oh, no, Dr. Adams. These are all respected people, community leaders who are vitally interested. It would be a good opportunity to promote your ideas."

"What's the format?"

"Each person will make a ten-minute presentation followed by a thirty-minute discussion period, and then we'll take phone calls from listeners. One hour total."

In spite of my doubts and suspicions I agreed to appear. The scientific establishment had chosen to ignore me. Perhaps common people could do what intellectuals could not.

Ruth was excited when I told her. She said she would get all her friends to listen.

The program started at eight o'clock PM the following week. Professor Wells was pleasant enough and looked distinguished with well-groomed, gray hair and moustache. I could see why he had impressed the radio people. He was tall, handsome and athletic. The others were ordinary looking, and I neither knew nor recognized any of them. One, an evangelical preacher, also tall and husky, had eyes that could bore a hole through you. He said little, apparently waiting his turn.

The moderator, a pleasant young woman, started the program by introducing the panel members in a voice that smiled. I was the only scientist. A short, chubby man, a math teacher in a parochial school, seemed meek and frightened. An elderly woman who taught science in a public high school asked to speak first. The moderator politely told her that Professor Wells had organized the forum and would present the issue first. "You can speak right after him," she said. The woman looked anxious as she fidgeted with her purse and finally laid it on the floor beside her.

Wells began: "I have appeared on the radio several times over the past months, and many of you already know my hypothesis. However, for those of you who don't know I will summarize it. I believe the phenomenon we call the long day was an illusion produced by aliens who somehow spread a light, hitherto unknown chemical element that has penetrated our brains to produce the illusion. The sun did not stand still; the earth did not stop rotating; time did not stop. It was all illusion. These aliens are taking over the planet unobserved. To those of you who wonder where they are, the answer is simple: the light element has rendered us unable to see them."

The fidgety woman did not wait for an introduction: "I'm Mildred Garcia, and I teach high school science. I have never seen or read of any reliable evidence for aliens or unidentified flying objects, although some people seem to love the idea. Of course, the thought that we are not alone in the universe is seductive, but where is the evidence? Why have the government and the science establishment ignored them? The only answer is they don't exist. But in answer to Professor Wells' theory that the apparent long day was an illusion: how could everybody on earth have had the same illusion? Those aliens, Professor

Wells, must be plenty smart and thorough. Your theory is nonsense, Sir. I believe that long day was simply a quirk of nature. The universe is a beautifully complex machine, and its mechanism failed temporarily, as all machines do occasionally. I have no idea what the failure was, but it apparently corrected itself. I think that's all there is to it."

"Professor Adams," the moderator said. "What do you think?"

As much as I wanted to describe Stan Starr's idea of the contracting universe, I knew it was half-baked and no better than Wells'.

"First of all, neither of these explanations is a scientific theory or even a hypothesis. A scientific theory must be testable. That means we should be able to use it to predict something observable. If the theory fails to do that, you must find another. Mr. Wells' idea cannot be tested because the aliens have rendered all humans incapable of perceiving them or the motion of the sun. His so-called theory precludes any testing or verification. Besides that, Mr. Wells, there cannot be an unknown, light element. Hydrogen is the lightest element in the periodic table. There is no way, within atomic theory, to account for an element lighter than hydrogen. If any such element were found the entire atomic theory would have to be scrapped. At any rate, because this element is imperceptible, it has no observable properties, so we can never hope to isolate or study it. So his hypothesis precludes the possibility of finding either the element or the aliens. As for the aliens, I know of no credible scientists or other professionals who have seen them. Only amateurs and crackpots have reported seeing them.

"Mrs. Garcia's suggestion that the universe merely had a temporary failure suffers from the same fault: it is not testable or verifiable. Her idea is not a theory either. It is merely a story that offers a false feeling of understanding."

"What do you propose, Dr. Adams?" the moderator said.

"I have not been able to devise a testable hypothesis. And that's what makes this event so frightful and fascinating. When someone offers a real theory, we will be on the road to understanding that day."

"Doctor Adams," Wells said, "I would appreciate it if you would refer to me as Professor Wells."

"In your radio interview you said you did not hold a university faculty position. You also said you do not have a doctorate."

"That is insulting!"

"The truth often feels that way. Call me Mr. Adams or Joe if you like. I don't mind."

"I expected to come here for an intellectual discussion, not a personal attack."

"I'm offering rational and scientific facts. It's your ideas I'm attacking, not you personally."

"Reverend Watkins, you have something to say?" the moderator said. "Go ahead, Reverend."

"It's clear to me that you are all looking in the wrong places. It is not difficult to see the cause of that day if we have eyes to see. Only God could produce such an event. In his universal benevolence, God has performed a miracle for the entire world to behold." He looked upward and paused a moment before continuing. "What is there to understand? What more do we need to know? His warning is clear. The Lord has stopped the sun for a reason. What reason can He have but to warn us? We have become a complacent and Godless society. Just look around at the disasters our cities have become: havens of divorce, abortion, drugs, crime and countless other sins. And what has science done but lead us out of the path that God prepared for us. Science claims to explain everything, but in truth, it explains nothing. Science is the Devil's work, carefully crafted fabrications pasted together with lies.

"Our scientist friend here wants a theory. What theory can explain God's will? This is not the first time God has intervened in the workings of the natural order. In the midst of battle Joshua said, '. . . Sun, stand thou still upon Gibeon; and thou, Moon, in the valley of Ajalon. And the sun stood still . . . in the midst of heaven, and hasted not to go down about a whole day. And there was no day like that before it or after it.' Yes, God works miracles and always with a purpose. We may not yet know God's purpose in this case, but that He has one cannot be denied."

Mr. Devon, would you care to comment?

I felt sorry for the poor meek man. He looked so nervous and out of place straightening his tie. Finally he began in a slow, raspy whisper: "We are the wrong people to be discussing this phenomenon," Mr. Devon said. "None of us can claim expertise in astrophysics. Dr. Adams is right about theories, and I wish he had one. Everything he said is correct, in contrast to the other panel members, but we seem to be stuck with whimsical, bizarre explanations that can be neither verified nor falsified. I am not an astrophysicist either, so I have little to offer, except this: No one has brought up the question of evidence. What actually happened that day? Mr. Wells says nothing happened. I think the first item of business is to determine precisely what happened. And the only way we can do that is to measure the effects of that day. Trouble is, there were no effects. None whatever! Not the disruptions in weather or changes in motion and inertia. With no effects to observe, it is very difficult to say that anything happened. The NAS Commission members were forced to conclude that nothing happened. Logically their conclusion is valid.

Mr. Devon's statement made me feel hollow. "Mr. Devon," I said. "I appreciate what you said. And I understand that without effects we have nothing to grasp except superstition, religion and quackery. But I'm not ready to give up the way the NAS Commission did."

"You see, even the NAS Commission agrees with my theory in part," Wells said. "I mean that it was an illusion."

"I read their report," I said, "and they never mentioned either aliens or perfuming the planet with light elements."

"Just a moment," Mrs. Garcia said, "If the universe were to break down again, what could anyone do to fix it? Nobody, no nation in the world, controls the universe."

"That's what we're trying to understand, Mrs. Garcia," Mr. Devon said. "Your suggestion is a nice idea, but it doesn't help. The only answer to your question is that only God can fix the universe when it breaks down."

Mr. Wells broke in, "I see this panel is not as open-minded and unbiased as I had hoped. We'll get nowhere as long as we bicker about falsification and verification.

Feeling overwhelmed, the moderator broke in. "I think we've heard the panel's views. Let's take some phone calls. Our lines have been busy since we started. Hello, welcome to our panel on the long day."

"Hello. Am I on?"

"Yes, go on, please."

"Well I'm sick and tired of these high falutin' scientists talking about things nobody understands and then telling us what to think. The reverend's right. God can do anything, What right do we have to dispute Him? And furthermore, like the reverend says, God has a purpose. He's telling us to mend our ways or be damned! That's what I believe and that's all I have to say."

"Thank you," the moderator said. "I don't think that call requires a response. Our next caller is a young man. How old are you?"

"Seventeen."

"Go ahead please."

"I'm in Mrs. Garcia's general science class, and I want to tell you she's great. She explains science for us real good. I really like her, and I think you all should listen to her."

"Do you have any opinion on the long day?" the moderator asked.

"No, Ma'am. We got a day off from school, though. It was pretty nice."

Before she dismissed him I interrupted: "Young man, from your age I guess you must be a senior."

"Yes, sir."

"I also assume that you didn't take chemistry, since you're in general science."

"No way! Chemistry ain't for me. Mrs. Garcia gave us two weeks of it, and it was awful. I don't think anybody understood it."

"Yet you like Mrs. Garcia as a teacher?"

"Sure. She gives us stuff we understand. You know, like ecology and stuff like that. You know, how we're all part of the ecosystem of animals and plants, and how we all live off each other."

Reverend Watkins could not hold back: "Young man, God made the animals and plants for man's use. Man is special and should not be grouped with animals, let alone plants."

"I beg your pardon, reverend," Mrs. Garcia said. "Ecology is an important body of knowledge, and we better pay attention to it if we're going to survive on this planet."

"Oh ye of little faith!" the reverend said. "God provides for our needs."

"God helps him who helps himself," Mrs. Garcia said.

As Mr. Devon sat shaking his head and looking down at the table, I understood why Dr. Lazar resigned from the NAS Commission. The phone calls lasted half an hour longer. Most callers either subscribed to the notion that nothing had happened, or that it was a miracle that could never be understood. But the most astounding thing was how many of them talked to me as if I were evil personified.

When the hour ended the moderator summed up: "It is always interesting to hear people's opinions. I'd like to take this opportunity to thank you all for a very informative and entertaining discussion. And for our listeners, please stay tuned for more in our new series of enlightening and provocative discussions on timely topics. Again, thank you all."

When the broadcast ended I moved toward Mr. Devon to speak with him, but he was leaving. I left without comment or conversation. I'd had enough of popular opinion.

*   *   *

"You were wonderful, Joe," Ruth said. "At least four friends called to say you were the star of the evening. You looked so handsome on the screen."

"Maybe, but it's hard to beat dedicated ignorance. If you win, what have you won? If you lose, you lost to ignorance and stupidity."

*   *   *

Having failed at every turn and with nowhere else to turn, I presented a modest proposal to the chemistry department. In it I proposed only to set up a seminar on the subject of the long day and invite scientists and students from all relevant departments.

At a faculty meeting called to discuss my proposal, I gave an oral presentation. Harvey Baron was the first to speak, and from his comment the verdict was clear.

"Have you applied for external funding?"

"I've tried NSF, Department of Energy, the Army, the Navy, and Environment."

"Does your request for departmental support mean they turned you down?" he said.

"That's correct, but no one condemned it as unworthy of study; only that they had all their funds committed. They suggested I approach it locally, that's why I'm here."

"Odd," Harvey Baron said. "The way you described it suggests that the problem is world-wide. Why should it be a local problem?"

"What do you mean the way I described it? It was worldwide and everybody on earth saw it, including you."

"We really don't need to get into that. I'd like to keep the discussion on a rational and professional level."

"So do I. And I don't appreciate the suggestion that I'm not rational or professional."

Harvey Baron raised his eyebrows in mock surprise and looked around at our colleagues. "No offense, Joe. I simply meant that this is not a real proposal. You haven't presented an experimental plan. Without direction it would have little chance of success and will only drain our meager budget."

"The point of this proposal is to bring people together to work out a hypothesis. If one arises, then we can begin to tackle the problem."

"Why don't you pursue the public media? You made a start on TV the other night."

"That was awful."

"I agree," Harvey said. "Sounded like the lunatic fringe."

Before I could respond, George Buchner spoke with a hint of impatience: "Joe, you're asking us to devote departmental funds to pursue a project that only you find important. Have any colleagues shown interest?"

"I think some would if we had support."

"But to divert our attention to a questionable project isn't fair to the rest of us, is it?"

I looked around the room at my colleagues' faces. They looked like students afraid to be called on, most were looking down at their hands. "I have the department's answer. I withdraw my proposal, but I think we're making a mistake we'll regret some day."

I did not wait for the chair to adjourn the meeting, but rose and walked out. Charlie Hollowell followed me. "Come on, Joe. I'll buy the coffee."

When we sat down at an isolated table near a large window of the basement coffee shop he said, "I heard one of your students say you were going to schedule your final exam the next time the sun stands still, so they'd have plenty of time."

"To hell with them. They're stupid too. I thought you'd understand, Charlie."

"I understand that you're killing your chance for tenure."

"Damn it, Charlie, you remember that day as well as I do."

"Sure. Classes were canceled. We all had a day off and threw a party. Let it go, Joe. No one cares."

"The most important event in human history, and all it meant was a day off."

"It wasn't that much of an event, and apparently not one single person agrees with you." Charlie saw that I was teetering between anger and confusion. "OK, it happened—once." He put his hand on my shoulder. "Is it worth your job? Harvey and his ass-kissers say you've abandoned science for mysticism. They're trying to make you out a weirdo."

I felt dumb and powerless. A great injustice was being committed in plain view, my best friend didn't get it, and there was nothing I could do. Without comment, I left

Charlie sitting there, walked back to my office, turned off the light and walked home.

As I walked across the playing field at the edge of campus I saw a bird soaring high above. It certainly remembered nothing of that day. How carefree to fly through life worrying only about the day, staying alive, and caring nothing for the beautiful, the strange, the inexplicable. Just fly and feed and live until your days run out. Sure, Charlie's right.

*   *   *

When I appeared on the back porch Ruth looked surprised. "What happened? It's only eleven-thirty."

I sat in a recliner beside her and remained silent for a moment. "Nothing . . . no, that's not true. My colleagues think I'm nuts. And so do my students."

"Nobody thinks that, Joe."

"I know. I worry too much about useless things."

"Everyone sees the world through different eyes. Other people don't or can't see what you see. Your mind's eye peers into the unknown. What do you see, Joe? I mean besides that day and the beautiful sun rigid in the sky like a gold medal? Sometimes I feel you see too deeply. Not like the others. They don't have your faith in the order of nature."

"Faith, is it?"

"Probably. Think of the spectacle of an immobile sun and the horror it conjured. I can see why people might convince themselves it never happened."

"What could Dad have meant, Ruth?"

"You'll never know. Does it matter?"

"It does to me." Anger was beginning to swell. "He meant something. It was s-u-n, not s-o-n. I'm sure of it. If only I'd been there. I'm always away at the wrong times."

"Come now."

"Like missing the award he got in New York for his work in astrophysics. It would have meant a lot to him."

"He understood."

"You know, Ruth, we had a big competition going between astronomy and chemistry all through my undergraduate and graduate days. I thought it was fun competing with my dad until I realized it wasn't fun to him. He was a member of a group of a few hundred astronomers. There are hundreds of thousands of chemists. His field was tiny compared to mine. He was well known worldwide, but I think he felt sheepish about it."

"Why would he?"

"Big frog in a small pond, maybe. I was swimming in an ocean of scientific sharks. When I finally realized it I stopped enjoying the competition. I always respected his work, though, even when I didn't understand it."

"It would be nice to link his name to this greatest of all astrophysical events, wouldn't it?"

"That's not the reason, but . . . sure. I suppose so."

Ruth always surprised me. Here she had spotted a kernel in a bushel. She had cracked the outer shell of a buried feeling I was not even aware of. When I took her hand and said, "You're always right," she reached over and kissed me.

"You've been running yourself into the ground, Joe. That's what worries me. You have so much talent and energy. It's a shame to waste it on a fruitless fight when you have so much good work to do in chemistry. Not to mention our beautiful daughter."

After a few silent minutes I stood. "I'm going outside. The hedges need trimming."

"Good! I'll fix something nice for lunch."

*   *   *

The next morning I arrived at my lab remembering nothing between the time I left home and that moment. It was as if I had walked out of a dream into the bright light of day. My desk lay like a corpse shrouded by books, papers, and magazines, seemingly dropped there from the sky. At that moment I realized how much time and energy I had devoted to the long day at the expense of my legitimate research. That pile of papers, journals and books formed the chaos I had to dig out of. I realized then that people were right: I had spent enough time embroiled in things I did not understand at the expense of those things I had worked toward all those years. Hardly knowing where to start, I dug through the pile, separating out journals I had not read into a stack and returning books to the bookshelves. Then I lifted the top journal off the stack. It looked like a foreign object. I laid it down on the small piece of clear desktop and turned pages, scanning titles, until I came to one that sent a cold shiver through me. The article described a new, highly conducting organic polymer made from a semiconducting one. The authors claimed that it conducted almost as well as copper. I devoured the pages, rereading to make sure I had understood. A Japanese and an American, working together, had, for the first time, polymerized acetylene gas to make a semiconducting film. Others had tried and succeeded only in making dry powders. Polyacetylene film was exciting enough, for it was a good semiconductor. The authors exposed the semiconducting film to iodine vapor and converted it into a silvery, lustrous film that conducted an electric current like copper, except that it was plastic, light and flexible. They theorized that the iodine removed negative charge in the form of electrons from the otherwise rigid polymer molecules, creating positively charged "holes" for other electrons to move into. Electrons from an electric current could then move through the film by jumping into holes leaving new holes behind them for more electrons to move into. The explanation was simple, clear, and beautiful!

I finished the article and looked through my chemical agents for iodine crystals and a sample of one of my polymers that conducted slightly. I put the polymer sample in a wide-mouth jar beside a few iodine crystals and covered the jar with a glass plate. Within minutes purple iodine vapor filled the jar, and the sample began to turn reddish and lustrous, like copper. I took out the sample and tested its conductivity. It conducted like mad! But as it stood on the lab bench the sample reverted to its original, nondescript cream color and its conductivity dropped off. I repeated the experiment inside a large dry box that I kept free of moisture and atmospheric oxygen. This time the sample's conductivity was even higher and did not diminish nor did its color change as long as it stayed in the dry box. I spent the entire afternoon exposing samples of all my polymers to iodine vapor and measuring their conductivity in the air and in the dry box. Some showed improved conductivity and some didn't, but I felt reborn. As five o'clock approached I called Ruth to say I'd be late for supper.

"What's wrong?"

"Big breakthrough. Tell you later. Gotta go."

When I got home two hours later, I ran in and picked her up. I could barely get the words out: "Right under my nose, Ruth. What a breakthrough!"

"That's wonderful. It was time for a breakthrough."

"Tomorrow I'll try some other agents. There are countless oxidizing agents, you know."

"This calls for a celebration. And I have a bottle of the same champagne we drank on the long day. Remember?"

"What are we waiting for?"

*   *   *

Over the next few weeks I experimented with other oxidizing agents and found several that worked even better than iodine. Working late every day I managed to submit four papers to the journal before the end of the semester. Requests for reprints soon began to pour in. One was a phone call from a French electrochemist named Marcel Moré in Paris who wanted to apply for a travel grant to visit my lab and asked if I would support his application

"Of course, Dr. Moré. I've read all your papers."

"Good. I would like to spend a month in your lab to learn about conducting polymers. I believe we can make them electrochemically."

We talked for a long time about the possibilities and agreed that Marcel Moré would travel as soon as he could get approval from his department and the French government.

Two months later I picked him up at the airport and drove him to the university, where I had reserved an apartment for him on campus. Marcel brought several boxes of equipment. "I thought you might not have access to these, and I did not want to waste time ordering them."

After dropping off his bags at the apartment, I drove him to the chemistry building and showed Marcel my equipment and some of my polymers and how we measured conductivity. Then I helped him set up his electrical equipment.

He assembled his delicate electrolysis apparatus and explained how it worked. I called two of my graduate students to watch. Marcel dissolved my starting compound in a solvent that would conduct electricity. He then poured the solution into a special glass tube fitted with two platinum electrodes. Controlling the voltage carefully, he turned on the electric current so it passed through the solution. As the current flowed, a coating began to form on the positive electrode.

We watched with fascination as the electrode changed color. Marcel explained: "The simple molecules around the positive electrode lose electrons to the electrode and bond to the electrode. When another molecule approaches, it donates the electron from the attached molecule and thereby becomes bonded to that molecule. The process continues until we have a long string of conducting molecules connected to each other—the polymer."

"Beautiful," I said, as the electrode changed to shiny black.

"And this polymer should be a good conductor already because it has been conducting electrons from the individual molecules into the electrode," Marcel said.

He then disconnected the cell without exposing its electrodes and solution to the air and moved it to the dry box, where he opened the cell, peeled the film off the electrode, washed it with a non-conducting solvent and dried it by blowing dry nitrogen gas over it. I then measured its conductivity.

"Slightly better than the same polymer we made using iodine vapor," I said. My students could not stop staring at the product and asking questions. Finally Marcel reached into his briefcase and handed each of them copies of his latest papers on the process. "Read these, and then we will talk."

After we had made several more samples using Marcel's apparatus, I called Ruth to say I wanted to invite Marcel to dinner.

"Of course. I'm fixing a roast."

When Marcel and I showed up, Ruth put out her hand to shake his, and he took her hand, leaned forward and kissed it. She blushed and tried not to appear shocked. "Come in. We'll have cocktails first. What would you like?"

"In America, always martinis."

"Come, Marcel. It's my turn to teach you my technique."

Ruth moved out of my way and put the roast in the oven. "How do you like your beef?" she asked.

"Done to perfection."

"Me too," I said.

"You two aren't much help," she said as I added vermouth and gin to ice in the shaker.

"You won't believe what we did today, Ruth. What took us a week, Marcel accomplished in minutes. Pure films that conduct like metal. Amazing. We'll set the field of conducting polymers on its ear."

"It is new for me also. I have never worked with plastics."

"How do you like Florida?" Ruth said.

Beautiful, warm and green. It is quite chilly yet in Paris."

"And your wife? Will she be joining you?"

"I am afraid not. We have two children in school. Next time, perhaps."

"Too bad. I'd like to meet her."

"You and Joe must visit us in Paris. We will show you the City of Lights."

"I hear it's beautiful."

"Incomparable. The most beautiful city in the world. Of course, I have a slight prejudice."

"And rightly so," she said. "Have you seen New York?"

"A mighty city."

"It may not be as pretty as Paris, but it's wonderful in its way."

"I like the wilds of Florida," I said. "It's primitive, but it's my birthplace."

"You speak English very well," Ruth said.

"I spent three years as a post-doctoral fellow at Columbia University."

By the time we had finished two martinis, Ruth had the roast out of the oven and we sat down to dinner.

*   *   *

The month of Marcel's visit could not have been more profitable for both of us with six joint research papers. His method allowed the graduate students to expand their research projects to the point where they submitted their dissertations the following year.

I had not mentioned my interest in the long day to Marcel, but on the drive to the airport I could not resist bringing it up. His eyes lit up when I started.

"It was truly astounding," he said. "I shall never forget it."

"You don't know what that means to me, Marcel. People here have ignored it completely. Did you read the NAS's report?"

"It was shameful."

"How about looking into it?"

Marcel's brows wrinkled. "I read some of your articles and letters, Joe. I wanted to write to you then, but it did not seem appropriate."

"Why not?"

"Two of my friends in astronomy wanted to study it, but the pressure against it was powerful."

"Politics?"

"One never knows for certain, but I think the government feared the religious extremists. Europe has always had problems with troublesome religious groups that cast doubts on science to gain support for their extreme views. People high in the government did not want to stir them up."

"I never suspected our government was involved. I blamed it on weak-willed scientists who saw only low odds of success."

"There was that, too, of course. If only someone had produced a viable theory."

* * *

I managed to set the long day aside, and by the end of the next year Marcel and I had applied for half a dozen patents on our process and on several useful materials we had prepared. My career was back on track. When I came up for tenure my resume was so good that even Harvey Baron didn't argue against it.

In one of my letters to Marcel Moré I wrote of the irony of my work: "The scientific community so readily accepts our work on molecules, electron holes, and other hypotheses that no one can ever hope to see, but they will not accept that day that everyone saw."

When he received my letter Marcel telephoned. After the usual pleasantries he said, "Joe, I have thought about the long day quite a bit since we spoke in Tampa. As enticing as it is, I urge you to put it aside. Consider this: if the cause became known, what difference would it make? We shall never duplicate the phenomenon. It has been years now and no ill effects have followed. Abandon it, Joe, and continue with the work for which we have been trained and for which you have an amazing talent. Let us keep in touch. I have a new paper on my desk. I will send you a copy for your comments before I submit it."

"*Merci, mon ami.*"

*   *   *

This is the section of Joe Adams's notebook where several pages have been ripped out. I am not able to determine why they were removed, but I assume they contained personal items that were unrelated to the issue at hand. I have indicated the gaps.

*   *   *

I heeded Marcel's advice, and my academic life proceeded with success that some might call astronomical. My research attracted attention that led to invitations to give seminars around the country as well as to give a plenary lecture at a national meeting. I easily attained the rank of full professor with the concurrence of Harvey Baron, which surprised me. I was on top of my scientific world, but I never lost the hollow feeling.

After our daughter Esther earned her Ph.D. in chemistry at Cornell University, she came to work in my research group. As a physical chemist she added an important expertise. She also stood to gain valuable experience in a burgeoning field.

During her first semester with me she met Frank Wright, a young electrical engineer who had just joined the engineering faculty. They were married the following summer, and she continued to work with me until the birth of her first child, a boy they named William. She took a few months off to take care of Billy.

(Three pages missing)

Before Esther was due to return to work she told me she was thinking of quitting, saying she and Frank want another child soon. Of course I was not happy with that. I told her how promising her career was, and what a shame it would be to abandon it. I even offered her a year or two off, hoping she would be ready to come back by then.

Her response was, "As much as I love chemistry, Daddy; I can't imagine walking out on that baby for any job."

Ruth later told me that Esther told Frank about my objection, and he became furious saying, "They raised their child; we'll raise ours."

(Eight pages missing)

Ruth and I dropped in to see Billy his first day home. Ruth went straight to the baby's room and found him awake and brought him to the living room saying, "Such a cute little bear."

Esther stood beside her and looked down at the child. His eyes were still sticky, and his arms flailed at random. I poked at him a little and then went out with Frank.

Ruth later told me she approved of Esther's decision to stay home with the baby. Esther told her that I didn't. To which Ruth said, "He'll get used to it. It's best for Billy."

Frank was showing me some citrus plants he had put into the ground. "Wish I had planted some," I said. "How long before they bear fruit?"

"Three or four years."

Unaware of Frank's strong feelings, I said, "Esther should be back to work by then."

"Hire somebody else, Joe. She's staying home."

"That should be her decision, Frank."

"Right, and she's made it."

"It's a shame to throw away her career."

"Not for Billy."

Noting Frank's tone, I dropped the subject and asked how his work was going. After a few seconds he said, "Took the entire year to get funded and equipment set up, but it's finally going. I'll be cranking out papers before long."

"Good. Stay with it. I wish I knew more about electrical engineering."

"Microelectronics is hot stuff right now."

"I know. I'm on another end of that field."

From that day on I never again broached the subject of Esther's career.

*   *   *

The blow came ten years later. In fact it was my thirty-fifth year at the university. My weekly graduate student research meeting was ending, and the department secretary stuck her head in the door to announce that Harvey Baron wanted to see me. I never understood how that humorless autocrat had managed to get faculty backing for the Chairman's job.

His office was next door to the conference room, and I went in. "Hi, Harvey. What's up?"

Skipping his usual, cool courtesies, Harvey Baron stood behind his large desk, passed his hand over his slicked down, sparse, dark-dyed hair, and looked over his glasses: "I called you in to talk about retirement. I understand you had your sixty-second birthday recently."

"I have no plans to retire, Harvey."

Ignoring my response he continued: "If you accept retirement this year, I am authorized to sweeten the pot with a $10,000 salary raise retroactive to the beginning of this academic year. Besides the cash amount, that will boost your retirement income significantly."

"Not interested."

"My offer is good only through this week. If you don't accept it by Friday, it will be withdrawn. I have the approval of both the dean and the provost on the offer and the conditions."

I was stunned. The well-oiled, political bastard was making no effort to sugarcoat the pill. He'd made up his mind to push me out and had the support he needed. Our differences started over the long day, and though we rarely spoke outside of faculty meetings we were usually on opposite sides. The mutual antagonism grew when he became Chairman, so I didn't expect sympathy, but I didn't expect such cold brutality. I hit him with all the logic I could muster: my research was going well and bringing credit to the department, I was still actively publishing and had enough ideas and funding to continue for several years more, students consistently ranked my teaching above average, I still had much to offer. Harvey's answer stripped his feelings bare: "With your salary, we can hire two young assistant professors with fresh ideas and lots of energy, people who won't keep the department stirred up. Whether you retire or not, we'll need half your research space this semester for the two new faculty members we just hired."

Harvey's eyes unveiled the core of his hatred. Knowing logic could never prevail over such feelings, I walked out and went to my office. Someone spoke in the hall as I passed; I didn't hear or see who it was. Memories of years of battling swirled me into a confused, angry vortex. All my years at the university focused like a laser on that blinding moment in Baron's office. I felt like the worn exhaust of a massive institutional machine with my archenemy finally in command. I considered refusing, perhaps suing the university. But win or lose, I knew I would end up the loser. I grabbed a blank sheet of paper, scribbled a cryptic memo accepting his offer, and walked it back to Baron's secretary. Then I started packing, as anger and frustration continued to build. My brain swirled as I filled trashcans and boxes with papers, notebooks, and records. In an eruption of aboriginal anger and frustration I threw out everything that reminded me of thirty-one years of warfare. I opened the file drawer containing my documents related to the long day and threw them out too. After souring my years in the university, that terrible day would mock me no longer. "If there is a God, why in hell would He do such a senseless thing?" I said to myself.

The sun was setting when I threw the last of my files into the Dumpster behind the chemistry building and dragged myself home. I told Ruth what had happened and what I had done, expecting her to be angry with me for being so destructive.

"That's wonderful, dear. I've been hoping you'd retire soon so we could enjoy each other more." I should have expected her response, but Ruth always managed to surprise me with her abiding generosity.

For the rest of the semester I worked out of my home and came to the department only to meet classes. I soon realized how much I would regret throwing out those files. That history would now live only in my memory like the stories of long-dead grandparents who still speak through our memories of them, though we can no longer touch or talk to them.

At first, retirement was not bad. I didn't miss the classroom or even my research much and the politics and committees not at all. Ruth was wonderful. With Esther married and in charge of her life, we took the European vacation we had long planned. Eventually, I began to collect my thoughts for a book about the long day. But everything stopped the day Ruth came home from the doctor's office with news of a devastating cancer. The next year and a half was a nightmare of surgery, radiation, chemotherapy, traveling to medical research centers, but mostly tortured waiting.

Finally it came. The world faded, and a gaping hole opened. Only the dull, gray, dissonance of the passing days reminded me that I still lived. Survival seemed impossible, worthless, and futile. I barely remember those days now, staring vacantly at the TV, hearing and seeing only the reverberations in my own mind. Charlie Hollowell called me for lunch a couple of times, but strangely, we had little to talk about. He was still working and talked about problems that no longer mattered to me.

A couple of months ago, my daughter prevailed on me to move in with her. She was afraid to leave me alone after I had two minor fender-benders in the same week. The day she talked about moving, I had left a stove burner on that caused a minor fire and burned a hole in a Tupperware bowl. I hated the idea of moving, but Esther was sincerely worried, and I didn't want to cause her grief. At least I would be near my grandchildren. It had become easier to talk with them than with adults.

While Frank and I were moving my things in, Esther called me aside for a cup of coffee. Standing at the coffee maker, she said, "Daddy, we don't think you should drive any more."

"Why not? It wasn't my fault either time."

"We don't want you to hurt yourself or anyone else, Daddy. You don't go out that often anyhow. We'll drive you

wherever you want to go. It'll be like having a chauffeur."
She handed me the coffee with a smile.

"I'd be stranded."

"Don't worry, Daddy. We'll take good care of you."

I was already regretting the move.

"Also, please, Daddy, don't mention that long day anymore."

"Why, for heaven's sake?"

"Just don't, please."

"Your mother understood. She never bought the popular denial; not her. She saw through the smoke screen."

"See, Daddy? You start ranting when you get on that subject. Frank and I think it will confuse the children and make them feel insecure."

"Esther, you were born nine months after that July day. You probably wouldn't be here if it had been an ordinary day."

"I know, Daddy."

"You heard about it when you were a kid. Did you feel insecure?"

"No, Daddy, but Frank was too young to remember."

"What's the harm in talking?"

"Please, Daddy."

It took a week to arrange my things. Happily, my room was big enough for my desk. I kept up with a few chemical journals and didn't go out much. Once or twice a week I'd wander through campus, but never the chemistry building. Sometimes I would spend the whole afternoon browsing in the library.

Returning from a walk this afternoon I overheard Frank in the kitchen. "He's getting crazier and refuses to let it go. We'll have to put him in a nursing home eventually; I say now's the time. Hell, he's seventy-five."

Before Esther could reply, I burst in. "I lived it. It's part of me. Why is it crazy to talk about something I lived through?"

"Because you seem to be the only person who lived through it," Frank said. "You're supposed to be a scientist, but you sound like a religious fanatic."

I stopped a moment to calm down. "Listen to reason, Frank."

"For Christ sake, even your generation doesn't remember it."

"Some people say the Nazi Holocaust never happened. How do you think the survivors feel about that?"

"How do I know there was a Holocaust? I wasn't there, and I don't know any survivors. As for your miracle day, maybe the day *seemed* longer; it was a hot July; maybe everything just slowed down. All I know is your long day is bullshit." Frank glanced at Esther with his lips curled around an angry smile and stalked out to the kitchen.

"Daddy, why do you rile him like that?"

I said nothing, and she went out to calm her husband. When she was gone I said aloud, "I won't give up even if I'm the only one left who believes it. Oh, Ruth. How could you abandon me like this?"

That evening, feeling I had little to lose, I sat my grandchildren beside me on the sofa and began to recount the details of the day that stood at the focus of my life. As I began, Frank said, "That does it. He's outa here." Then he walked out the back door and let it slam.

My voice quivered; Esther's face showed resignation and perhaps a trace of relief. Soon the telling began to calm me. I found myself basking in the sun's true light. Ten-year-old Billy and eight-year-old Ginny listened passively.

After I had told them about that day and the days that followed, I continued: "The blue silence had spoken, not in sounds, but in beautiful stillness. Through the years I have begun to sense its meaning—that you can know some things without knowing all things. Uncertainty and confusion spawn anger and hatred. Love demands certainty and simplicity, but, like the sun's presence, we can enjoy its beauty without understanding it."

Ginny had fallen asleep on my lap.

"That was a neat story, Grandpa. Tell another one."

Smiling through her tears, Esther embraced me and then went out to her husband. In summary, I can only say that the above is as true as anything can be in this world.

*   *   *

Quietly, I turned off my desk lamp, put on my robe and slippers, and went out to the back porch. Night was beginning to bleed into morning. I sat in the oak rocker with my notebook looking at the lake through the Spanish moss. The brightest stars were dissolving into the hushed celestial solvent. Out of the chaos, my thoughts fell upon Stonehenge, its tumbled monoliths a testament of the human desire to understand things beyond our reach. Certain that humanity sprang from this yearning I fell into a stilled rapture at the silent prelude, the almost imperceptible crescendo of new light. Then, in the immense climax that vaporizes the brooding web of fears, the sun burst over the world as it did on that July morning with a glory that never fades. I now see that the time between sunrise and sunset can vary. It can be a moment or a lifetime.

Joe Adams

*   *   *

The following postscript was handwritten by Joe Adams's daughter. Reading it, I assume it was the first time she had seen his notes.

*   *   *

329

I found Daddy still on his rocker. I had just put on the coffee and walked out to take in the beautiful morning and found him slumped over. I knew from the peaceful expression on his face that he was gone. He looked so serene that I did not disturb him. I sat beside him and took his hand and held it. The notebook into which he had been writing fell to the floor with his ballpoint pen. I picked up the notebook and read it through tears.

Using his pen I added these lines to complete what he considered his life's most important work. Out of love and respect for my father I shall not attempt to publish it, for the time is not right; I do not want him to receive further ridicule. Perhaps some day the world will remember the wonderful day they have pushed out of their memories. On that day Professor Joe Adams will finally be vindicated.

Esther Adams Wright.